To Audrey

Thanks, Such a great daughter!

GAMING FOR LOVE

Book #1 of The Griffin Brothers

BY CRYSTAL PERKINS

Hide the game controllers... or don't!

Crystal Perkins

ABOUT GAMING FOR LOVE

A young woman carrying the
weight of her world on her shoulders.

A man struggling with a devastating betrayal.

Love is a game they're determined to win...

Yasmin just wants to keep her family's Las Vegas bookstore afloat. She doesn't have time for anything other than trying to figure out how to pay the bills. When an incredibly hot guy with tattoos and piercings walks into her store, she's relieved to discover what a jerk he is once he opens his mouth. His bad behavior makes it easier to try and ignore the way her body responds to him. Trying is all she can do once he sets his sights on her, determined to win her over.

Computer genius Scott Griffin thought he was in love once, until he found out that it was all a lie. The crazy, pen loving bookworm he encounters sets him on fire like no one else ever has. When she stands up to him, he realizes that it's more than just her body that he's intrigued by. But, he can't have her, can't have anyone after what happened in Chicago. Or, can he? When she challenges him to woo her, he pulls out all the stops.

They embark on a romance filled with sweet gestures and steamy nights. Until a shocking revelation causes Scott to feel the sting of betrayal again while Yasmin loses everything, including the man she loves. A loving family and a loyal group of friends will try to help them find a way back to each other, but will it be too late to save them both?

For Niquey and Gabi...

The best daughters a mother could
ever hope for. I love you!

CHAPTER 1

<u>Yasmin</u>

The pile of bills in front of me is not getting any smaller. Especially with the new ones that arrived today. I'm not sure how I'm going to make this work. The money just isn't there. When my parents died 2 years ago, I was so caught up in my grief that I didn't think about how hard it would be to keep a bookstore open in this economy. Yes, I had the life insurance settlement and the loyal customers who had been shopping at I Heart Books for years, but soon it won't be enough. We can maybe stay open another six months if things don't change. As for me, I am not at the point where ramen is my only meal, but I am afraid that I will be soon.

Samantha, Danny and Erika have been there for me when I needed to cry or yell or just throw some books around. They listen to me, offer ideas and when all else fails, get me drunk. No one could ask for better employees *or* friends. I don't want to let anyone go but I am afraid it will come to that soon. I am also afraid that I won't be able to go back to college for my junior year. School starts in a couple of months, but can I really afford it? I have scholarships and I know that my parents wanted me to go, but I need to be here to keep their dream, this store, alive.

It gets to be too much to think about sometimes. Most 20 year olds are just thinking about their classes or what guy they want to get with. Wouldn't that be nice? To have nothing to worry about except living my life? A guy would be nice, too. I have been on a few dates in the last two years, but no one who I felt a special connection to. I want special. I *deserve* special.

Lost in my thoughts, I almost don't hear the door open. I look up into a pair of the most beautiful green eyes that I have ever seen. They are lighter than emerald but just as intense. As I tear my eyes away, I notice that there are actually three people in front of me. Mr. Green Eyes, an older woman in her late forties or early fifties and a teenage girl who looks around 16. The woman speaks first.

"Hello. We are new to Las Vegas and heard that your store is the place to go for books. My granddaughter loves to read and needs something new," the woman says with a friendly smile. She is petite with brown hair streaked with gray and welcoming blue eyes.

"Welcome to town. I'm Yasmin. I would love to introduce you to some new books and authors," I tell the girl. She looks up at me from where she was staring at the ground. I notice that she has the same green eyes as the man, but hers are tinged with sadness. A sadness that I recognize in myself. She is taller than her grandmother with long brown hair and a thin but curvy body. Even with the sadness in her eyes, she is breathtakingly beautiful.

"Can we move this along? I need to get back to work." The husky male voice belongs to Mr. Green Eyes and it makes my stomach flip.

I look up and am again momentarily captivated by those eyes. When I blink to clear my head, I take in the rest of him and nearly lose my mind at what I see. He is over six feet tall with jet black hair styled in a faux hawk. Both of his ears, his right eyebrow and his lip are pierced. His jaw is chiseled and currently hard set with a hint of stubble. And sweet Jesus, that mouth. Lush, sexy lips that seem set in a permanent smirk meant to drive a woman wild. Just thinking about what he could do with that mouth causes me to lick my own lips. As I run my eyes further down, I see his light blue t-shirt straining against the lean muscles of his biceps and chest. He isn't over muscled, just perfectly formed...at least from what I can see. He also has sleeves of colorful tattoos down both arms. Jeans and combat boots complete the bad boy look. I know I will embarrass myself if I don't stop looking, but I am not sure if I can make myself stop. Thankfully the girl saves me.

"You didn't have to come with us, Uncle Scott. I know how important your work is."

He reaches forward and cups her cheek, "Baby Girl, nothing is more important to me than you and the rest of our family. Never forget that."

There is a moment of uncomfortable silence while the three of them take each other in. It passes when the woman - his mother - speaks again.

"I can't wait to see what you suggest for Alex. I have to admit that I sometimes read her books!" she says with a sly smile. "Oh and I have somehow forgotten my manners. I'm Maggie and I think you have already heard that this is Alex and Scott." She reaches out her hand, nodding to her son and the sad, beautiful girl. I shake it, feeling a sense of calm and somehow knowing that I will like this woman already.

"It's great to meet all of you. What kind of books do you like to read, Alex? Our YA section is the largest in the store and I read many of them myself so I am pretty sure I can find something for you." I smile at her and wait for her answer.

Before she can respond, Mr. Green Eyes – Scott - says with a smirk, "You read those books? Trying to relive your own high school years, huh?"

"YA books are some of the most well written books around. Your *mother* just said she read them, yet you are making fun of me? And you don't look much older than me!" I spit out through clenched teeth.

"Scott Nathaniel Griffin, you apologize right now!" his mother says with fury in her eyes.

"I'm sorry," he mumbles. "I'm heading to the café next door for a coffee while you two shop."

I watch him walk out the door and notice how well he fills out those jeans. "Let's get started," I tell Maggie and Alex, walking toward the YA section of my store.

* * *

Scott

I had to get out of that store. I know I promised Alex and my mom that I would spend the morning with them. And I really wanted to see Alex happy, like she always is with a new book. Her smile has been hard to find since her parents, my sister and brother-in-law, were murdered in a robbery gone wrong. My parents and my brothers have been holding it together for her, but it is hard for me. If it wasn't for me, they would still be alive. Everyone says that they don't blame me. That I was tricked and a victim in the whole thing too, but I blame myself.

I also had to get out of the store because that woman, Yasmin, was making me feel something that was more intense than I have ever felt for anyone. When we walked into the shop, I noticed the funky, cool vibe of the store first. Handwritten signs, book posters, literary t-shirts and some cool pieces of art lined the walls. I was thinking my niece would love this place, when I looked over and our eyes met. Warm brown eyes met mine and sent an immediate shock to my system. What the fuck? I don't make connections anymore, I just don't.

So, I did what I had to do and acted like an ass. I noticed her checking me out which both turned me on and scared the shit out of me. I had checked her out already when my mom was talking to her and I don't think my body has ever reacted so fast in my twenty one years of life. Rich, dark brown hair that was almost black, was pulled back into a tight ponytail that reached past her shoulder blades, making me want to wind my hands around it. Those beautiful eyes, a pert nose and strong cheekbones, just daring me to caress them, met my eyes next. Then her mouth, damn what a mouth. Not too full but still luscious lips smeared with some kind of dark pink gloss were tempting me. I wanted to be on that mouth, I wanted that mouth on me. *All over me.* I don't know how I managed to tear my eyes away and look any further, but I did.

A graceful neck led to a positively sinful body. She wasn't super thin with fake tits like the society girls I had been fucking for years - or like my ex, Amber. No, lush breasts strained against a t-shirt that said something about reading irresponsibly. A trim waist and full hips, the kind you want to hold onto when thrusting in hard, led to a great ass and legs that went on for miles ending in a pair of black glittery Toms. She—Yasmin—was easily around five seven and with heels would be just the perfect height.

That's why I had to get out of there. I was ready to blow like a thirteen year old just looking at her. And when she fired back at me after my stupid comment, I wanted her in more than a physical way. What the hell is wrong with me? Let me get this *iced* coffee and think of my eighty year old high school math teacher so I can go back in there. I need to get my shit together and be there for Alex and Mom.

* * *

Yasmin

I really like Alex. After her initial shyness, she told me that dystopian books are her favorites. I took her to the section, but noticed her gaze kept straying across the aisle to contemporary fiction. I met Maggie's eyes and she shook her head, giving Alex a look filled with sadness and love. I started telling them about some of my favorite dystopian books. Alex had read a few but was excited that I could recommend some more to her. Before we left the section, I pulled my favorite funny contemporary off the shelf and asked her to try that one too, for me. Her smile wavered but then got a little brighter - just for a moment - as she nodded.

As I am walking them up to the register, Scott comes back into the store. He has sunglasses on and a swagger to his walk. I try to ignore my body's immediate reaction to him as I step behind the counter. I ring up the books - minus the contemporary one. I can't really afford to give it away, but I want to. I feel a connection to Alex in some unknown way and I want to help her. I give the total and Scott throws an AMEX Black card on the counter before Maggie can even get her wallet out.

"You don't have to pay, honey," Maggie says to him with a frown.

He looks at her, an intense look on his face. "Yeah, I do. Please let me."

She nods and I swipe his card. I hand him a pen and the slip to sign. After he signs, he sticks the pen behind his ear with another of those infuriating smirks.

"Excuse me, but are you really going to steal my pen?" I ask, irritated.

"Yeah. I think you can afford one less Bic pen."

"First of all, you don't know anything about me and what I can or can't afford. And second, I happen to *love* pens, any pen and nothing pisses me off more than some ignorant asshole taking whatever he wants because he thinks he's God's gift to the earth. Now give it back," I practically scream the words at him.

A moment of silence passes where I realize that I had just yelled at and insulted a customer. One I desperately need. I open my mouth to apologize when Maggie bursts out laughing. "I like you Yasmin. Expect us to become regulars here." She smiles at me. "Give the pen back, Scott."

"Crazy pen loving bookworm," he mumbles while slamming down the pen and storming out of the door.

"I like you, too," Alex says. "Can I call you when I read the books to talk about them? Or come in?"

"Of course! I love talking about books! You can call or come in anytime."

* * *

Scott

"Yasmin seems like a wonderful young woman," my mother says with a smile when we get back to her house. My parents bought this large rambling mini mansion when they decided to relocate the company headquarters. My mom has made it warm and welcoming despite the size, just like our Chicago home. My brothers got condos in City Center on The Strip but I chose to remodel the guest house and stay on property. I will never leave my loved ones unprotected again.

"She's an uptight bitch. I mean, who gets upset over a 10 cent pen?"

"She is most definitely not a bitch. She was great with Alex and actually made her smile. And how upset did you get with Luke for taking that *free* flash drive you got at CES last year?"

"She made Alex smile? Really?" Shit. Why couldn't she be a cold bitch? I *need* her to be a cold bitch. Then, she won't be of interest to me anymore. Yeah right. I couldn't forget her, even if I tried.

And I want to try. At least I can manage not to see her again. But, do I really want to not see her again? Fuck, fuck, fuck! What is happening to me? I can't do this, I can't. I need to get to my place and work on the new software I am designing.

My mom looks at me intently, like she is reading me from the inside out. She probably is - she always seems to know what we are all thinking before we can even say it. I love her so much and I can't disappoint her and my dad again. They have never come out and said that I have disappointed them but I know that I have. The tats, the piercings, nothing shook their love or faith in me. But what happened with Amber, yeah, that is unforgivable. I know it even if they have never said it.

"Yes, she made Alex smile. And she gave her a contemporary book to read. You know she hasn't wanted to read anything based on real life since..." She stops there, a look of such intense sadness in her eyes.

"Since I fucked up all of our lives and got her parents killed," I say through a haze of hurt and loathing.

"No. No, Scott. Do not say that. How many times do we have to tell you that it is not your fault?" She seems so sincere. But I know that she can't be. I destroyed this family.

"I *can* blame myself." I practically run out the back door without even saying goodbye. I had to get out of there. I will finish this software project and add to my family's wealth. God knows we don't need it-we have more money than we could all spend in ten lifetimes. But this is all I can contribute to my family, all I can give them. So I will. Even if I have to work day and night, I will. They deserve better, but this is all I have to give.

CHAPTER 2

<u>Yasmin</u>

"We really need to get an online presence. I know you wanted to stay small and just have the store. But, online could save us," Erika tells me and I know she is right.

"I know. My parents would have done it already. I don't even know where to start though," I tell her honestly. Give me a book and I am good. Technology, along with math and science, are foreign concepts to me. I mean I can use what I need to on my phone and computer, but don't ask me to do anything beyond basic.

"My friend, Sean, knows how to build websites. I bet he could help us get started for cheap. What would really help would be this new program that I have been reading about. It was previewed at CES and is still being worked on, I think. It's software for both computers and phones, through an app, that lets you put in a description, sentence or characters from a book and find matches to choose from. Amazon and Barnes and Noble are salivating over the thought of it."

"Wow. That would be awesome. But if Amazon and B&N are after it, there is no way I could afford it."

"Things are pretty bad, huh? If you need to let me go, I understand. You are my friend first and I don't want you struggling. I mean it."

"I know you do and I love you for it. Things *are* rough, but if we can get the website up, maybe that would help. I was thinking that we could do recommendations and link in some of the bloggers I've met. Maybe make it both a social place and a place to shop."

"That sounds great! I'll call Sean and have him get started!"

"So, tell me about this *friend*, Sean." Erika turns red and starts blushing. She is saved by the store phone.

"Thanks for calling I Heart Books, this is Yasmin. How may I help you?"

"Hi Yasmin. It's Alex. Do you have time to talk?"

"Alex! Yes, of course! I'd love to talk to you! Did you finish one of the books?" It has been a week since she came into the store and I am really hoping that she read and liked one of the books. I head back to my office to take the call, mouthing to Erika that I will be back on the floor soon.

"I read *all* of the books and I loved them so much! They were exactly what I needed." She proceeds to tell me what she liked about each book and we talk back and forth for over half an hour before she tells me, "I especially liked the contemporary book. I-I haven't read a contemporary in about nine months. I haven't wanted to read anything based in the real world since..."

I wait patiently, not wanting to push her when it seems like she's struggling with how much to tell me.

"Since my parents died."

"Oh, honey, I am so sorry." My heart breaks for this beautiful girl. Just like my heart broke inside of me the day *my* parents died.

"Everyone says that but no one understands," she says with a hint of bitterness.

"I understand," I tell her gently. "My parents died 2 years ago. This was their bookstore. They loved it like it was a second child and when they died, I took it over. Every day since their car accident, I miss them and sometimes I can hardly bear to be in this store. But, books have always helped me escape and I can't imagine not being able to talk to customers and friends about the books here in the store."

"Oh. You *do* understand. I didn't know and I'm sorry for you, too. It doesn't sound like it gets easier. I want it to be easier, but I don't want to forget them either."

"It *does* get easier, but you never forget. Some days I almost forget that they are gone and go to call them when something good or bad happens. Then, I remember that they are not here. I know that they would want me to live my life and be happy. So, I'm trying and most days, I succeed."

"I think my parents would want that for me too. I stopped reading contemporary books because I didn't want to read anything real. I couldn't stop reading but I thought if I read something that was futuristic or in a fantasy world, I could get lost in them. Especially because my mom loved reading contemporary books - YA and romance especially. But, the one you gave me was fun and good and I think when I come in again, I want to get some more."

"Oh, sweetie, I am so glad to hear you want to read contemporary again. They *are* reality based for the most part but you can still escape in them. Not in another world, but with a hot guy who has a tender heart or by seeing a character go through a rough time and get through it. You know those books have saved a lot of lives and brought happiness to many people.

I will confess that like your mom, I read contemporary romance and now New Adult books when I'm not reading YA. I like to escape into them and imagine that some hot guy would want to romance me. I know that's not going to happen. A book store owner is not sexy to most real men. But, at least I can pretend that it might happen when I am reading."

"So, you don't have a boyfriend? Really? I mean, I think you're awesome and gorgeous."

"Aww thanks. No, I don't have a boyfriend. I haven't had much time to date, but my friends have been bugging me to make time. I think you are awesome and beautiful, too. I want to see you smile more."

"My grandparents and uncles tell me that, too. I want to try to be happier. Are you working tomorrow? I'd like to come in and get some more books. And see you. I think one of my uncles can bring me."

"Yes, I'll be here. I can't wait to see you." We say our goodbyes and hang up. I can't stop thinking that I would do anything I can to help this girl through her grief like my friends helped me.

The next day, I am talking to Sean on the phone about the website when Alex comes in with who I think is one of her uncles. He has those same amazing green eyes, black hair and facial features as Scott but that is where the similarity ends. This guy is in an expensive looking charcoal suit with a deep purple shirt unbuttoned at the collar. His black hair is a little long on top but styled in a controlled way and he is wearing fancy shoes that could probably pay my rent for a few months. He is also seriously built, his muscles fighting against the expensive suit that holds them. I tell Sean I'll call him back and hang up.

Alex runs right over to me and gives me a hug. "Yasmin, this is my Uncle Ryan. Uncle Ryan, this is Yasmin."

"Hello, Yasmin. It's great to meet you. My mom and Alex haven't stopped talking about you all week," he says with an easy smile and a little sparkle in his eyes.

"It's nice to meet you, too, Ryan. Your mom and Alex are great!" I reply honestly, thinking that he's a really nice guy.

I can't explain the instant connection I have with this family. Well, except for the connection with Scott. That is easily explained as pure lust at first sight. Until he opened his sexy mouth. Then it was irritation at first sight. But, the other three members of his family that I've met so far are really nice and friendly. I would love to see Alex and Maggie outside of the store. Maybe I can ask them to lunch. Wait, I can't afford lunch. Damn it, yes I can. One lunch won't decide the fate of this store.

I must have been spacing out for longer than I thought because Alex says, "Yasmin, are you okay?" I snap out of it and tell her I am fine, just thinking and that I can't wait to show her some books.

"I am heading over to mystery while you girls do your thing. I think Harlan Coben has a new book out," Ryan says with a sheepish smile.

"He does and it's awesome," I reply and point him in the right direction.

Alex and I lose ourselves in contemporary YA books for over an hour. Thankfully, Danny is in today and can handle the few customers we have. A few stop to say hi as we are curled up in two of the comfy chairs I keep around the store. We are laughing and talking about our favorite YA boys when Ryan comes over to tell us he has to get back to the office.

"I don't want to leave yet," Alex tells him. "I'm having fun."

"I can see that, honey. If I didn't have a meeting in an hour, I would let you stay here all day," Ryan tells her, regret written all over his face.

"I could bring her home," I say without thinking.

"That would be awesome! Please Uncle Ryan, can she?" Alex looks so happy my heart almost bursts.

"It's really not too much trouble for you?" Ryan asks me, hope in his eyes at seeing his niece smiling.

"Not at all. I am off at 5." I look at Alex then. "I do have some work, sweetie, so I can't stay here and talk to you. You are welcome to stay, though."

"I would love to stay. And I can help you if you want," she says shyly.

"I never turn down free help."

Ryan watches our exchange, a look of curiosity on his face. "Why don't you stay for dinner when you come over? We have a Friday night barbeque every week. It's one of the only times our family gets together all at once. We have been doing it for years but this will be our first since we moved here."

"I wouldn't want to intrude on your family time," I tell them although I really want to say yes. I would love to see Maggie. Not Scott. Okay, yes Scott. Maybe he can keep his mouth closed while eating.

"You wouldn't be. Oh, please come!" Alex pleads.

I meet Ryan's eyes and he nods. "Alright, then, I would love to have dinner with your family."

"Put your number into my phone and I will text you the address." I do as he asks and then we say our goodbyes until later.

I spend the afternoon catching up on emails and bills while Alex reads and helps shelve books. Right before we are set to leave, I receive an email from Erika with a link to the software program she was telling me about. I print out the info and stuff it into my purse without looking at it. Alex and I say our goodbyes to Danny and head to her house.

* * *

Scott

I made some great progress with the software today. If I can just work out these last couple of bugs, I will definitely be done in time for my dad and Ryan to launch it before the fall semester starts at the universities. I want to make my parents proud and bring good publicity to the company. It's not enough but it's something. Anything I can do is worth it.

I head out of the guest house - my house, I remind myself -into the backyard. My brothers are all there, along with my parents. We all got my dad's green eyes but while Ryan and I have his black hair, Owen and Luke are brunettes like my mom. Erin had my dad's black hair too. The thought sends an arrow into what's left of my shattered heart, but I push it away as I notice that Alex is missing.

"Where's Alex?" I ask as I head over to the table.

"Yasmin is bringing her. Alex didn't want to leave the bookstore so Yasmin said that she would drive her home when she got off of work. Ryan invited her to dinner with us," My mom says with a smile.

"Excuse me? You left Alex with some chick we don't know?" I stalk towards Ryan.

"Alex was laughing and happier than I have ever seen her. Yasmin seems great and I don't think she would do anything to hurt Alex. She was excited to see Mom again, too," he fires back.

"Yasmin's great? And you invited her for dinner? Keep your dates away from our family meals." I have never once in my life felt jealous about anyone, not even Amber, who I dated for a year. But the thought of my brother dating Yasmin makes me want to tackle him into the pool.

"This isn't a date, although now that you mention it, I *should* ask her out. She is a little young for me, but definitely gorgeous." He looks at me in amusement when he says it and I am afraid that my jealousy is showing. I try to school my features into indifference but I'm not sure it works.

"Damn, Scott, do you like this Yasmin girl? Because you didn't even react to Ry saying that Alex was laughing," Owen tells me, looking at me like he's trying to figure me out. Good luck with that.

"I. Do. Not. Like. Yasmin," I spit out, a little too forcefully.

"I don't like you either so I guess we're on the same page," I hear her sexy, melodic voice say from behind me. I whirl around to see Alex and Yasmin standing by the patio door. Yasmin looks pissed and well, so does Alex.

"What is wrong with you, Uncle Scott? Yasmin is my friend. She understands about mom and dad because her parents died. Why can't you be nice to her?" Now she looks like she wants to cry.

Shit. I need to fix this before the tears start. "Alex, honey, don't cry. I'll be nice, I promise. Just please don't cry." I wrap my arms around her as she starts to sob.

I look up to see Yasmin fidgeting and looking like she wants to get the hell out of Dodge. I can't really blame her. My niece needs her, so I swallow my pride.

"Please stay. I'm sorry that I have been an ass. I will be nice to you." I pull away from Alex and reach into my pocket. "Look, I've even got a pen you can have." I hold it out to her, hoping that she will take it and stay. For Alex. She needs to stay for Alex. And me. NO! Not me. Who am I kidding? I want her to stay so that I can get to know her better. I shouldn't, but I do.

* * *

Yasmin

Scott's holding out a blue pen to me. It looks like the kind businesses give out. I still feel like I might want to run but a big part of me is yelling in my head that he remembered that I love pens and is offering me one. I reach out to take it. It says "Tech Boys Do It Better" and has the name of some company I've never heard of on it.

"Do they really?" I ask him before I can stop myself, blushing instantly.

"What?" He says looking confused, until he sees the pen he gave me. "Oh, yeah, definitely." And the smirk is back.

Thinking of being with him makes me want to melt right there on the ground. I'm not a virgin or a prude, but it *has* been awhile. Maybe too long. My friend, Candi, tells me I need to get something battery powered to pass the time, but I only want body parts in there. And yes, lately that means my fingers while thoughts of a certain green eyed bad boy run through my mind.

"Your parents died?" I'm snapped out of my thoughts -thankfully since I am standing in front of my fantasy and his family for God's sake - by the question from a brown haired, green eyed guy who looks younger than Scott and seems to favor his mother in looks and coloring, but is no less stunning.

"Owen!" an older looking version of Scott and Ryan with salt and pepper hair says sharply. He turns to me with a kind smile. "Please excuse my son, he sometimes lacks manners. And a filter. I'm Gary and it is great to meet you, Yasmin. You know Maggie, Ryan, Alex and of course Scott, already. These are our two other sons, Owen and Luke." I nod at them and notice that Luke looks like his mother as well.

"It's nice to meet you all. And Gary, Owen's question is okay." I look over at him. "Yes, my parents died two years ago in a car accident. A drunk driver ran them off the road. I took over the bookstore when they died."

"You own the bookstore?" Maggie asks looking a little shocked.

"Yes, I do." For now at least, I add silently.

"You're pretty young to be running your own business. From what my wife says, it is a wonderful shop," Gary tells me.

"It *is* wonderful. It was my parent's dream and I'm carrying it on for them. I'm 20, so yes, I am young, but I love it as much as they did."

"Well, that's what's important, doing what you love. And thank you for helping our girl smile again." He looks over at Alex with eyes full of love when he says this.

"It's my pleasure, really," I tell him.

"Enough with the sappy stuff, can we eat now? I have a party to get to," Luke says with a smile, lightening the moment.

I walk over to the table with Alex and Scott to sit down. Alex sits in the spot next to her grandparents so I take the last spot, next to Scott. I don't want to sit next to him, but I have no choice. Oh, who am I kidding? I *so* want to be next to him.

They start passing the food around and it looks amazing! As usual, I load up on carb-filled sides. I know that I should eat more protein instead but the potato salad and mac and cheese look too good to pass up.

"Are you really going to eat all of that?" Scott looks at me incredulously.

"Umm, yes?" Oh, God, did I take too much? Do I look like a pig?

Scott must sense my unease because he leans in close to me and whispers, "I think it's sexy as fuck that you want to eat all of that. I hate women who won't eat in front of guys."

What I said about melting earlier? Nowhere close to this. I am basically a liquid form in this chair. What's this guy doing to me? And can he do more?

The rest of the night flies by. Everyone is so nice and funny. I love to hear them tease each other. They all make an effort to include me in their conservations, even Scott. *Especially* Scott. He asks me about myself and what I am studying at school. He tries to talk to me about what he does, but I tell him that I am pathetic when it comes to anything having to do with computers. He seems to find that funny and teases me, bumping my shoulder with his. I catch the other members of his family smiling at us from time to time. When Maggie brings out brownies for dessert, Scott puts the largest one on my plate with a smile. He jumps up to walk me to the door when I say that I need to get home. He tells me that he hopes I had a good time and kisses me on the cheek. Maybe he isn't such a jerk after all.

CHAPTER 3

<u>Scott</u>

It's the morning after the barbeque and I wake up rock hard. I could pretend that I don't know why or that it's just normal morning wood but I know better. I was dreaming about Yasmin. About how sexy she looked eating last night, how she moaned after her first bite of my mom's mac and cheese. I want to make her moan like that while I'm sucking on those hot tits of hers and thrusting my cock into her. Shit, I want to do that so bad, I could barely stop myself from throwing her over my shoulder and carrying her to the guest house. Especially when I leaned in to whisper in her ear last night. She smelled like something floral but musky at the same time and I was even harder than I had already been, if that's even possible. Well, I guess it is. I was hard the minute she asked me about the pen with that sparkle in her darkened eyes. Yeah, I think she wants me to.

When I kissed her cheek last night, she flushed red and her lips parted slightly. I wanted to kiss her mouth, too, but I held back. I shouldn't have even kissed her cheek. Talking to her all night and then that small kiss made me realize that I want to get to know more than her body. I want to get to know *her*.

But, I can't go there. My family seems to love her and she is bringing my beautiful niece back to life. I can't use her for a one night fuck. I know that it would be a use-the-entire-box-of-condoms kind of night, but I can't do it. I would have to see her again. I *want* to see her again. One night wouldn't be enough with her.

Shit! I can't think like this. I don't deserve more than one night and I can't give more than that. I already learned that once. She seems nice but what if she's like Amber and just wants to use me and my family? What if someone gets hurt again? I couldn't live with myself. Fuck if I don't want her, though.

I can use her to take care of my cock myself, though. I start stroking and pulling, thinking about her. Her tits stretching another book t-shirt last night, her tight ass and those hips. I grip myself faster and thrust harder into my hand as I imagine that it's her hands on my cock. And her mouth. Yes, that mouth that I think was made for me, sucking my cock in and out. That's it. Just that image is enough to make me come harder than I ever have on my own. Holy fuck, I am done for.

As I lay there panting, my phone starts to ring. I stretch over to grab it and see that it's my mom. "Hey Mom, what's up?" I ask, trying to make my breathing sound normal.

"Hi Scotty," she says, using my childhood nickname. "Luke wants to have a pool party this afternoon but I want to make sure he doesn't bother you if you are planning to work."

"No, it's cool." A pool party for Luke means plenty of college girls in barely there bikinis. Just what I need to get my mind off a certain bookworm. I think that maybe it's time to get back in the saddle, so to speak.

"Great. Your dad and I are going to take Alex shopping and stay at Owen's condo so that you boys don't have to worry about her."

"You mean so you don't have to worry about us corrupting her!" I say with a laugh.

"We love you boys and support your choices, but yes." She chuckles into the phone.

"I get it. And thanks for always supporting us. I'll stop up at the house and give Alex some money so she can get whatever she wants."

"You don't need to do that, Scott."

"Yeah, I do," I tell her, remembering why I need to find a quick fuck and forget about Yasmin. I can't have her. I won't let myself.

* * *

<u>Yasmin</u>

I'm sitting at home, deciding which sexy romance book I want to read since Sam and Danny have banished me from the store today, when I get the text from Ryan.

My brothers and I are having a pool party. You should come if you're not busy. It starts at 2:00.

I look at it and think about how to respond. When I drove up to their house last night, I nearly fainted. I mean, I know Maggie has a huge rock on her finger and everyone I had met in the family had been dressed nicely, but I had no idea that they were *rich*. Like, seriously rich. But they were so nice and down to earth that my unease went away immediately.

I think of my books and then I remember the cabanas with comfy looking couches that surrounded one side of their pool. If I could snag one of those, they would be perfect to read in. I saw ceiling fans and misters in them so I could be comfortable in the heat.

Making my decision, I text back a quick reply.

Sure, I would love to. Thanks.

I decide on the book and then think about what to wear. I have some skimpy bikinis but I don't want to look like I'm looking to get laid. Although if I'm honest, and if last night's dream is any indication, my body would like nothing more than to have Scott sink into it. Still, I'm not going there. I choose a more modest purple bikini with a bandeau top and boy short bottoms. I'll wear a maxi over it, because what if no one is swimming at this fancy pool party?

I realize my mistake as soon as I pull up to the house at 2:30. The cars in the driveway are not fancy and the music and yelling from the backyard is deafening. I ring the bell but no one answers so I try the door which is unlocked. I walk to the backyard and take in a scene that looks straight out of a 80s frat movie. Girls in skimpy bikinis and college age guys are flooding the backyard. A few of the cabana curtains are closed and I can only imagine what is going on inside. I am ready to turn around when I hear my name.

"Yasmin! Glad you could make it!" Luke shouts from the pool.

I look over and see him surrounded by girls, all of whom shoot me death glares at his acknowledgement. I wave and as I turn to the left, I see Scott, also surrounded by girls. Our eyes lock and his seem to darken. I'm frozen again, but then he looks away and I see one of the girls next to him pouting and thrusting up her fake looking breasts at him. She is blond and super thin - the complete opposite of me. He smiles and starts talking to her. I know then that I was misreading him and stupid to even fantasize about him. Obviously, his tastes run to size zero not six (on a lucky day).

I look around again and see the cabana closest to the deep end is vacant and doesn't seem to have anyone's stuff in it to lay claim. This is probably because most of the party is centered around the shallow end of the pool where everyone can stand and party more easily. I make my way over, plop down on the couch - it *is* comfy -

and start to read. Ryan and Owen come over to say hi and ask if I am okay over here by myself. I assure them that I'm fine and perfectly happy to be reading my book, alone. They bring me water and snacks and tell me to find them if I need anything else. I thank them, thinking that I really do like this family. Well, most of it.

I am at a *very* good part in my book, with the main characters about to finally have their epic sex scene when a guy comes over to the cabana. He's around six feet tall with wavy blond hair and a surfer's body. Board shorts ride low on his hips. He is cute but I'm not interested and *really* want to read my book.

"Hey, what is someone as hot as you doing here all alone *reading*?" he says, laughing in a mocking way.

"I like to read and this couch is comfortable," I tell him and look back down at my book, hoping he takes the hint.

Which, of course he doesn't. "You're dismissing me? Really? Do you know how many girls out there would love to be alone with me?" he says, waving his hand out toward the pool.

"Well then maybe you should go back out there and find one."

"Listen, bitch - ," he starts to say, the expression in his eyes frightening me, when the voice from my dreams cuts in.

"No you listen, *bitch*. She made it clear that she's not interested and now you need to step away."

I look up to see Scott, dripping wet, looking menacing with his piercings and tattoos, glaring at this guy. He also looks hot, like really hot. Most of his chest is covered with tats and I want to explore them all with my hands. And Okay, my mouth and tongue too. Damn, I need to control myself before I jump him.

"Whoa dude, I didn't know she was taken. Sorry man." Surfer boy makes a hasty exit.

"What are you doing here, Yasmin?" Scott asks looking angry at me now.

"Ryan invited me," I tell him defensively. I'm honestly a little hurt that he doesn't seem happy to see me after last night. I thought... I don't know what I thought, but I was obviously wrong.

"So, what, you come here in a *dress* with a book to read at a pool party?"

"I was planning to read today and I saw how comfy these couches looked last night, so why not? And, not that it's any of your business, but I have a bathing suit on under my dress."

"Well, then you need to get in the pool and have some fun." And before I can think about that, he reaches over and picks me up in his arms, runs for the pool and jumps in the deep end.

I push to the surface, my book floating somewhere behind me. Scott surfaces in front of me. "What the hell was that for?" I ask him, treading water.

"I wanted you to have some fun."

"I *was* having fun!"

"Reading? You're at a pool party and reading is more fun?"

"I was at a *really* good part in my book!"

"A good part?" he says grabbing my book from behind me. Looking at the cover, his smirk is back. "Yasmin, I would happily do anything to you that you read in one of these books."

What? Did he just say what I think he said? He *is* moving closer to me. We are about an inch away from each other now and the tension is almost too much to bear. I want him to kiss me. I *need* him to kiss me. All over my body. Oh God, he's leaning closer. Yes please.

"Scott," I whisper, pleading with my eyes for him to kiss me.

"Yeah, baby. I know." He moves his head toward me when all of a sudden he is hit in the head by a beach ball. I look past him and see the bikini girl smiling like she just won something.

And she did win. The spell is broken. Scott looks at me like a scared, cornered animal and then quickly swims to the shallow end and grabs bikini girl to dunk her under the water. They come up laughing. I can't believe how stupid I am. Did I really think that he would kiss me when he could be with her? I can't compete with her or any of the other girls at this party.

This is my cue to leave. I pull off my dress, grab my book, swim to the ladder and climb out of the pool. Ryan comes over to the cabana as I am toweling off and gathering my things.

"Are you okay? Scott can seem like an asshole sometimes, but he doesn't mean it. It's been a rough few months for all of us. You don't have to go. I will keep him away from you if you want." He's so sincere and I hug him tightly.

"Thanks, Ryan. But this isn't really my scene and I'm not in the mood to see Scott hooking up with someone else who I obviously can't compete with," I tell him honestly, instantly regretting it. Did I actually just admit to Ryan that I like Scott? What is wrong with me? He doesn't make fun of me or tell me I'm right.

Instead, he looks at me curiously and says, "You like him. I thought you did last night, but now I know. Give him a chance, Yasmin. I think the two of you would be good together. Like I said, he's really not the asshole that he seems to be sometimes. And as for competing with that girl, she has nothing on you. You look smoking hot in your bikini. There is not a guy here who wouldn't want to have a chance with you."

I look past him to see Scott in the pool with Bikini Girl. She is on his lap on the steps with her mouth latched onto his neck. He is looking straight at me while he rubs her back. He looks mad. What is *he* mad about? He reaches down and pulls her in for a kiss, looking at me the whole time.

"There's one who doesn't want to have a chance with me," I say as I try not to cry.

Ryan notices the stricken expression on my face and turns around to look behind him. "That little fucker." He turns back to me. "I'm sorry, Yasmin. There is no excuse for my brother or his behavior. Please don't let it influence your opinion of the rest of us. We all really like you."

"You don't need to apologize for him. And it's not like we are together or something. We had a good conversation last night and I thought that he was interested. But, I guess I was wrong. And I guess he felt the need to show me just how wrong I was. I really like everyone else in the family, too." I look at him. "How come no one has snatched you up, Ryan? Although I'm not interested in you that way—no offense—a girl would be lucky to have you!"

He laughs heartily and then turns serious. "No offense taken. There was a girl once and she pretty much shredded my heart. I don't let myself get close to anyone anymore. Not just because I am afraid of getting hurt. No one has ever come close to comparing to her, no matter how much she hurt me."

I reach out to touch his cheek. "I'm sorry, Ryan. You deserve to be happy. I'm glad that we are becoming friends."

"Me too, Yasmin. You're a cool girl." We both look over to where Scott is. He pulls his mouth away from Bikini Girl long enough to smirk at us and then he kisses her again, moving his hands under her bikini bottoms as she squirms.

"I *really* have to leave now," I say and Ryan nods, looking disappointed. I wave goodbye to Owen and Luke, who look at me a little sadly, and then I'm gone.

CHAPTER 4

Scott

I wake up to the mother of a hangover, alone in my bed. Thank God I wasn't drunk enough to let that girl in with me. She tried but I couldn't even kiss her after Yasmin left, let alone get it up. I shouldn't have kissed her while she was there, but seeing Yasmin in that sexy bikini, hugging Ryan with a smile made me want to kill my brother. I wanted to be the one hugging her but I knew I couldn't. I had to make sure that she didn't think what almost happened in the pool was going to happen again. So, I pretended to be into whatever her name was. I must have done a good job of convincing her because she left right away.

I *wanted* to want that girl and I tried to play along even though I felt nothing with her. Every time I tried, I saw Yasmin, with her lips parted and eyes going almost black when I told her I would do what those guys in romance books do for their girls. What the fuck was I thinking? Oh yeah, I was thinking that I needed to fuck her more than I needed my next breath. I would have, too, if whatever her name is hadn't hit me with that ball. Jealous little bitch stopped me from tasting those hot lips that I think of all day and night.

I should thank her, really I should. She wanted me to thank her in a carnal way last night and I thought about it, really planned on it. It wouldn't have been here, though. I don't bring anyone into my home, my bed. It is always their place or a hotel or even their car. Never mine. Not even Amber. I am saving my places, if not myself for the "one." I know it sounds cheesy, but I want what my parents have. I want someone special who is in the relationship just for me and nothing else.

Someone like Yasmin.

Fuck, I can't think like that. I barely know her. But I know that she is saving my niece and my family loves her. And I want her so bad that I can't even get it up for another, willing girl.

Maybe I do need to just fuck her. I could get her out of my system. I still don't think one night would be enough. We could go to her place or a hotel for a weekend. I would need a Costco size box of condoms. Or two. Shit, I'm about to come just thinking about it, about her. Time for a cold shower. Or maybe a hot one, while I think of her in my arms for those few seconds.

After my shower, which lasted longer than planned since I had to take care of myself twice to avoid being rock hard for the rest of the day, I head outside. Luke and his buddies are just about done cleaning up the backyard. Even though we have a shit ton of money, my parents make us clean up after ourselves. We don't leave extra work for anyone who works for us.

Blaine is one of the guys helping clean up and just seeing him makes me rage with jealousy and protectiveness. When I saw him go to Yasmin's cabana yesterday, I wanted to go all alpha on his ass. I know she's not mine and I don't want her to be, but she is not going to be anyone else's in front of me. That's fucked up, I know, since I was all over someone else in front of her. But, I can't help how I feel. As I walked up behind him and heard her trying to get him to leave, I wanted to protect her so much it hurt. I only ever feel that way about my family. And, she is not my family. I need to figure this shit with her out and fast.

"Hey man. What was your deal yesterday? You had Britt hanging off of you so I thought that cabana girl was fair game. Then you flip out on me, jump in the pool with her and get right back to Britt. Why were you cock blocking me if you didn't want her for yourself?" Blaine says, trying to look intimidating.

It's not working for him. "She was telling you to leave her alone and you weren't listening so how was that fair?" I spit out.

"Whoa, wait. Cabana girl? Was he messing with Yasmin?" Luke asks me.

"He was trying to."

"Dude, you stay the fuck away from her. I mean it. She is helping my niece and she doesn't need to deal with your shit." Luke turns on Blaine.

"What about your brother's shit? He is the most fucked up of all of us and he can touch her, play mind games with her? She's a hot piece of ass. I bet I could turn her no into a yes and make her scream my name all night if I tried a little harder. I would be okay with a no, too, if you know what I mean."

As Luke and I both lunge for Blaine, Ryan and Owen run out of the house and grab us, holding us back. "Get the fuck out of my house and don't come back!" I yell.

He looks between me and Luke. "You heard him," Luke says.

"You just fucked up, Luke. You won't get in now." He turns to the guys around us. "Come on. He's not going to be in the frat so you don't have to help him. Unless you and your brother want to apologize, Luke."

"Just go, asshole," Luke tells him, but I can see that he is upset.

When they are gone, I turn to Luke. "I'm sorry, bro, I had no idea that was going to happen."

"I know. It just sucks. I was set in Chicago but here I have to earn it all again. But he's a dick. You and Yasmin are more important."

"She is. I'm not. I'm not worth it."

"Shut the fuck up, Scott. How many times do we have to tell you that no one blames you for Amber? We *love* you. Why won't you believe us? You need to forgive yourself," Owen tells me and his eyes are glassy.

"That asshole was right about one thing. You can't play with Yasmin. When you left her in the deep end and went back to what's her name, she looked like someone kicked her puppy. If you want to be with her, go for it. But if you just want to play with her and use her, think again. We may not have known her long but I like what I know. And I know she is not one of your quick fucks," Ryan says, giving me a stern look.

"Yeah, I could tell how much you liked her. She liked you too, it looked like. The way she was all over you in her bikini." I am jealous again and I hate it, but that's how I feel.

"All over me?" Ryan reaches forward and grabs my shirt. I work out but I am no way delusional enough to think that I could hold my own with my brother. He's like a block of marble. "She gave me a hug because I was being nice to her. She was very clear in the fact that she is not interested in me, even if I wanted her. Which I don't. I *thought* that I wanted her with you, but after you practically fucked that girl in front of her and let her walk away, I am not so sure anymore. What the hell were you thinking?" He shoves me backward, looking pissed. I look around to where Owen and Luke are both standing with their arms crossed, glaring at me.

I know that they aren't going to stand for some bullshit answer so I give them the truth. "I-I think I may want to be with her. I mean, really be with her. Not just for a one night fuck. But I'm afraid that she is going to use me like Amber did. Or I'm going to fuck up and hurt her. Then, she won't be there for Alex. So, I thought that if I looked like I was getting it on with someone else, she would stop looking at me like she wanted me to kiss her."

"First off, Yasmin is nothing like that psycho bitch Amber. We all hated Amber and I don't think any of us feel that way about Yasmin." Ryan looks to my brothers who shake their heads. "She's really cool and smart and doesn't put up with your behavior, which is just what you need. Second, I don't think she is the type of person who would abandon Alex if things go south with you. She may not want to come around if that happens, but we could take Alex to her. And third, you need to have a better opinion of yourself. You may try to give off the asshole vibe, but we know you better. Like Owen said, *no one* in this family blames you for what happened. It was not your fault. Please believe that, Scott. As lucky as you would be to have Yasmin, she would be lucky to have you, too."

"You all hated Amber? You were nice to her when I brought her around."

"We were nice to her because we wanted you to be happy. Even Mom couldn't stand her. We were afraid that she was using you, we just didn't know how much. *We* carry guilt for that, for her, too, you know." Luke and Owen nod at that, too. How could I not have known? And they feel guilty? Wow. Before I can process what he told me, Ryan continues. "Now, are you going to man up and go for it with Yasmin?"

"Yeah, I think I am." I tell him, taking a deep breath. "Can I have her phone number, Ry?"

"Hell yeah," he tells me taking out his phone.

"We'll help you if you need anything," Owen says.

"Yeah, you know Owe and I are better with the women than you two old guys," Luke says with a laugh. I know my brothers would help me and would be there for me no matter what. Maybe it's time I start realizing that I deserve their love. I'm not quite there yet, but I have hope. That's something that I thought I lost nine months ago.

* * *

<u>Yasmin</u>

It's been a busy day at the store. Sundays always seem to be a big book buying day. I need it.

The website is coming along and Erika keeps telling me to read that article but I haven't had time. She thinks that maybe I can get a small business loan to buy the software when it is ready. I don't know if I could get a loan, but if this software is really that good, I could sell my house. It wouldn't be a great choice, but to save the bookstore I would do it.

Sam arrives, so I head to my office to grab my purse so I can get something to eat. As I walk in the door, I grab my phone and notice a text had come in a few minutes before.

Unknown: Hey Yasmin. It's Scott.

My breath catches in my throat.

Unknown: Are you there?

Me: I'm here now. What do you want?

He replies almost immediately.

Unknown: Honestly, I want you. Will you go out with me tonight?

Is he kidding me? He was just with another girl *in front of me* yesterday and now he expects me to go out with him?

Me: What about bikini girl?

Unknown: Bikini girl?

I don't answer him. If he can't figure it out, that's his problem. I start to leave the backroom when he texts again. I guess he got it.

Unknown: OH! She's a non-issue.

Me: Really? Because you couldn't get away from me fast enough to make your way back to her yesterday. You looked pretty busy with her tongue down your throat when I left.

Unknown: I couldn't get away from you fast enough because I wanted to kiss you more than I wanted my next breath and that scared the shit out of me.

Me: I wanted to kiss you too. And it scared me too. But I didn't run away to be with someone else in front of you.

Unknown: I shouldn't have done that. I was hoping that I could make you not want me anymore if I acted like an asshole. I didn't want to be with her. I wasn't with her after you left. I only want you.

Me: You have a really funny way of showing it.

I swallow and finish typing, deciding to just lay it out there. What do I have to lose at this point?

It hurt. Seeing you with her really hurt me. After the barbeque Friday night, I thought that you liked me. I didn't know if you would be at the party, but I was hoping that you would be. I wanted to see you again.

Unknown: I DO like you, Yasmin. I am SO sorry that I hurt you. I can't promise to never hurt you again. But, I'll try my best not to. Please go out with me.

Me: I want to but I can't. I don't trust you. I saw the girls you were with at the party. I can't compete with them. You may think you want me, but I'm just something new and different for you. You'll realize it and then walk away for something better. Someone thinner. I'm sorry, but no.

Unknown: You can't compete with them? Are you kidding me? They are nothing next to you. You were the hottest girl at that party. Every guy there wanted to be with you. I don't need someone "thinner." I mean WTF ,Yasmin.? You have to know how perfect your body is. How can I prove that? I'll do anything. Well, almost anything. As long as it's legal :)

Me: Thanks for the compliments but I don't know what you can do. I have always wanted to be wooed, though. Maybe you could do that? If you want...

Unknown: Wooed?

Me: Yeah, you know, romance me. Make me feel special.

Unknown: Umm, you ARE special but no one has ever called me romantic. I am not sure how to do that. You mean flowers and shit?

Me: It could be flowers or it could be whatever you want. It would just show me that you really are interested and that I am worth putting in a little bit of effort for. If you don't want to, that's fine.

Unknown: You ARE worth it and I definitely want to show you that. I'll think of something :) Can I keep texting you while I attempt this romance thing?

Me: Yes, yes you can. I would like that.

Unknown: I'd like that too. I better go now so I can try to plan this out. Talk to you soon.

Me: I can't wait to see what you come up with :)

I close my eyes and resist the urge to jump up and down. Maybe I wasn't wrong about him Friday night. I walk next door for lunch with a smile on my face.

CHAPTER 5

<u>Yasmin</u>

Scott's texted me several times a day since he first started three days ago. Mostly just asking how I am doing or what I am watching on TV at night. Oh, and if I am reading anything sexy that I want to tell him about. I keep saying no to that. I'm not ready to share that with him, although every time he asks, a shiver runs through my body. It's become comfortable and fun, but there has been no formal wooing yet. Although the multiple texts a day do make me feel special, I can't help thinking that he has given up. It makes me a little sad, but at least we're friends now, I guess.

Scott's texts have also been taking my mind off the problems with my store. I'm still keeping a steady stream of customers, just not enough to make up for the slow periods we've been through. Sean is almost done with the website and my friends Sarah and Lisa from Girls with Books have promised to promote the new website on their blog and Facebook page. Sam has set up a Facebook page for the store and she is posting when new books arrive and about local author events. I really need to book a major author event but my store doesn't have that kind of clout anymore. My parents used to have major authors and celebrities in monthly but that dried up a few years ago when one of the local Barnes and Noble stores became an event store. I know we aren't a huge volume place, but our customers would support an event. I just have to figure out how to get one!

I'm hanging out in the front of the store with Erika when Alex and Gary come in. I introduce everyone. Alex needs new books and Gary wants to pick up a new football book. I point Gary to his book and head over to YA with Alex.

"How are you doing, sweetie?" I ask her, noticing that she looks tired.

"I'm fine ...no, I'm really not," she tells me, sitting in one of the chairs. "My mom's birthday is in a few weeks and I'm not sure if I can handle it."

"Honestly, my parent's birthdays aren't hard for me because I still celebrate those days for them. I invite my friends over and we eat their favorite foods. Now, the day that they died is different. I can't really function on that day. But I choose to celebrate their lives on their birthdays," I explain to her, stroking her hair.

"Wow, I never thought of it that way. I can do that, I can celebrate them. I don't have any friends except for you, though. Would you come over and be with me and my family?"

"Of course I will! When is it?"

"June 30," she tells me, looking excited now.

I take out my phone and enter it into my calendar. "Done. I'll be there. Anything else I can help you with?"

"Actually, there is. I'm so bored at home. Could I help you here?"

"Oh Alex, I would love to have you help me. But I can't afford to take on any more employees right now. I'm sorry."

"You don't have to pay me. Could I just volunteer? Maybe help with story time or shelve books?"

"I would love to have you volunteer! Are you sure it's okay with your grandparents?"

"Is what okay with her grandparents?" Gary asks from behind me.

"Alex was asking if she could volunteer here to get out of the house," I explain.

"That's a fabulous idea! Just coordinate the days and times and we'll make sure she's here. You always manage to bring a smile to our girl's face and I would love to see that more often."

I'm about to tell him that she makes me smile too when I spot Hank from Office Depot entering the store. I excuse myself and meet him by the cash wrap. "I didn't order anything this week Hank."

"This is a special delivery for you today," he says with a smile motioning to the box he has placed on the counter.

"A special delivery" I ask in confusion. "What is it?"

He opens the box with a flourish while he says, "One of every type of pen in our store!"

I look inside the box in shock seeing everything from the expensive ones I have salivated over to the cheap ones that I have passed up. And oh holy hell, there is every color of Sharpie and Sharpie pen imaginable in there. This box is a thing of beauty.

As I am still standing there with my mouth open, Hank tells me, "This goes along with the box." He hands me an envelope.

Yasmin is written on it. My heart starts beating and I know who it is from before I open it.

My Dearest Yasmin,

I am hoping that this letter finds you well.

OK, that is all the fancy shit I can write. I know you want to be wooed but you said that I can do it my way so here goes.

I didn't want to get you flowers yet because I can't decide what kind I want to get you and I don't know what you like. The same with chocolates. I don't know what you like there, either. But, I DO know that you like pens, all pens, you said. So, here are lots and lots of pens. I hope you put them to good use and don't just keep them in the box looking pretty. Can pens look pretty? Fuck if I know. But I guess they may be pretty to you. I do know you're gorgeous to me and I hope this gift makes you feel special. Text me when you get this—if you want...

Scott

Oh my God! I am being wooed, really wooed and he started with pens! PENS! I could probably die happy from this right now. Okay, not really, because he hasn't even kissed me yet, but I feel like I could burst with happiness. I am definitely going to text him, but first I have a letter to write.

"Can you guys take a letter to Scott for me? It should only take me a few minutes to write it," I ask when I walk back to Alex and Gary.

"Sure," Gary says to me with amusement in his eyes.

"Was that box from Uncle Scott? It looked like it was from Office Depot," Alex asks me with confusion on her face.

"It *is* from him and it is also from Office Depot. He bought me pens, lots of pens. Let me grab one and I'll get that letter written!" I smile at her as I turn to go grab a pen. But, which one?

"Are you and Uncle Scott going out?" Alex asks me as I search through the box.

"No, we aren't. We're just friends right now." I grab a green Sharpie from the box and turn to her. "If we did decide to date, though, would that be alright with you?"

"That would be awesome!" she replies. I look up at Gary, who smiles back at me.

"I think it would be awesome, too," he tells me.

"Great. I just wanted to make sure. I mean, I don't know if we will, but I wanted to make sure it was okay and not weird and now I'm rambling." I can feel myself turning red.

"Why don't you go write your letter while we pick out our books, Yasmin?" Gary says, kindly. I take the Sharpie back to my office and do just that.

* * *

Scott

I got a one word text from Yasmin. "Thanks." That's it, just thanks. I thought the pens would make her happy. And the letter, I thought that was good. I thought I was on the right track. What the hell am I going to do now? I must really suck to just get that one word.

Shit! I need to finish this software but I want to win this woman over. I may have to postpone this wooing thing until the software is finished and I can focus solely on her, but I don't want to wait that long. It could be two months or more. No, not more. I will get this done in my two month time frame. I have to. But, I also have to have Yasmin. I drop my head in my hands as it all overwhelms me.

"Hey son, I rang the doorbell but I don't think you could hear me over this music," my dad says as he enters my lair. "Are you okay? Is this project too much for you? We can push it back. Lord knows we don't need the money."

"No Dad. I can do it. I promised you and Mom. I won't let you down. Again." I can't look him in the eye as I say this.

"You have never let us down! How many times can I tell you that what happened to your sister was not your fault? The only thing I need from you is for you to forgive yourself. I love you, son."

I look up to see his eyes glistening. Mine are wet too. I know he means it. My mom said it. My brothers said it. And now my dad said it too. I don't think that they would all lie to me, so maybe I need to believe it myself. "I love you too, Dad."

"Now, let's see if I can put a smile on your face," he says, handing me an envelope.

Scott

That one word makes me stop breathing for a moment and fills me with hope.

"Enjoy your letter. I'll let myself out," my dad says and I barely register him leaving as I open the envelope.

Wonderful, sexy Scott,

I LOVE my pens SOOO much! I can't believe you did this for me. I feel special and properly wooed. I can't imagine that you would be able to top the pens, but I wanted to help you with some of your questions. So, here are some things that I like:

Milk chocolate and caramel

Cupcakes - chocolate with white frosting, red velvet and lemon are favorites, but I'll try almost any kind. Except bacon. Bacon and pastries just seems too weird.

Blue, purple and white colored flowers. Tulips are my favorite. I like flowers that have a meaning to them, although roses are good too!

Blue and purple used to be my favorite colors but green, especially the almost emerald colored green of a certain someone's eyes, is becoming my favorite color now.

Handwritten letters. I never before realized how special getting a handwritten letter can make a person feel. So, thanks for that.

Oh, and you, I like you.

Yasmin

Holy shit! I didn't suck. She liked it and she likes me! Yes, oh fuck, yes! I haven't felt this good in, well in forever. Even before the murders, before I knew what Amber was and what she did, I never felt this happy. And it's all because of a sexy, pen loving bookworm. Who would've thought? I grab my phone and text her.

Me: Hey beautiful. Are you busy?

Yasmin: No. It's slow right now in the store. Did you get my letter?

Me: I did. I loved it. You're right about a handwritten letter making you feel special. I feel special now. I can't remember the last time I felt that way.

Yasmin: I 'm glad that I could be the one to do that for you, to make you feel that way.

Me: Me too. So, you like my eyes, huh? Do you think about them often?

I can't stop myself from teasing her. And I really want to know the answer.

Yasmin: Oh God, I knew I shouldn't have told you.

Me: But you did and you didn't answer my question.

Yasmin: Yes, I think about your eyes. Are you happy now?

Me: What do you do when you think about them? Do you get yourself off?

Please say yes, I think to myself. I want to know that she gets off to thoughts of me like I do to thoughts of her.

Yasmin: I am turning off my phone now. Goodbye.

Fucking A! What is wrong with me? Asking her if she gets herself off by thinking of my eyes. Who says that to a girl before even taking her out for a date? I know I'm not experienced at all with this wooing thing, but I thought I had some common sense. But, no. I am such a dumbass, letting my throbbing cock think for me. How am I going to fix this one? Well, I can start by looking up flowers and what they mean. Particularly purple, blue and white ones. Dammit. I hope it's enough.

CHAPTER 6

<u>Yasmin</u>

I still can't believe the text conversation with Scott yesterday. I thought we were on the same page and then he has to get crude with me. Yes, I do get myself off when I think of his eyes. And lips. And hot body. But I wouldn't tell him that in a text. What if someone saw it on my phone? Or his. God, I would die of embarrassment if Maggie or Gary saw that. Maybe I was expecting too much and he's really just trying to get me into his bed for a night.

I need to stop thinking about Scott and start focusing on what I need to do. The website launches today and I am hoping to see orders start coming in. We can't compete with Amazon but I think we have good prices. Sean did a great job with the design and Sarah and Lisa have been promoting us like crazy. I should look at that article from Erika, but I can't yet. I know if she thinks it's so great, I will too. Then I'll be forced to make the hard choice and put my house on the market.

The house that I grew up in and my parents loved. It's a beautiful Craftsman style home off of Alta Drive. That used to be the

place to live here in Vegas. Before Summerlin and Seven Hills became so popular. Some celebrities and politicians live in the area
still. My parents bought the house years ago when there was no
Barnes and Noble *or* Borders in town and the store was successful.
It was paid off 10 years ago. Through the thin times over the last 5
years, they took out a mortgage on it to pay the bills. My dad said
that other than me and the store, he was the most proud of buying
the house for my mom. The thought of selling it makes me sick,
but I can't bear to take out a second mortgage and run the risk of
not being able to pay. Then I would lose the house *and* the store. I
will have to decide soon. Erika says the software comes out in 2
months.

I start to reach for the article when the door opens and Alex
comes in for her first day of volunteering. And she's not alone.
Could this day get any worse? I am happy to see Alex but not *him*.
I'm not going to forget the text conversation that easily. Bikini Girl
would probably like something like that, but not me. I mean, we
haven't even been out on a date yet. Yeah, I know it's my fault that
we haven't, but that doesn't mean I should be treated like a slut.

"Hi Yasmin! I can't wait to do story time today! I printed out coloring sheets and brought cookies and feather boas for the kids to
wear while I read Fancy Nancy!" Alex says with a smile, carrying
an overflowing box.

"Are you okay with that big box? Let me help you!"

"I'm great. I've got it. I'm going to head back to the kids area to
set up." She is practically skipping down the aisles and it makes me
happy to see. Not happy enough to let Scott off for not helping her
though.

I whirl on him. "How could you not help her?"

"I have my hands full," he protests as he whips a large bunch of
purple flowers from behind his back. "They are hyacinths. They
mean I am sorry and please forgive me. I *am* sorry. I didn't mean to
make you uncomfortable with my texts yesterday. Or cheapen

what we have been sharing. Our conversations mean a lot to me. Even though we haven't known each other long, *you* mean a lot to me."

I take the flowers from him and look up into his eyes where I see the remorse there. He also looks a little scared. His words touch me and I want to put him at ease, so I do what we do best and joke with him. "What, no letter?"

He smiles the biggest smile I have seen from him and it turns his eyes a sparkling green. "Of course there's a letter. This wouldn't be a proper wooing without a letter." Reaching into his back pocket, he withdraws a small envelope, with a small stuffed bear attached to it. "Or a pen," he adds while pulling the head off of the bear to reveal a pen inside.

One of my last walls falls at my feet and I can't stop myself. I drop the flowers on the counter and throw myself at him. He catches me in his arms in a crushing hug. Our bodies are pressed together in all the right places and it feels better than anything I can every remember feeling. My nipples harden while pressed against his firm chest and I can feel him harden again my stomach. I am glad that I wore my high wedges today instead of my usual Toms. We are breathing hard and I am not sure I will be able to resist him, regardless of the fact that we are in the middle of my bookstore. I don't *want* to resist him. We start to turn our heads to each other.

"Yasmin, do you have markers I can use? I left mine at home," Alex shouts while coming around the corner. We jump apart like we've burned each other and I try to get my breathing under control.

"Yes, they are in the stockroom. There's an entire cabinet of supplies for story times and kids parties. Just ask Danny and he'll show you. Do you remember the code that I gave you for the door?"

"Yep. Are you okay?" Alex looks at us curiously. "You both look a little out of breath. Were you fighting? I thought you would like the flowers, Yasmin. Uncle Scott said that he made you mad and was trying to apologize." She looks at him intently. "Did you not apologize? Is Yasmin still mad at you?"

"We're good, Baby Girl. She liked the flowers. I better get going. I have a ton of work to do. Someone will be by to pick you up." He kisses the top of her head and turns to go.

"You're not coming back to pick her up?" I ask, disappointed when he shakes his head no. "Oh, well can I have my letter and pen?"

He looks down, like he forgot that they were still in his hands. When he looks up again, his trademark smirk is back. "Of course. I wouldn't want to deprive you of anything that you want." He hands them to me with a wink and saunters out the door.

I sag against the counter as Alex looks at me with amusement in her eyes. "You've got it bad. But, so does he," she tells me as she skips off laughing.

I look down at the envelope in my hands and slowly tear it open.

Beautiful, sexy Yasmin,

If you're reading this, I hope that means that you've forgiven me (or are at least considering it) and I haven't yet done anything else to upset you. I love that you wrote back to me and I hope that we can keep these letters going. I'm really liking putting a pen to paper for you. My life is surrounded by computers and I have always believed that technology was better. But, at least in this case, I think the old fashioned way may be better. I'm not going to stop texting you, though, but I'll try to behave. :)

In your letter, you told me things that you like. I want to return the favor, but I'd rather tell you things I hate. I'm just that kind of guy. So, here is my list:

I hate people who use others. It is the one thing that is unforgivable to me. I would rather have someone ask me for something outright than use me.

I hate being proper. My family is being honored at a fancy ball in a few months for our charity work and advances in technology. Our company's PR people have told me that I have to wear a regular tux with a tie and take out my piercings. So, no tats or piercings showing. Oh, and I have to let them style my hair into something conservative. My parents love me, tats and all, so why can't I be me?

I hate fancy food. Give me a burger and fries or some mac and cheese any day!

I hate that my family had to move because of me and my actions. That's all I can tell you now. Maybe one day, I can tell you more, but I just can't right now.

I used to hate myself but there is a beautiful pen loving bookworm who is starting to make me believe that I am not all bad.

I hate that I haven't kissed her yet and I hope to have the chance to do that soon.

Scott

I am swooning. Seriously, honest to God swooning. I want to find Scott right now so I can comfort him, assure him that I don't want anything but him from him, tell him that I think he is awesome the way he is and oh yeah, kiss the fuck out of that gorgeous mouth of his.

I notice that some texts came in while I was reading the letter. I swipe my finger over the screen to read them.

Scott: I'm sorry that I had to leave and I can't come back later. I have to finish this project in the next two months and it is seriously kicking my ass. I would rather be with you. Having you in my arms for even just those few seconds felt AMAZING!

Scott: Yasmin, are you there? Please don't be mad!!

Scott: Yas? I'm so sorry I left. I can come back. Just tell me we're OK, please.

Shit. I hope he isn't on his way back. I don't want him to think I am upset. I'm not at all.

Me: I'm sorry--I just saw your texts. I was reading your beautiful letter. I 'm not mad. Go take care of your work while I write your letter.

Me: Oh and I like that you called me Yas :)

Scott: Whew! I was worried, but glad you liked my letter. I can't wait for yours.

Scott: Yas, Yas, Yas, Yas....

Me: Will you call me that when I see you in person next time?

Scott: Definitely. When can I see you? I mean, can I ask that? Shit, I don't know how to act around you.

Oh, hell. I've done this to him. I don't want him to act differently around me. Okay, maybe a little less cocky would be good, but I don't want to change him.

Me: Please don't try to act differently around me! I mean it, I like you just how you are! Well, maybe don't kiss other girls in front of me again, but everything else about you is pretty wonderful and sexy.

Me: As for seeing me, I could bring Alex home tonight if you think you can take a break from your project.

Scott: Thank you for saying that. I like you too. And I definitely won't be kissing any other girls in front of you OR when you're not around. You're the only one I want to kiss.

Scott: Yes, please, please come find me tonight. I'll let everyone know that you are dropping off Alex.

Me: OK. I will see you then. Don't work too hard :)

Scott: I have to work hard but I can't wait to see you. Goodbye Yas.

Me: Bye.

I close my phone thinking about what I am going to write in my letter. The day seems to drag. Alex does great at story time and helps Danny in the backroom. I pay some bills—and watch my bank account dwindle—and fill some orders from the website. I'm excited to see us getting business from there, but my mind is on Scott and seeing him later tonight.

* * *

Scott

I've been working my ass off all day trying to break through the latest obstacle that popped up for the software. I want to be at a good stopping point when Yas gets here. I finally figure out what I need to adjust in the programming for this particular part of the program when I hear my doorbell ring. I jump up and then look down. Shit! I was planning on changing before she got here. I tend to get caught up in my work and frequently spill coffee or food on myself. You can't completely disguise the nerd with some muscles. I also wear my glasses when I work instead of contacts. So, here I am, in a coffee stained t-shirt, frayed jeans and my glasses. My hair is a mess from running my hands through it, too.

The doorbell rings again while I am trying to figure out how fast I can make it upstairs. Fuck it, I tell myself. If I don't answer the door, this worry will all be for nothing anyway. I'll let her in and then tell her to wait while I go change. I practically run to the door.

"Hey!" I say as I swing the door open. But, Yasmin is already crossing the backyard. Dammit, I'm an idiot. "Yas," I yell.

She turns and smiles a relieved smile when she sees me. "I thought maybe you weren't home or you were too busy to answer. I didn't want to bother you," she says, worrying her lip between her teeth while she walks back to my door.

"No, no. You are never a bother. A welcome distraction, but no bother. Besides, I finished what I needed to before you got here."

"Why didn't you answer the door then?" She looks worried now.

I reach out and run my thumb over the crease between her eyes. "I realized that I look like shit and was trying to figure out if I could run upstairs fast enough before answering the door. I finally decided to answer it first and then change after. Guess I wasn't fast enough."

"Oh. Well, you don't look like shit. Maybe a little rumpled, but still good," She tells me as we move inside and I close and lock the door. I love my family but I need some alone time with this beautiful girl.

"Really? My shirt has like four coffee stains on it!"

"You could just take it off," Yas says and then clamps a hand over her mouth.

"You want me to take off my shirt?" I ask, feeling my cock harden at the thought of her wanting me out of my clothes. I reach behind me and grab my shirt but stop to wait for her to say it.

"I can't believe I said that out loud." Not the answer I wanted and I start to let go of my shirt. "But, yes, I do want you to take your shirt off. I want to see your tattoos."

I am now hard as a piece of steel as I remove my shirt and see her eyes darken. I stand still and let her look her fill. She steps forward and starts to extend her arm out, but stops. "You can touch me. In fact there is not much else that would make me happier than having your hands on me. If you want to touch me, you don't ever have to ask, Yas." I know my voice is husky because I can barely talk with how aroused I am by the thought of Yas and her hands on me. I wait patiently while I see her making her decision, the choice clear when her eyes darken and she reaches forward.

CHAPTER 7

<u>Yasmin</u>

I nearly moaned out loud when Scott said that I could touch him anytime and then called me Yas. My parents used to call me Yassie but no one else has ever shortened my name. In Scott's husky voice, it is the sexiest thing I have ever heard.

I move forward and take his right wrist in my hand, turning his arm to the side. His forearm is covered with a skyline that wraps around his arm and covers him from wrist to elbow. There are colors here and there making the buildings come to life. A lake wraps around the bottom.

"Is this Chicago?" I ask as I run my fingers over the lake, moving up to the buildings and then the night sky.

"Yes. I got it before we moved. I had been trying to decide what to put there and it just seemed right." He is biting his lip ring into his mouth as I caress his forearm.

I nod and move my fingers further up his arm to the anchor with "Gary" curved over the top.

"For your dad." I smile and meet his eyes, which are enclosed in glasses. They somehow manage to make him look even hotter, especially with his eyebrow piercing peeking out over the top of them.

"Yeah. He was a Navy SEAL."

I move over to his other arm because I am afraid if I touch his chest, I won't be able to move away from it. This forearm is a mix of video game characters as well as characters from Star Wars *and* Star Trek. I run my fingers over Yoda and tell him, "I love Star Wars *and* Star Trek, too! I'm not much for video games but this is one cool tat."

"Really? You like them both?" His eyes are on fire, but with more than just desire, turning them a bright green. I nod yes and he continues to talk as I move my fingers to trace the outline of Spock. "Video games were my best friends when I was in high school. I was the nerd in school, always bent over a computer or playing a game. Math and science fascinated me. Girls interested me, but they didn't know I existed, other than to copy my homework. My older and younger brothers were all big men on campus, but not me. I wasn't bullied physically because Ryan would have beaten the shit out of anyone who touched me, but being ignored wasn't exactly fun. So, my games became somewhat of a lifeline for me."

I lean over and place a kiss on Mario. "Well then, I'm going to have to start playing some video games to thank these guys for being there for you. How did you get like this?" A shiver runs through him as I gesture to his hot, muscled body.

"Like this?" He cocks that pierced eyebrow and I know that he is teasing me.

"You know what I mean. You *know* how hot you are. And I was at the pool party, remember? You were swarmed by girls. If you don't want to tell me, that's fine."

"You think I'm hot?" I roll my eyes and start to step back. He reaches out to stop me. "Things changed in college. I roomed with an exercise freak, Brent, who convinced me to actually leave the room and work out. I didn't become as hard core as him, but I developed some muscles that the girls seemed to appreciate. Working for my parents' company didn't hurt, either. The Griffin name is as much an aphrodisiac for some women as my muscles are. The tats and piercings came later but seemed to add to the appeal. Chicks dig a bad guy."

"I don't think you're a bad guy."

"That's because you don't know everything about me. One day I will tell you. But, I can't right now."

"That's fine. We haven't even been on a date. I don't expect you to spill all of your secrets to me yet."

"Thanks. And FYI, this is a date. At least to me."

I smile at him. "Me too and FYI, it's a great first date so far."

My fingers continue their journey and I see the names Erin and Dave above and below "Never Forget." From my talks with Alex, I know that these are her parents. I lean in to kiss this one too but Scott stops me. "Don't. Please don't," he tells me in a strained voice.

"Okay, I won't. I'll stop touching you." I lower my head, hating that I messed this up.

"Fuck, no, don't stop. Your fingers feel amazing." He lifts my chin and looks me in the eye when he says, "I don't mean to be an asshole. That one just hurts too much. I don't want you tainted by it."

"You're not being an asshole. I shouldn't have tried to kiss it. You told me I could touch, not kiss, and I already did it once without asking. But for the record, I want to give you comfort if I can," I tell him sincerely.

"Let me clarify." The smirk is back along with the dark emerald color in his eyes. "You may touch me *and* kiss me anytime you want on any part of my body. And, you just being here with me is a comfort," he adds, the smirk replaced by a soft smile.

"I might just take you up on that."

"Please do."

I move around to stand behind him. The entire span of his shoulders is covered by his mother's name. I trace the letters and tell him how awesome I think it is. Below that is a tattoo of a giant griffin. The mythical half lion, half bird looks fierce and proud. The colors and detail are incredible.

"Wow, this is amazing." I start to trace it with my fingers but instead lean in and trace it with my tongue.

A shudder runs through his whole body and he jerks forward. "Jesus, Yas, you almost made me come like a horny teenager."

I give the griffin one last kiss and step back. "I'm sorry but I had to do it. My fingers wouldn't do it justice."

"I'm not complaining. I just want you to know how you affect me."

"You-you affect me, too." And he does. I never thought of a back as being sexy but damn if his isn't. All those lean muscles under that tight, hot skin are making me a little weak in the knees.

"Are you wet for me?"

I hesitate and then answer honestly. "Yes, I'm always wet when you are around."

"Fuck. I didn't think I could get any harder but damn if that didn't do it."

"Is this too much? Should I stop touching you? I mean, we haven't even kissed and I'm not going to have sex with you tonight."

He hangs his head and doesn't say anything for at least a minute and I start to back away. "Don't stop. Please. It *is* torture for me, but I want your hands on me. I can take care of myself later."

I move forward and trace the words that cover his lower back.

We must learn to live together as brothers or perish together as fools. -Martin Luther King, Jr.

"I'm guessing that this is for your brothers but I am surprised by an MLK quote."

"When we were younger, my brothers and I fought so much that my mom finally told us that we were fools for not appreciating each other. I saw the quote one day and it reminded me of that."

"You guys are closer now, I mean you seem to be," I say as I move back to the front of him. He nods.

I look him in the eye as I trace his last name, which covers him from one shoulder to the other, just under his collarbone. "This one is self-explanatory," I say with a chuckle. His jaw is clenched so tight that his teeth must be grinding and his lip is red around his piercing from where he was biting it. I want to reach up and lick it better, but we aren't at that point just yet. "Only two more. Is it still okay?"

He gives me a terse nod and I move my fingers to his right pec. His body is truly a work of art and not just from his tats. He is lean but still beautifully muscular. There is a light dusting of black hair on his chest, but not enough to distract from his tattoos. He also has a six pack that I will be touching very soon and I'm not sure how either of us is going to survive that. For now, I focus on the swirling words just above his currently hard nipple. "Alexandra Marie." Ahh, this is for Alex. I'm not surprised at all. I know how much he loves that girl and I love that he has inked her name on him. I want to kiss this one but I am afraid it will snap the tension that is barely keeping us in place.

Instead, I move down to the rows of numbers covering his stomach from the top of his ribs to the edge of his low slung jeans. They are all 0s and 1s. "This is called binary code, right?" I ask as I feather my fingers across the ridges of his ribs and then his glorious abs. As I move lower, he grabs my fingers.

"Yes. It's part of the first program that I created for our company." He continues to hold my hands in his. "I'm sorry but I have to stop you. I can't take any more."

"Thank you for letting me know about your tats. I'm sorry that I–I did this to you. I really can't have sex with you tonight. I'll go now." I start to turn, but he grabs my arm.

"I don't want you to go, Yas. I just need to cool down a little. How about I go change like I planned but I'll throw in a cold shower? Will you wait for me and we can grab some dinner from the main house or order something?"

"I don't want to leave either. How about I go up to the house and grab us some food. I can bring it back while you're showering and then we can eat."

"If you go up there, you'll get stuck with my parents and Alex for a little while at least."

"So, take a warm shower and not a cold one." I tell him, giving a meaningful look to the bulge in his jeans.

"Fuck, Yas, you need to go now," he grounds out as I slip out the door.

* * *

Scott

I barely make it to the shower before the need to take my cock in hand overwhelms me. Yasmin touching my tats was one of the most erotic things I have ever experienced. Damn, her hands felt good on me. I relive those hands—and her mouth—while I tug and pull myself to completion. As usual when I'm thinking of her, it's intense and nearly brings me to my knees. I need to have her soon. She told me not tonight, but now that I have her in my house, I want her in my bed.

Wait, what? She's in *my* house. I don't ever let a woman in my house. Shit. It's too late now, I can't make her leave with some lame excuse. I tell myself that it doesn't mean anything and it is good that she doesn't want to fuck. I don't know how I would explain the need to go outside to do it. That would be a big mood killer for her, I think. No, I know it. She wanted to be wooed so kicking her out of my house before fucking her senseless would guarantee that I don't see her again. And despite my fuck ups and hang ups, I want more than one night with her.

I have to get myself off two more times before I'm under control enough to go back downstairs. As I come down the stairs, Yas is coming in the door with the food. "Here, let me help." I bound down the stairs and grab some bags from her. I take them to the coffee table and start unloading them. "They sent enough to feed an army. I'm glad that you have a good appetite."

When she doesn't answer or move into my line of vision, I turn to find her frozen in place with tears glistening in her eyes. "What's wrong? Did you want to eat in the dining room? I just thought we could hang out here and it'd be more comfortable." She shakes her head and I am even more confused. "Tell me, Yas, what did I do?" I'm feeling a little panicked now.

She swallows hard and closes her eyes. "I'm *not* going to eat all of this food. I mean, I know I'm not thin and hot like the pool party girls, but I don't eat that much. I didn't even eat much when I came to the barbeque. Some big helpings of sides but not much of anything else. I told you I couldn't compete with the skinny girls." Tears are rolling down her cheeks and she is shaking now.

What the fuck have I done? I made this amazing girl cry by making a stupid remark even though she *had* told me that she couldn't compete with those skanks at the party. But hadn't I told her that she was so much better than them? I must not have been convincing enough.

I place my hands on her arms as I speak. "Look at me." She doesn't respond and I move one hand under her chin to tip it up to me. "Open your eyes and look at me Yasmin. *Please.*" The please seems to do it and her eyes open. Tears are still falling from her eyes and I catch as many as I can with my fingers.

"Baby, I'm so sorry for making you cry. I didn't mean anything by what I said. I told you once before that I like it that you have a good appetite. I also told you that those pool skanks meant nothing to me. You mean something to me, though." I think she may mean everything to me but I'm not ready to tell her that yet.

"You say that but you haven't seen me in a bikini or, umm... naked."

"I *did* see you in a bikini. At the pool party. I may not have been next to you, but you looked pretty damn hot from where I was sitting. I haven't seen you naked, but I *have* felt you pressed against me and I know how good that felt. I also know that I couldn't even get it up for Bikini Girl, as you call her, but I just had to jack off three times in the shower because you were touching my tats while you were fully clothed. So, don't ever think that you are not hot to me."

She smiles then, a big bright smile that lights up her whole face. "Three times? Really?" I smile back and nod. "Wow. I'm sorry I fell apart. I obviously have some body image issues. Although, I'm not willing to stop eating good food so I can be thinner."

"You could work out with me. I mean, I definitely don't want you to lose any of these hot curves," I tell her while gripping her hips. "But if you want to get fit, I can help."

"I'd like that."

"Cool, we'll figure out a schedule later. For now, let's eat. Do you want to watch the new Star Trek movie?" I let her go and move to my Blu Ray collection.

"Yes! I love that movie." I seriously think that I could fall in love with her.

CHAPTER 8

<u>Yasmin</u>

We settle in on the couch to eat and watch the movie. I finally have my wits about me enough to look around. This is definitely a guy's place. Dark wood floors and black leather couches dominate the living room. There is some cool comic book style artwork on the walls and a few family pictures. It is an open, loft style floor plan with a small dining area leading to an open kitchen with an island. The appliances are all stainless steel and the countertops are black marble. I know Scott's bedroom and bathroom are upstairs since he said he was going there to take a shower, so his workspace must be down the hallway. I would love to see where he works.

"Umm, do you have a bathroom down here too or only upstairs?" I ask, sounding kind of like an idiot. I can't tamp down this urge to catch a glimpse of his workspace. I feel like it will show me more of him than this part of his place.

"Yeah, it's down the hall to the right. I'll get the movie ready if you need to use it." He gives me a sweet smile.

I practically jump off the couch. "Great, thanks."

I head down the hall and note that the door across from the bathroom is open. I peek in and hit the jackpot. It's definitely his workspace with computer parts and papers everywhere. Several desktop computers and laptops—all different models and brands— cover counters that run the length of the guesthouse. The upper shelves contain what looks like every book ever made about computers and computer programming. And then there are the toys. Pop! figurines of video game and Star Wars and Star Trek characters are everywhere along with models of the U.S.S. Enterprise and the Millennium Falcon. There are Mario figures that look like they came from a Happy Meal and-

"What the fuck are you doing in here?" Scott's voice roars from behind me.

"I-I just wanted to see where you work and the door was open."

"You wanted to see where I work? Who sent you? Who are you working for?" he asks, grabbing my arm.

"Wh-what? No one sent me! I knew that your workspace would be more 'you' than the living room and I just had to see it. I'm sorry. I should have just asked you." I wrench my arm out of his grasp and head for the front door.

"Yeah, you should have. I would have said no, though." I whip my head around as he continues. "No one except my family is allowed in there. The project that I am working on is wanted by our competitors who are racing to try and put out something similar. Plus, it's my personal space. I don't let anyone outside of my family into my personal spaces."

"You let me into your house."

"Yeah, I did. I still don't know what came over me." He sees my look of horror and his face softens. "No, I didn't mean it like that. It's just that I invited you without thinking about the fact that you would actually be coming into my place. I'm always so careful and with you, I just asked you, I didn't even think about it."

"I'm glad you did and I'm sorry that I went in there without permission. It's so cool, though. I loved all of the figurines and models mixed with those computers and computer books."

He gives me a shy smile. "Yeah? You thought my nerd's paradise was cool?"

"I did. Oh, and I should also mention that you look even hotter than usual with those glasses on. I think it's time for me to give you my letter."

"You like my glasses, huh?" I nod. "What's this about a letter?"

"I owe you a letter and now is the perfect time to give it to you." I reach into my back pocket and hand it to him.

* * *

Scott

Scott

This one's purple. Hmm. I turn it over and slip the paper out of the unsealed flap. There are only four words on the paper, but they are some of the best words that I have ever read.

Kiss me please.

Yas

I turn and place the paper and envelope on the hall table. Then, I reach out and cup her cheeks. "My pleasure," I whisper as I lean in and press my lips to hers. She immediately kisses me back and it stays gentle and closed lipped for a few minutes, our heads angled, lips slanted and eyes closed. I'm holding her hips and she is clutching my biceps.

As she's catching a breath, Yas slips her tongue out and swipes it across my lip ring, then sucks the ring into her mouth. I let out a low growl at how good it feels. I let her play with it for what seems like hours but is only minutes. Some of the hottest minutes of my life. I can't take it anymore and thrust my tongue into her mouth on her next breath. She sucks my tongue in just like she did with my piercing and then tangles her own tongue with mine. Her hands move from my arms to my neck and she curls her hands into my still damp hair, scratching at my scalp as she loses some control. We stumble to the couch and kiss for at least an hour. I am not checking the clock or anything but I know my lips are bruised and my body is on fire. Fuck if this girl doesn't taste even better than I imagined that she would.

I remove my lips from hers and she whimpers in protest until I nudge her chin up and start to trail kisses along her jaw, sucking and nibbling on her ear and then that graceful neck of hers. I have to resist the urge to mark her. I want the world to know she is mine. Wait. Mine? Where did that come from? I have never wanted to claim a woman as mine, ever. Amber was the closest I came to feeling anything like that. Even with her, I wanted to be with her only and I even considered marrying her, but I didn't feel the need to claim her. Can I do this? Can I fucking make someone belong to me? Can I belong to someone else? I don't know. Or maybe I do.

Lost in my thoughts, my mouth has stilled on her neck. "Scott, is everything okay?" Yas asks nervously.

I move my hands back up to cup her cheeks, place my forehead against hers. "Yeah, it is. In fact it's perfect. You're perfect, Yas."

"Perfect? No, I'm not. No one is." She laughs as she meets my eyes

"I think that you may be perfect for me," I reply honestly, the words coming out before I can think about what I am saying or stop myself. Shit! What if I scare her? We haven't known each other long. We had an instant connection and I feel it getting stronger every time I see her. But, still, what guys says something like that, especially after only one date? This is more than just a normal date, though. I even let her into my house. I'm still a little freaked out by that and annoyed that she was in my workroom, but I'm not sorry that I invited her in.

She looks surprised for a moment, but then that beautiful smile of hers returns. "I think that you may be perfect for me too. Too perfect, though."

"Too perfect? Am I that spectacular?" I tease her.

She rolls her eyes and says, "Well, your *mouth* is spectacular. As much as I would like to find out about the rest of you, tonight is not the night. In fact, I should probably go while I still can."

She pulls away and I feel the loss immediately. What the fuck is happening to me? "Can I see you tomorrow?"

"Yes. Do you want to come over to my place? I can make you dinner and we can watch a movie." I don't answer right away, so she continues, "I mean, if you want to. We could go out somewhere instead." She looks unsure of herself and I hate that. She should know how amazing she is. Not just with me but with how she is helping Alex.

I reach for her hands. "Look at me Yas," I tell her and then wait for her to raise her head and meet my eyes. "I would *love* to be anywhere with you. We can go out or go to your house. Whatever you want. For the record, though, I would *really* like to go to your house and see your place."

She leans up on her toes and kisses me lightly on the lips. "My house it is then. I'll text you the address. Is seven okay for you? Oh, and is there anything you don't like to eat?"

"Seven is great. And I will eat pretty much anything." I give her one last lingering kiss and she heads out the door.

I watch her walk around to the side gate of the yard and then I remember the pen. Dammit! I picked up a pen for her when I was at the gym this morning. They had some out on the counter and I grabbed one. I run back inside and grab the pen, then head to the driveway, hoping that she is still here.

As I round the corner to the front, I am relieved to hear her voice. What she is saying stops me in my tracks.

"Candi, do you think your friend can get me in for a waxing in the morning?" My mouth goes dry and my cock gets even harder than it already was. "Yes, I know it's been awhile and I don't know if I am going to *get any* but I want to be prepared." She listens for a few seconds. "Great, I'll see you then! Bye."

She turns toward her car and spots me where I am finally un-frozen. Her eyes get wide and her cheeks turn red. "Di-did you hear that?" She sees the heat in my eyes and covers her face with her hands. "Oh my God, you did. This is so humiliating."

I decide to put her out of her misery as I walk up to her. "Don't be embarrassed. It's extremely hot to know that you want to be ready for me. Although, you don't need to get waxed if you don't want to. I'm more than happy with you however you want to be." She turns redder and for some reason, I get more turned on. "Oh, and if I am the deciding vote on whether you *get any* tomorrow, consider this a hell yes." I pull her to me and kiss her passionately for a few minutes.

She finally pulls away, both of us breathless. "I *really* need to leave. Was there a reason you came out here?"

"Oh yeah. Yeah there was. I got this for you today." I hand her the pen that reads "Books make great weights."

"What the fuck? Who says something like this?" She looks at me with a hint of anger.

"Some group advertising at the gym? I don't know but I saw it and it said books and it's a pen and yeah, I should have looked closer at what it said. It sucks doesn't it? Shit, I suck!" I bow my head and scratch the back of my neck.

"The saying on the pen sucks, but you giving it to me doesn't. And neither do you. Thanks, Scott." She pulls my hand from my neck and kisses my palm. "I'll see you tomorrow."

CHAPTER 9

<u>Yasmin</u>

The day flew by even though I expected it to drag. I went and got waxed with Candi. She tried to convince me to visit the sex shop but I reminded her that I am not the kind of girl who can just walk into one of those places and be comfortable. I eventually convinced her to back off, but had to promise to give her some details of my date. I stressed the word *some* with her, because I want to keep things for myself.

Work was good too. We had a pretty steady stream of customers and a good amount of internet orders today. I felt like I could breathe. I am extra happy about that because I don't want to be stressed when Scott gets here. I have chicken baking in the oven and rice and veggies cooking on the stove. I stopped by Drago Sisters Bakery and picked up a variety of treats for dessert. Now, I just have to figure out what to wear.

I don't want to be too dressy, but I can't be in a t-shirt and jeans. Well, I guess I could. I mean, Scott was in a stained t-shirt, jeans and those sexy glasses when I went to his place. But, I want to put in some effort. I finally decide on a fitted purple boat neck top paired with a dark denim flared skirt that hits just above my knees. I slip on some strappy heels and forgo any jewelry because I don't want to have to worry about it getting in the way later. Underneath, I have a strapless satin bra and matching boy shorts in a teal blue. I hope they are sexy enough. I like the color and I didn't want to be too obvious about wearing something that screamed sexy. I'm worrying a little and thinking I should maybe put on something lacy when the doorbell rings. Too late now.

* * *

Scott

When I pulled up to Yasmin's house, I was surprised. It is a rambling one story with lots of wood and windows. I didn't think the bookstore was a big money maker, honestly, and expected her to live in an apartment or a small home. It's beautiful, though the grass is a little overgrown.

"Hi," Yas says as she opens the door. She is dressed semi casual and I'm glad that I did the same. I picked a short sleeve white button down and tan cargo shorts paired with Vans.

"Hi yourself. You look beautiful," I tell her and I mean it. I love that she has her hair down, flowing over her shoulders in soft waves. The fitted top and loose skirt emphasize her curves and those heels are the things of fantasies.

"Thanks. You look pretty good yourself. Come on in." She moves aside and I walk into the house. I want to kiss her, but I don't. I want to show her that I can be respectful and not just attack her, even though I *really* want to do just that.

"Your place is pretty amazing," I tell her, taking in the high ceilings and large open living room.

She looks sad for a minute. "My parents bought it years ago when the bookstore was doing really well. They loved this house." She looks like she is going to cry.

"What's the matter, Yas? Is something wrong with the house?"

She seems to collect herself and puts on a smile that doesn't quite reach her eyes. "No, nothing's wrong with the house. It's per- fect. Dinner should be almost ready. We can eat in the dining room, on bar stools in the kitchen, out here on the couch or in the enclosed porch. Which would you prefer?"

"Hmm. How about the kitchen. I've always loved sitting on a stool at the kitchen island while my mom was cooking."

"Umm, okay. But just to warn you, I am not as good a cook as your mom. I'm not bad, just not at her level," she tells me honestly.

"Not many people are, but I am sure that I will love whatever you made." I would eat rocks if she cooked them and tell her it was the best meal ever. I really have it bad.

We walk into the kitchen, which is open and airy with a big cen- ter island and windows overlooking a big backyard. She checks some pots on the stove and then turns off the heat and moves them to the back burners. Then she bends over and takes a pan out of the oven. The sight of her bent over sends images to my mind of my flipping up that skirt, yanking down her panties, grabbing her hips and taking her from behind right there against the stove. I shake my head as I realize that she's speaking to me.

"Scott? Did you hear me?"

"No, sorry. I zoned out for a minute. What did you ask?"

She looks a little sad when she says, "I asked you if you wanted me to make you a plate or if you wanted to do it yourself."

"Oh, I can do it." I round the island, trying to keep my back to her to hide my erection and grab the plate out of her hand, holding it in front of me. "This looks great. Thanks again for having me over," I tell her, kissing her forehead. If I kiss her lips right now neither one of us will be eating dinner.

* * *

<u>Yasmin</u>

What a disaster. I don't know what I did, but obviously I'm boring Scott and he is not into me. I mean, he didn't even hear me talking to him and then he kissed me on the *forehead*. Now, he picked the furthest stool possible from me and angled his body away from me. He doesn't need to worry. I can take a hint. We'll eat and then he can get out of here and find someone who interests him. I should have known better than to think that he would really want to be with me.

Maybe I should have worn something sexier, but I was in jeans and a t-shirt when he kissed me yesterday. Obviously, I'm the problem. I just need to make it through dinner and then go cry in my room. Because, although we haven't known each other long, I know that I am going to cry over this man.

"This is really good," Scott says, still facing away from me.

"Thanks," I mumble back.

He must hear something in my voice because he turns toward me with a worried look on his face. "Is everything okay?"

He's really going to ask me that after he tunes me out and then won't even sit next to me much less look at me? What the fuck? "No, Scott, everything is *not* okay!" I jump off the stool and face him. "I thought that this was a date. I *thought* that you were into me. But it took less than ten minutes in my house before you were tuning me out and sitting as far from me as possible. You haven't even looked at me once since you started eating. Why did you come here, Scott? *You* asked me if we could see each other today. I told you I was fine with going out if you didn't want to come over. It's obvious that you want to leave, so why don't you? Just go and find someone who you *want* to be with." He sits there staring at me, not saying a word. Tears are now threatening to spill out of my eyes and I realize that I need to get away from him.

"Just show yourself out!" I cry as I start to run from the kitchen.

* * *

Scott

I am momentarily shocked as Yas yells at me and then my stomach drops as she starts to leave the kitchen. Jesus, she *really* thinks that I don't want to be here with her. That couldn't be further from the truth. I sat away from her because I wanted to eat this dinner she cooked for me. I knew that if I sat close to her and breathed in her scent, I would throw her onto the island and take her fast and rough. That's how hard I am for her right now.

I grab her hand as she runs by me and place it on my crotch. "I want to be with you. Feel how much I want to be with you." Her eyes grow wide and her lips part as she feels how much I want her. "When you bent over to get the chicken out, I wanted to grab you and take you from behind *hard*. I sat away from you so that I could control myself enough to eat this wonderful meal that you cooked for me. I'm sorry that I made you feel unwanted. Know that I can't imagine a time when I will not want you. I want you so bad it literally hurts."

She strokes my cock through my shorts. "It hurts?"

"Yeah, I'm so hard that it hurts," I growl out as she continues her slow torture.

"Can we go the bedroom or does it have to be in here?" she asks, biting her bottom lip.

"What?" Now it's my eyes that go wide.

She takes a deep breath. "I want you to live out your fantasies, *within my boundaries*, but I would like our first time to be in a bed. Will that work for you?"

"Oh, hell yeah. That works. And I want you to stop me if something isn't good for you. Promise me that, Yas. I promise *you* that I won't be upset if you don't like something that I want to do."

"Oh. Well maybe we should talk about this. I mean, I'm pretty tame when it comes to sex and there are some things that I just won't do. I would rather tell you now."

"Okay, go for it. Tell me what is an absolute no for you." I reach out to hold her face so that I can make sure that she looks me in the eye and doesn't back down.

"Well, I don't want anyone else to be with us." She swallows as I nod. "I don't want any S&M. I mean I *might* be okay with playful tying up or a playful slap on the ass, but nothing hard core or involving safe words." I nod again and she continues. "And no, um, no anal." She tries to turn her head but I hold her in place.

"Well, I don't want to share you with anyone, male or female, and I don't want anyone but you. I *would* like to tie you up sometime but I think it would be fun for you and I am definitely not into it hard core. You could tie me up, too, if you want. Spanking is *not* really my thing and anal *definitely* is not. I want to be in your pussy, feeling all of your natural wetness. That is going to be more than enough for me. Now, I won't lie and say that I haven't done any of those things. When I hit college and girls started paying attention, I experimented a lot. It helped me figure out what I like *and* what I don't. So, I think we are on the same page. The things I mentioned you might not like are different positions. I think that I would like to try all different ones with you but I don't want you to be uncomfortable, okay?" She looks relieved and the fire is back in her eyes, darkening them again. I need to get to her bedroom now.

"Yes, okay. I-I would like to try different positions with you too." She leans in and kisses me and I am gone.

* * *

Yasmin

I'm glad that we got all of that out, even if it was embarrassing for me. I didn't want to give Scott any expectations that I couldn't follow through on. Thank God he didn't want to do any of that extra kinky stuff. I grab his hand and lead him from the kitchen down the hall into the master bedroom. I put my parents' bed in storage last year and finally took over their room. It's pretty feminine now and I'm a bit nervous about him seeing it.

I pause outside and turn to him. "My room is, umm, pretty girly. I hope that doesn't turn you off."

"Well, I wasn't expecting your room to be manly," he says with his trademark smirk. "And I don't think anything could turn me off right now. Open the door, Yas."

I do as he asks and try to see the room from his point of view. The walls are a dove grey with deep purple moldings. The king size bed has a tufted grey headboard and is canopied with sheer silver panels. The bed itself is covered in a deep purple comforter and pillows in varying shades of purple as well as white and silver. Hanging over the middle of the bed is a crystal chandelier, not an old-fashioned one, but one with vertical drops of sleek, square gems surrounding the light in the middle. The bedside tables and dresser are mirrored and there is a white leather tufted loveseat and ottoman underneath the bay window. Plush, deep, dark purple carpet covers the floor. Yep, definitely girly.

"Holy shit, Yas," Scott says as I flinch. "This is the sexiest bedroom I have ever seen."

What did he just say? "You like it? Really?" I stammer out.

"Fuck yeah. And thinking about you in that bed. Damn, I *need* you to be in that bed, like now."

I lead him over to the edge and kiss him. I let go of his hand to curl mine in his hair. I love the soft feel of it. He moves his hands up and down my sides as the kiss deepens. They skim the sides of my breasts but never stop where I want them. I reach between us to unbutton his shirt and he lets go of me long enough to help pull it off. I press a kiss over his heart before he pulls my mouth back to his. I'm rubbing my hands up and down his abs and chest while sucking his lip ring into my mouth when he moves his mouth away from mine. I try to capture it back, but then he's sucking on my earlobe and licking my neck. He bites down a little hard on that special place behind my ear and then immediately runs his tongue over it. His hands have finally found my breasts and his thumbs are running over my pebbled nipples through my shirt.

"I promised that I would do whatever you wanted me to do from those romance books of yours. So tell me, what do you want?" he whispers huskily into my ear as I arch into his hands. He nuzzles my neck and I love the feel of his eyebrow piercing as it rubs against my shoulder while his lips feather over my neck.

I don't answer. I can't. What I want is to have his mouth on me. Licking my clit and fucking me with his tongue. That's what I want. But, how can I ask for that?

"Baby, tell me. Don't be embarrassed. Tell me what those book boys do to drive you ladies wild." His lips leave my skin as he looks into my eyes.

"They-they. Oh hell, they like to go down on the women and make sure that they come a few times before they, you know, have sex." I'm blushing now and looking at the ground as his hands go still on my breasts.

"Seriously. They really do that?"

Now I am completely mortified. "Yes, yes, they do. But you don't have to. Just forget that I said it. Just, just do what you want. Or don't." I try to move away from him but he grabs my waist.

"I never said that I didn't want to do that or that I wouldn't do it. I'm just surprised. Most of the girls I've been with, I was just in it for me and they didn't seem to be upset about it because they liked my fingers and cock just fine. I *have* gone down on girls before.

Not a lot, but I've done it when I was going through my experimental phase. I don't hate it, but it has never been something I love or think about doing. I didn't realize so many women wanted that. It just hasn't been my experience."

Again, I try to get away from him so that he doesn't see me die of embarrassment right here in front of him. And again, he doesn't let me. "I *told* you I don't need you to do it. In fact, *I* don't want you to do it. It shouldn't be a chore. You should do it because you want to. If you do it just because I want you to, I'll be able to tell and it won't be good." I can't meet his eyes and I just want to get past this.

"You *do* want me to or you wouldn't be so upset," he says moving his mouth to my ear. "Tell me what they say in the books about why they want to do it."

I shake my head no. I am not going to tell him that. Sure, the women in the private romance groups I belong to online talk about it a lot and even make special posts with passages that they like. But there is no way I want to say it to him.

"Tell me, Yas. Tell me what they say in those books that turns you on. Please."

He looks sincere, so I answer honestly. "They say that they want to taste them and that they love the taste of them."

"Of their pussies?"

"And their mouths, skin, breasts. They like the taste of all of them."

"Well, I'm already addicted to the taste of your mouth and your skin. My mouth is watering thinking about your breasts, too. So, how about I taste those and more of your beautiful body. If my mouth ends up between your thighs, then I'll try to make it good for you. Okay?" he asks as he starts to pull my shirt up. I nod as I help him pull it up over my head.

CHAPTER 10

<u>Scott</u>

When Yas's shirt comes off, I nearly lose my mind. Her full breasts are barely encased in a blue strapless bra. I can see her nipples poking through the fabric. I can't stop myself from leaning over and sucking the left one into my mouth through her bra.

"Scott," she moans arching into me. My name has never sounded sexier.

"You like this, baby?" I ask while moving on to her right breast to give it some attention. I give it a little bite when she doesn't answer me right away and she rocks her hips into me. "I guess that's a yes." I chuckle.

"Yes, don't stop."

"I have a dilemma now." I say as I take a step back and look at her breast thoughtfully.

"What? What's the matter? Why did you stop?" She opens her eyes in alarm.

"Well, your tits look so good in this bra that I'm not sure if I want to take it off. I mean, I want to taste you but watching them heave up and down while they almost pop out is one of the hottest things I have ever seen."

She looks me in the eye and reaches behind her before I have a chance to react. She unclasps her bra and lets it fall to the ground. "Problem solved."

If I wasn't already half in love with this girl, this one act would have gotten me started. Fuck, but that was hot. And now I am getting a full view of one of the best set of tits I have ever seen. Seriously. They are full and heavy looking with dusky pink nipples that are standing at attention. And they're real. That is probably the sexiest part of all. Sure, fake boobs are big and pert, but they don't *feel* like Yasmin's did when I cupped her through her shirt. I move her backwards toward the bed until her knees hit the edge. I lay her down, following her but bracing myself on my forearms so I don't put all of my weight on her.

"I want to spend awhile with these beauties but I am not sure my cock is going to agree with that idea. I need to taste them, though. I know I sound like one of your books right now, but it's true." I lick my lips and bend over. The first flick of my tongue has her hips lifting off the bed. God, I love that she is so responsive to me. "Easy. I haven't even gotten started yet."

I put my hands under both breasts, lifting them up. I decide that the left one gets to go first again. I suck it into my mouth while my other hand kneads the right one, pinching her nipple between my thumb and forefinger. Yas starts to writhe beneath me, rubbing against my length while she becomes more out of control. I alternate between her two breasts and when I bite the nipple on one while pinching the other, she explodes beneath me.

I look up and see her watching me as she tries not to scream. I lick and suck until she comes down. "You just fucking came only from me playing with your tits?" I ask in wonder.

"Yes." She is panting hard. "It-it's been a long time for me and my breasts have always been sensitive. I'm sorry." She turns her head sideways, looking embarrassed.

"Sorry? What the hell are you sorry for? Knowing that I did that to you makes me feel...well makes me feel like the shit."

She smiles up at me. "Your mouth and tongue are pretty spectacular. Your teeth and fingers too."

"Spectacular huh? Let's see if I can keep up my reputation with you."

I move my hands down her stomach to the side zipper on her skirt. I undo the button and slowly pull down the zipper. How I'm managing to do anything slowly when I really just want to rip her skirt and panties off and fuck her until she *does* scream is beyond me. But I know she deserves to have as much pleasure as I can give her and I want to be her best ever. Especially since she told me that it's been awhile. Yas lifts herself up so I can pull off her skirt and she is left in satiny boy short panties that match the bra she removed a few minutes ago.

I stop to look her over from head to toe and can't believe how lucky I am to be here with her. "Do I need to take those off myself, too?" she asks me in amusement.

"How much do you like these panties?" I ask her huskily, while I hook my fingers into each side.

Her eyes widen and then the surprised look in her eyes turns hungry. "I could care less about the damn panties."

"Good answer," I say as I yank and rip them off of her.

Now she's fully bare to me and fucking beautiful everywhere. Her breasts are still damp and swollen from my attentions, her slightly rounded stomach and hips are sexy as fuck and her pussy is pink and glistening. And bare. "So I see you made your waxing appointment," I tease and she nods, smirking at me. "Your body is so amazing, Yas. I mean it. I could look at it all day. Not today, though. I need to touch you and kiss you some more and then bury my cock in you until we both scream."

"Yes. Please do that. But I want to touch you, too." She reaches for me but I pull back.

"Not yet. I'm the guest in your house so I get to go first. Plus, if you touch me now, it will be all over before I even make it inside of you."

"That's okay," She says trying again to reach for my crotch. "You jerked off in the shower three times in like thirty minutes. You can recover pretty fast."

I dodge her again. "I want my cock in your pussy or your mouth when I come the first time with you."

"My mouth?" Her eyes light up and she dives forward.

I catch her wrists to stop her. "Pussy. I meant pussy."

"But you said mouth. You don't want me to suck and lick you off?" She pretends to pout.

Her words make me jerk forward as my cock tries to bust out of my shorts on its own. "Of course I want that," I say through clenched teeth. "What guy wouldn't want that? But, I also really want to explore the rest of you. So, please let me. *Please.*" I think the please is what gets through to her so she backs up and lays down again.

I lift her right leg up and contemplate removing her heels. I decide to leave them on but start kissing her ankle above the strap. I move up to her calf and a shiver runs through her. I look up to see her eyes, dark and hooded, watching me. "You like to watch me put my mouth on you Yas?" I ask as I move up and turn her knee to kiss the sensitive spot on the back.

"Y-yes," she stammers.

"Good. I like you watching me." I reach her thighs but instead of going higher, I drop her leg and grab the left one, making the same trail up her leg. This time when I reach her thigh, I don't stop this time as I kiss, lick and suck on her supple flesh. I go back and forth between the two and she is in a frenzy by the time I pause.

"Please Scott, if you don't want to go down on me that's fine, but at least touch me. *Please*." Just like my please had an effect on her, hers affects me too. I pause and look up at her, see the begging in her eyes and I know that I am going to use my mouth, tongue *and* fingers to take care of her ache. As I am bending down, I realize that I am not just doing this for her. I *do* want to taste her. I'm not going to say it like in a cheesy romance novel, but I want it just the same and I can show her just how much.

* * *

Yasmin

After I beg him to touch me, I see Scott lower his head. A second later, his tongue slides over my slit and his mouth sucks my clit in. I fly up off the bed so he moves a hand up to rest on my stomach, holding me down. His other hand moves to my center and he slips a finger in. He moves it in and out in time with his tongue swirling and his mouth sucking. My hands are twisted in that silky hair of his and I scratch his skull as he takes me higher. I am getting closer when he slides a second finger in, twists them both and bites down on my clit at the same time. I scream his name and come harder than I ever have in my life. My orgasm goes on and on, probably because it *has* been so long and my body needed the release. He keeps licking and sucking and pumping, going slower and gentler as I finally come back down.

He lifts his head, smiling like the Cheshire Cat and starts moving up my body, kissing my stomach and then biting my hip, hard. I yelp and he starts kissing and licking it to make it better.

"I'm sorry. I have just been wanting to mark you and I knew you wouldn't like it on your neck where everyone could see."

"Mark me? Am I yours now?" I smile at him lazily, still sated from my two orgasms.

"I hope so. Will you be mine?" he asks, looking me in the eye.

"Yes. If you'll be mine. Do I get to mark you too? I mean it's my turn, right?" I ask, sitting up.

"Fuck yeah, Yas. You can mark me anywhere." He moves over me and lays down on the bed with his arms behind his head.

"Hmm. You are wearing too many clothes for me to decide where yet." I say as I reach for his belt buckle. I pull his shorts and boxer briefs off together because I'm impatient. I can see him in his underwear later. He kicks off his shoes and is totally bare to *me* now.

I take him all in and he is so hot and beautiful that I think my eyes are going to permanently cross. His chest and abs lead into those perfect "V" oblique muscles and then down to his thatch of black hair. Pointed straight out at me is a magnificent cock. It's big, but not scary big, and thick. My mouth is literally watering at the sight but I make myself keep looking. His thighs are leanly mus-cled like the rest of him and he has light hair on his legs, just like on his chest. I am SO glad that he is not hairy. A little hair is okay, but I am not a fan of hairy guys. I want to touch and kiss him ev-erywhere but first I have something that I need to tell him.

"Scott?" I look him in the eyes and continue. "Thank you for... well for...you know." I blush and look down.

He rears up to sitting and tilts my chin up to look in his eyes again. "You don't have to thank me, Yas. I didn't do that just for you." He holds up a hand when I open my mouth. "And that's all I'm going to say about it. But don't be surprised if I do it again." His eyes, which are incredibly dark now, sparkle as I push him back down.

I kiss and lick both of his nipples for a few minutes as he growls and plays with my hair and then trail kisses down his ribs and abs. I lick both of his obliques and he comes up off the bed. "Easy. I have barely even started." I tease him with a version of his own words.

I could kiss up and down his legs like he did to me but I don't have his patience. I kneel down between his legs and bend over. I see the pre cum glistening on the tip of his cock and I look up at him as I lick it off. His eyes are so dark green that they are almost black and his fists are now clenched tightly in my comforter, twisting it. I move my head back down and lick him from base to tip and then take him into my mouth. I fist my hand around the bottom of him and move it in time with my mouth. Almost immediately, he starts thrusting into me. I reach down with my other hand and massage his balls. I can feel him getting closer when he wrenches me off of him.

"I need to be inside of you now," he growls as he flips me onto my back in the middle of the bed. He starts to leave me and I protest. "I need to get condoms out of my pocket, Yas."

"In the bedside table. I just bought some today," I pant.

He opens the drawer and draws out a strip. "Some? You must have over 100 in here. Feeling optimistic?"

"I didn't know what kind you would like," I say defensively, then add. "But yes, I was hoping that you would want me more than once tonight."

"I like whatever will get me inside of you. Brands and styles don't matter. And I plan to be inside of you as much as you'll let me tonight. You said it's been awhile for you and it has been for me too. So, I'm not sure how many times we can go and still be walking tomorrow. But, I'm game if you are." He quickly covers himself.

"You better not leave this bed unless you're crawling out of it," I shoot back and reach for him while I spread my legs wide.

I position him at my entrance and he starts to slowly move inside while holding himself up above me. It hurts a little since it's been so long and I involuntarily flinch.

"Are you okay?" he asks, stopping. Worry is in his eyes and all I want to see is desire. I am already adjusting to him and the pain is going away.

"Yes, I just had to get used to you. Please start moving." I know that I have begged a bunch of times already tonight, but I don't feel self-conscious with him.

"You don't have to beg for anything from me, Yas. If you want something just tell me and I'll give it to you. I mean it. I'm not just talking about when we are in bed, either."

His words bring tears to my eyes. "Me too," I sniffle. "I'll give you anything I can. And don't look so worried, these are happy tears. Now, I am going to ask you again without begging. Can you start moving? I'm going crazy here."

"Your wish is my command," he says as he thrusts into me fully. I arch into him and start meeting him thrust for thrust as I wrap my legs around him and use my heels to urge him on. He is still being too gentle although I can feel myself building. I want more.

"Harder, Scott, *harder.*"

"You sure?"

"Yes, fuck me hard. I need it." This spurs him on and he drives me hard into the bed, gripping my hips to hold me in place. I feel like my bed is going to collapse any minute now.

"I'm close, Yas. Where are you?" he asks between kisses.

"I'm getting there." That must not be the right answer because he removes his mouth from mine and bends down to latch it on my breast. He also takes one hand off my hip and moves it down between us. The sensations of his cock pounding into me, his mouth sucking and nibbling my nipple, and his fingers circling my clit send me skyward. I come screaming his name and then reach out and bite his shoulder, hard.

That sends him over with me. "Fuck Yas! Fuuckk!" he yells as his body shakes along with mine.

He collapses on me and immediately apologizes. "I'll get off of you in a minute, baby. I can't move yet." I run my fingers up and down his spine.

"Take your time. I'm not going anywhere. Oh and I'm sorry about your shoulder." I add as I look at the teeth marks I have left in him. I'm surprised that I didn't break the skin.

* * *

Scott

I look over when Yas apologizes and see the mark forming over the imprints of her teeth on my shoulder. I lift up a little and smile down at her. "I told you to mark me wherever you wanted. And that was one of the hottest things I have ever experienced. Leading into what I can honestly say was the most intense orgasm that I have ever felt."

She smiles up at me shyly. "Really?"

"Was it not that good for you?" I ask her, frowning.

"Umm, hello. You made me come three times and the last time was so intense that I bit you. It was more than good, it was fucking amazing." She kisses me and I feel myself getting hard again inside of her.

I jump up because I need to get the used condom off of me—and put a new one on so I can start round 2. If she's ready, that is. "I need to get this condom off. I know you could feel me getting hard. I've never recovered this fast but I am more than happy to have you again if you're ready. If you're not, we can wait." I head to her bathroom while I wait for her answer.

"I'm ready, but this time I want to *have you.*" she yells to me.

"Have me?" I ask as I walk back in the room.

"Yes, I want to ride your cock. Can I?" She has a condom in her hand already and is tearing it open.

"I'm pretty sure you know the answer to that question," I tell her as I climb onto the bed and rollover onto my back.

"Oh, I think I do," she says as she leans over to roll the condom on my now fully hard erection. She straddles me and sinks down onto me slowly. She is so hot and wet for me, like she was the first time. And so tight. I slide in easier this time but her walls are still hugging me tightly.

"God, you feel so good."

"So do you," she tells me as she moves faster rolling her hips back and forth as she rides me. I pull her down a little so that my mouth can play with her tits. The angle pushes her clit against my cock as it moves in and out. She puts her hands behind me and holds onto her headboard as she moves faster and harder on me, close to her release.

"Scott!" she yells out as her body starts shaking and her walls start milking me from the inside. "Yes, oh God, yes." And then, she screams again.

I tighten my grip on her hips and thrust up into her as hard as I can. I'm a little worried about hurting her but I know it won't be long. My spine is tingling and my balls are tightening. And then, I'm going over the edge, my body as still as it can be while my cock is jerking inside of her.

I'm in trouble, big trouble, because that time was even better than the first and I can't imagine that being with Yasmin will ever be less than amazing.

CHAPTER 11

Yasmin

I wake up blissfully sore with my head on Scott's chest and his arms around me. I don't know what time it is and I'm not sure that I care. We were together four times before falling asleep and then woke each other up another two times in the middle of the night. We used our hands and mouths on each other those times but the orgasms were no less explosive. The man is a sex God and by his reactions to me, I think that I may be a sex Goddess.

"What are you smiling about?" that sexy voice asks me. "Are you thinking about my cock?"

I tip my head up and see his matching smile staring back at me. "Yes, I am. Your mouth, too." I should be embarrassed to be saying that but, after last night—and early this morning—I'm feeling bold.

I stretch and turn to get up. "Where are you going? I thought we couldn't leave the bed until we were crawling out of it," Scott protests.

"I know, but that was because I was a little distracted and not thinking about work." I let the sheet slide off of me and head toward the bathroom.

"Play hooky. You're the boss. You can take a day off."

I want to, I really do but I know that I can't. "I can't. I want to but I really can't. Besides, don't you want to work on your secret project?"

He chuckles. "It's not really a secret and yes, I do want to work on it. But for the first time that I can remember, I would rather be somewhere else than in front of a computer."

"I would rather be with you too, but I really have to go in. First, I need to shower."

"What a coincidence. I need a shower, too." He smirks and starts to get up.

"Oh no. If you come in here with me, we will never leave. Plus you have no clothes here." I put my hands flat on his chest to keep some distance between us as he steps up to me.

"You don't want to shower with me?" He turns on puppy dog eyes—a look I haven't seen on him before—and pouts.

"After last night, you *know* that I would love to do pretty much anything with you that involves no clothes. But, we can't this morning." It's hard to stay firm when I have my hands on him, but I have to. An idea comes to me and I tell him, "How about I come by your place after work and we can take a nighttime shower there and try out *your* bed."

He looks scared and takes a step back. "No. I told you that I don't let anyone but my family into my place."

"But, you let me in yesterday and I thought that after last night...I mean you said that I was yours and you were mine..."

"I did and I meant it but you can't come over. I can come here again tonight. I'll bring dinner." He engulfs me in his arms and places a kiss on my head.

I want to sink into his arms but his words hurt me. I knew that I wasn't good enough, but he made me believe that he felt differently. Now, I know. "You should go. I'll text you later to let you know if I'm free tonight."

"*If* you're free? What the fuck do you mean by that?" His eyes are flashing with anger as he looks at me like I grew a second head.

"I mean that I'm not the type of girl who is fine with being treated like she isn't good enough." I turn away because I can't hold back the tears anymore. "Just leave."

"I can't leave like this. Turn around and talk to me." I shudder with a sob and strong hands grab my shoulders to turn me to him. "Are you crying? No, Yas, no. Don't cry. There are things you don't know, reasons why I'm the way I am. It has nothing to do with you how I feel about you. I promise you that. I don't want you to ever say or think that you aren't good enough. You are. You're more than good enough. I don't deserve you, but I'm not willing to let you go." I look up into eyes filled with sincerity.

"You can tell me anything. Can you tell me about those things? I-I care about you, Scott. I now we haven't known each other long, but I do care about you."

"I care about you, too. But, I don't know if I can tell you. It's so hard for me to think about, I don't know if I can say the words out loud. I'm sorry. Can you be patient with me while I try to work my shit out?"

"I can try. But I don't want to be dating you for a year and not be allowed in your house."

"A year. You can see us a year from now?" He smiles at me.

"Yeah, I think I can," I reply honestly.

"Me too," he tells me. "Now, I better go or I am going to make sure neither of us leaves the house today. He kisses me lightly and then scoops up his clothes from the floor and dresses quickly. "So, tonight?"

"Yeah. I'll see you tonight." As he leaves, I realize that he never said that he would be letting me into his house a year from now. I can be patient but I *do* have my limits.

* * *

Scott

I pull up to my house and get out of the car.

"Well look who made it home," Owen says, walking out the front door of the main house. "Good to see you back in the saddle, bro."

I flip him off and walk around to the backyard and my place. I go inside and head up to take a shower. While I'm soaping up, I think about Yas.

Not in a sexual way, though. I think about her crying because I wouldn't let her come here. I did that to her. I know I'm normally a bastard to girls but I don't want to be like that to her. How can I tell her about Amber, though? She won't look at me the same. Even as I tell myself that, a part of me shouts that that's bullshit. I think she would still like me—care about me if she knew what happened. My brothers and my parents have said that I need to forgive myself because they don't blame me. I think that Yasmin could help me with that. She comforts me just by her presence. I know that I have to tell her if I want to save whatever this is that I have with her. I still don't think that I can say the words to her. Then it comes to me. I don't have to *say* the words in order to tell her. I can write them.

I get out of the shower and towel off then throw on a t-shirt and shorts. I go downstairs to sit at my desk and start to write. It's not easy, but it's not as hard as I thought it would be either. Once I'm done, I feel a little lighter. I grab my keys and head out the door to set up the next delivery to the bookstore.

* * *

Yasmin

I'm going to have to make some hard decisions soon. The online business is helping the store but I don't know how much longer I can keep all three employees on. It's starting to wear on me and I don't know what to do. We have such loyal customers who shop as much as they can, but new business isn't coming in. I've called every publicist I know and even some I don't but as much as I begged, they couldn't send me a big author for an event. Some of them were apologetic, telling me that they just couldn't send someone big to a small store. Others dismissed me when they heard me say "Las Vegas." I wanted to scream at them and say that Vegas is not all about The Strip and showgirls. We have a thriving reading community here. I wish that they would take a chance on me, but I understand. They have their bottom line too.

"Hey Yasmin," Sean says to me as he walks into the store. "Is Erika around?"

"Yes, she is. Let me call her for you," I tell him with a smile and a wink.

I call Erika out from the stockroom and a glowing smile takes over her face when she sees Sean. "Hi."

"Hi," he says back and then adds, "I was wondering if you were free for lunch."

"Umm, I'm not sure if I'm taking a lunch. We have a lot to do in the stockroom." She glances my way and I immediately step in.

"You're taking a lunch and I think sharing it with Sean would be a great idea."

"But, we have the online orders and you had to cancel Danny's shift," she protests.

"I can handle it for an hour—or two. Go have lunch, Erika. Enjoy yourself. Besides, Alex should be in soon to help out."

"You're sure?" I nod and she turns to Sean. "I would love to have lunch with you, Sean. Let me grab my purse."

We both watch her head to the back and then Sean turns to me to ask, "Are things not better, even with the website?"

"They're better, but it's not enough yet. I'm not sure if it ever will be."

"Did Erika tell you about the new book software that is being developed? From the latest interview that I saw with the CEO of the company, they are looking to sell to indies first before going to Amazon and Barnes and Noble."

"She did tell me. She gave me an article but I haven't had time to read it. She didn't say anything about the indies, though. I would hope that they would make it more affordable for us little guys. Maybe I *could* try for a loan and not have to sell my house to afford it when it comes out."

"You should definitely look into it," he tells me as Erika returns.

"Look into what?" she asks.

"We were talking about that software you told me about."

"Did you read the article yet?"

"No, but I have it in my purse and if it stays slow, I'll grab it to read up here by the register. Now go enjoy your lunch!"

"We will." They both say it at the same time and I can't help but smile.

It does stay slow. Ryan drops off Alex and I put her to work shelving. I also ask her to write some recommendation tags for YA. She's doing a great job and is smiling more and more every time I see her. I hope that I have contributed to that in some way. I think I have.

I'm just getting ready to grab that article when a delivery person comes in with a huge basket of chocolate. "Are you Yasmin?"

"Yes, I am," I tell him, noticing the thick envelope among the candy bars. **Yas** is written on it and my heart skips a beat.

"These are for you and the tip is already taken care of. Enjoy," he says, handing me the basket.

"Thanks," I tell him, looking over the basket. It has everything from Hershey's bars to Lindt, Ghirardelli and Godiva. Hershey's Kisses are sprinkled liberally throughout the basket as well. Looking closer, I notice some candy themed pens mixed in there. My heart flips thinking of him buying me pens, keeping that up. As much as I love chocolate and pens, it is the envelope that tempts me the most. I pluck it out and realize that it must have several pages in it. I think that I'll have to wait for Erika to get back so that I can go to my office and read it in private.

"Wow. Did someone send you all of that candy?" Alex asks coming up to the register.

"Yep. Would you like some?"

"Can I have the Godiva, it's my favorite?"

"Yes, you can. I have simpler tastes," I say, reaching for a Kiss.

It seems like hours before Erika returns when it is really only about 15 minutes. I tell her that I'm taking a break and to call me if she needs me. I go into my office, then close and lock the door. I have a feeling that whatever is in this envelope is going to change my life. I don't know if it will be for the better or the worse, but I need to find out.

I open the envelope, take out the papers and start to read.

Yas,

I know that I hurt you this morning and I need to apologize again. I also know that I need to tell you why I can't have you over to my place and need to keep our relationship a secret from my family. I know that I didn't tell you that part this morning and you're probably not happy at the moment, but don't stop reading. Last night, we promised each other that all we had to do is ask for something and we would do it for each other. I am asking you to read this letter to the end before deciding that you can't

be with me. I meant it when I said that I care about you and I really need you to understand.

I told you about high school and how I was a nerd and never had a date, much less a girlfriend. I also told you that when I was in college, I did a bunch of experimenting and slept around. I am not really proud of that, but it is what it is. I can't go back and change it. I can't change anything, no matter how much I want to.

Senior year of college, I was walking across campus distracted by a new programming code that I was trying to perfect. I bumped into someone and nearly knocked them over. I looked up to apologize and saw one of the most gorgeous girls I had ever seen smiling at me. She told me that instead of an apology, she would love to share a cup of coffee with me. Her name was Amber.

We laughed and joked while drinking our coffee and I couldn't believe that she was interested in almost everything I was. She even played video games and loved Star Wars. She didn't like Star Trek, though, I need to tell you that. Anyway, I was beyond happy to meet a gorgeous girl who was as much of a nerd as I was. I asked her if I could see her again and she said yes.

Amber became my first girlfriend. She hung out with me while I worked and came to Friday night barbeque at my parent's house. My family seemed to like her and she said that she loved me. I thought that I loved her too, so I said it back. I was protective of my place even back then. So, although I took her into my dorm room, I never took her to my apartment in downtown Chicago or to my work space at my parent's house. We spent a bunch of time at her apartment, though. I'm not going to lie to you. I was extremely happy and thought that she was the "one."

We were together for almost a year when I graduated. She said that she was one class short of graduating but would do so over the summer. I bought us tickets to Paris for when summer session was scheduled to end. She told me that she always wanted to go there and I couldn't wait to be there with her.

My sister Erin was so proud of me for graduating Summa Cum Laude. Even though she was 12 years older than me, we were very close. She was my dad's daughter from his first marriage but my mom had always raised her as her own. My brothers and I never thought of her as our "half" anything. She was our sister and even though she was older, we all were protective of her. We used to interrogate her dates when they came to the house. Can you imagine showing up to pick up a girl and having four little kids interrogate you? The guys usually thought that we were nuts, but she told us that she loved having her little guys looking out for her.

Like I said, most guys thought we were crazy, but Dave was different. The first time that she brought him home, he shook each of our hands. He promised to respect and cherish our sister. He said if he upset her in any way, he would lie down and let us all punch and kick him as much as we wanted to. They became exclusive and he became part of the family. He even came over to play video games with us and spent time with us when Erin wasn't home. I loved him as much as I love my blood brothers.

Right after their high school graduation, Erin found out she was pregnant. You've met my parents—they are open minded and accepting. Dave's parents weren't. They had big plans for their son to attend his father's alma mater and one day take over their business. They were upset that Dave's trust fund was released and he wanted to invest in our business—which was struggling back then—and use the rest of his money to make a life with Erin and their baby. Dave stood up to them, told them that we were more of a family to him than they ever were and walked out of their lives. He and Erin were married in my parent's back-yard in a family only ceremony. Erin didn't need a big ceremony. She said that the marriage was more important than the party or the dress.

I was 8 when Alex was born and I loved her at first sight. I was an uncle and I took my responsibility seriously. I knew that I would protect that girl with my life, just like I had pledged to protect my sister. She grew up and we all watched over her. We were happy, too happy I guess.

Dave's investment infused much needed capital into our business. We were able to expand into computer software and I am proud to say that the first program I designed— the one that is partly represented by my tattoo—was a big success. Dad insisted on paying Dave back his investment and along with other investments he had made, Dave was worth over a billion dollars.

Erin and Dave wanted to host my family graduation party. I brought Amber, of course. Everyone had a great time and we laughed and drank late into the night. Erin, Dave and Alex were leaving on a vacation to Disneyland the next day and they gave me a key and the security code to the house so that I could walk their dog. He didn't like the kennel and I offered to do it. I went home happy to have the love of family and of Amber. I had invited her to come to my apartment a couple of days later and I was planning on proposing to her. I went back to Amber's apartment with her that night and stayed again the next night.

I woke up two days after the party happy until I realized that the program that I had been working on was missing from my messenger bag. I had put it in there so that I could go straight to work because I needed to present it at a press conference. I started freaking out because I needed to now run to my workroom at my parent's house to get the back up. This program was going to bring more money and prestige to our company and part of the reason I chose that night to let Amber into my home was that I was wanted to celebrate the announcement of the program too.

Amber saw that I was stressed and offered to go to Erin's house and walk the dog. I was grateful to her and gave her the key and alarm code. The press conference went well and I was on cloud nine heading home with Amber's favorite Chinese takeout that night. She texted to tell me that she would be late. I was a little disappointed but I told myself that at least she was coming over. I was letting her into my heart and I knew that she would say yes. I was wrong.

While I was waiting at my apartment, Amber and her REAL boyfriend were robbing Erin's house. As if that wasn't bad enough, Dave had gotten food poisoning so they had come back to Chicago early. Alex was dropped off at my parent's house so that Erin could take care of Dave. Erin and Dave came home in the middle of the robbery and they were both shot dead by Amber. She didn't get away, though. The neighbors had seen her car in the driveway and knowing that Erin and Dave were on vacation, they called the police.

When she was taken into custody, Amber admitted that her relationship with me had all been a setup. She purposely walked in front of me so that I would bump into her. She never liked video games or Star Wars or me. I was just a means to an end to get close to my family. The one time I saw her, she told me that my sister begged for her life, but I'm hoping that she was lying. Like she lied about so many other things.

That all took place nine months ago. I have been blaming myself for being so stupid and causing my sister's death. My brothers and my parents have finally started breaking through to me. They told me that I need to forgive myself and that I was a victim. I know this but I've had a hard time believing it. I am starting to, though. Because, I have a reason now to want to be happy. I have you.

At least I hope I still do. I want to shout from the rooftops or jump on a couch to tell everyone that you are mine. But, I can't. My family told me that they didn't really like Amber and although I know that they like you, I can't bring a girl home yet. It feels too soon, like I haven't mourned enough. I also hope you understand now why I can't let you into my house yet. I tried that once. I know that you are not Amber, but like you said, we haven't known each other long. I want to trust you and I do to some extent, but I can't show you off or bring you home. I'm sorry, Yas. I know you deserve better than this and really, better than me. But, I can't give it to you now. I want to keep exploring this thing between us and I hope you do too.

I know I put a bunch of hope in this letter, but that is one of the things I feel when I'm around you, hope. I know you may not be ready to talk to me right after reading this but if you could text or call me when you can, that would be great.

Yours,

Scott

Tears are rolling down my cheeks as I finish the letter. I can't believe what Scott—and his family—had to go through. I ache for him while at the same time I want to fly to Chicago and beat the shit out of that bitch, Amber. How could she do that to him? No wonder he can't trust me yet. Or maybe ever. No, I won't think that way. I would never use him and he'll see that.

I think hard about what I want to say and then send the text.

Me: I understand and we can keep "us" quiet. Or at least as quiet as we can. I think Alex and your dad might suspect that something is going on with us. I am glad that you are realizing that it was not your fault. You are an amazing man.

Almost immediately my phone buzzes.

Scott: Thank you, Yas. If my dad and Alex ask you about us, tell them the truth. While I'm not ready to show you off, I don't want you to have to lie. You're an amazing woman and I will try to work this out as fast as I can.

Me: I know you will. Thanks for saying that I don't have to lie. It would be hard for me to lie to your family. I'll see you tonight?

Scott: Yeah, you will.

Me: OK, bye until later.

Scott: Bye.

CHAPTER 12

<u>Scott</u>

Things have been going great with Yasmin the last two weeks. I've stayed at her house every night. Waking up with her in my arms is one of the best things I've ever experienced. It is even better when I can convince her to go into work late and stay in bed with me longer. I know keeping our relationship from my family is bothering her, but she doesn't say anything. She's trying to be patient, but I am going to have to man up soon if I want to keep her. And I *do* want that.

It's not just the sex, although that is as incredible as ever. She is the hottest fucking woman I have ever met and being with her is a gift. I know she feels the same way about me since she touches and kisses me as much as I touch and kiss her. We are insatiable and it totally rocks.

But, it's our talks that make me feel like she is capturing my heart, piece by piece. We talk about everything but work when we're together. Other than Star Wars and Star Trek, we don't really have any common interests, but that seems to make us better. We go to the gym together a few times a week. She does some cardio while I lift and then we jog the indoor track together. She thought that she was out of shape, but she holds her own. Lifting all of those books must keep her in better shape than she thought.

I explain video games to her. I bought her a PS4 and she's started playing it with me. She talks to me about books and some of the YA ones sound interesting. I am starting to understand what people mean when they say that someone "completes" them. We are like two halves of a whole. I'm falling in love with her and, surprisingly, it doesn't scare me.

Tonight is going to be different for us. Alex invited her to a special dinner where we're going to celebrate Erin's birthday and she said that she didn't want to say no to her. Yas gave her the idea, telling Alex that she does it for her parents too. Alex has been so excited and she's been doing so much better. I am still not ready to tell everyone that we are together and I know it will be torture to be near her and not touch her. I am going to need to sit as far away from her as possible to maintain control.

* * *

Yasmin

I arrive at Maggie and Gary's house with Alex. I've seen everyone briefly when they drop off Alex at the store, but I haven't been back to the house in a couple of weeks.

"Yasmin! It's great to see you!" Maggie envelops me in a hug as we step out onto the back patio, which is full of balloons and streamers. Gary, Ryan, Owen and Luke all come over to hug me as well. Only Scott stays away from me. It hurts. I'm not going to lie. But, I told him that I would be patient and I'm trying.

"We have all of Mom's favorite foods, just like you suggested, Yasmin. See, there is cheese pizza, mini spinach and mushroom omelets, Grandma's mac and cheese and fried chicken too. We have red velvet cake for dessert."

"It all looks amazing. Thank you for letting me be here with you." I give Alex a big hug and feel my phone vibrate in my pocket.

I take it out to check the text as we sit down.

Scott: Thank you for helping her, Yas.

I look up hoping to see Scott across from me, but he's at the other end of the table. As far away from me as he can possibly get. I take some deep breaths to stop myself from crying. I agreed to this. And he has been wonderful to me. We talk and laugh when we're not kissing or making love. I don't know if he thinks of it as making love, but I feel like it's more than sex or fucking. He's still giving me random pens every few days and writing me letters. I could say that I am falling in love with him, but deep down I know that I have already fallen. I just need to stay strong and give him the time that he needs.

The dinner is great and everyone goes around the table telling their favorite stories or saying what they are thankful to Erin for. When they get to me, I tell them honestly that I am thankful to Erin for Alex. I've come to love her like my own niece and she's told me that she loves me too. I hope that we will always stay in touch, no matter where she goes for college or later in her life. She's a special girl.

After the plates are cleared from dinner, Gary comes back outside with an envelope in his hand. He has a look of sadness in his eyes when he turns to Scott. "Son, this came for you today. I didn't want to spoil the celebration but you need to make plans."

"Plans?" Scott asks him with a puzzled look as he takes the envelope from his father. His eyes grow wide and his hands start to shake. "Is-is this what I think it is?"

"Yes, Scott. Doug called this afternoon to say that they moved up the trial to July 13. He just found out and also heard that a subpoena for you was coming. I know we hoped that this wasn't going to happen, but the prosecutor really wants your testimony. He thinks that it will help take any sympathy away from Amber that her lawyer will try to drum up," Gary tells him as next to me, Alex sits up straighter and reaches out to squeeze my hand. I look over to her and ask if she's okay. She tells me that she is, she just wants justice for her parents. I nod.

I look up and see that Scott has gone pale and started shaking his head. His body is shaking. "No, I-I can't. I can't do it."

I don't even think as I rise up and move around the table to the other side. I reach him, saying, "Yes you can, Scott. You can do this."

"Yasmin, I know that you want to help Alex and you seem to have some grasp of the situation, but you don't fully understand," Maggie tells me in a kind but stern voice.

I ignore her and turn back to Scott, forcing him to look up at me. "I'll go with you if you want me to."

"Baby? You'll go with me?" When I nod, he reaches out to grab me around the waist and pull me to him. His head is against my stomach as my hands move into his hair and scratch his scalp the way he likes me to.

"Apparently Alex is not the only one Yasmin has been helping." I hear Gary say from behind me. I look up and am met with some surprised faces. I give them a small smile and start to turn back to Scott.

"I knew. They were kissing against the bookshelves in the Horror section last week." At my look of shock, Alex continues, a look of mischief in her eyes. "I know you thought that I was next door getting coffee with Sam, but I forgot my wallet. I didn't want to interrupt you. You looked really into it."

I blush deeply as Scott starts shaking again, this time from laughter." We *were* really into it so thanks for not interrupting, Baby Girl." He takes a few deep breaths and then looks up at me loosening his hold a little. "What about the store? I know that you haven't wanted to take time off or even go in too late in the mornings."

"Do you want me to go with you?" I ask, looking down into his eyes.

"Yeah, I want you to go. I fucking *need* you to go, Yas. I meant it when I told you that you comfort me."

"Then I will figure something out for the store," I tell him, leaning down to lightly kiss his lips. I try to lighten the mood a little by adding, "Besides, I've never been to Chicago. Even if I only see the inside of a courthouse and a hotel, I'll be able to say that I was there, right?"

Scott looks up at me. "We could go a day early and I could show you around a little if you want. We could even go to Windy City Tats so you can meet my tattoo guy, Zane." He smirks as he adds, "I know how much you enjoy his work."

I blush and playfully swat him on the shoulder. "I *would* like that. I've always wanted to go and see the paintings at The Art Institute. But are you sure it would be alright? This isn't going to be a fun trip for you."

"It's not going to be fun. In fact, I think it will be my own personal version of Hell, but I would really like to show you the city. I grew up there and I love it, even if I can't imagine ever going back there permanently."

"Well, it's settled then. I'll arrange for you to fly out on the jet two nights before the trial. Do you have a hotel chain preference, Yasmin?" Gary asks me.

"Umm, no. I guess whatever is cheap but nice. I can't afford a fancy hotel," I tell him honestly, feeling a little embarrassed.

"We're not staying in a cheap hotel. Can you have us booked into the W, Dad?" Scott asks, taking my hands in his.

"We? You're going to stay in the hotel with me?" I ask before Gary can respond.

"I've woken up with you in my arms every morning for the last two weeks and it's fucking awesome. I don't plan to stop doing that anytime soon."

"Scott! You parents are here. Oh my God, did you have to say that?" Now, I am beyond mortified and can't look anywhere but down.

"I hate to break it you, Yas, but my parents have four kids and none of us were the product of an Immaculate Conception. So, I don't think the fact that we are having sex is going to shock them." He laughs as he pulls me onto his lap and kisses me passionately.

I break away as soon as I can, which admittedly takes longer than it should. Having his mouth on me makes me lose my mind a little. Okay, a lot. I turn to look back at everyone else so that I can apologize. I find them all looking at me with wonder and happiness in their eyes.

"The W it is," Gary says with a twinkle in his eyes. "I'll tell them one bed is all you need."

"Th-thanks," I say as I bury my head into Scott's shoulder. He's shaking with laughter again and plants kisses all over my bent head.

As we get ready to say our goodbyes later, Maggie asks if she can speak to me privately. "Of course," I tell her. We head into the house while Scott stays behind with his brothers. Gary and Alex had abandoned us earlier for a long standing chess game.

* * *

Scott

"Okay, spill," Owen says to me with a smirk as I watch Yas head inside with my mom.

"Spill what?" I try for an innocent look.

"You know what, asshole," Luke chimes in. "You and Yasmin. Have you really spent every night with her for the last two weeks?"

I look around at my three brothers and know from the looks that they are giving me that I am going to have to tell them something. I won't tell them everything, though. Some things are just between Yas and me. I won't cheapen what we have by talking about her that way. "Yes, I've been with her for a little over two weeks and I am happier than I've ever been in my life." There, I said it.

"Over two weeks? Wait, is she the one you were with when I caught you doing the walk of shame that morning?" Owen asks with a smile.

"Yes, she is who I was with. But, there was no shame. I'm not ashamed of being with her."

"Are you sure about that, bro?" Ryan says and the look in his eyes is skeptical as he continues. "You haven't mentioned her once in the last two weeks, you didn't greet her when she got here and you sat as far away from her as possible during dinner. If she hadn't jumped out of her chair to comfort you, none of us would have known that the two of you are together. That doesn't seem like you not being ashamed of her."

Fuck! I should have known that Ryan would pick up on all of that. "I am definitely not ashamed of her. But, you're right, I didn't want any of you to know about us. I-I just didn't want anyone to think that I was getting involved with someone again too fast or worrying about what she could want from us. I also didn't want you guys to pretend to like someone just for me again," I admit with a sigh.

"Dude, really?" Luke says. "Are you fucking serious? Yasmin is nothing like Amber. She's great and no one is pretending to like her. We all *do* like her. She's helped Alex and apparently you so much in such a short time. There is nothing fake about her at all. And, she's *smoking* hot."

"Don't talk about her like that!" I growl as I move towards him.

"Calm down, man," Owen says, stepping in front of me. "We're not blind and you have to know how hot Yasmin is. He didn't mean to be disrespectful, he was just being honest. I think he even meant it as a compliment to her."

"I did, Scott, I mean it. I wouldn't disrespect her, even if she wasn't with you. I told you that we like her." Luke looks remorseful now.

"She's awesome and I'm happy for you, Scott. You deserve someone like her. I can't believe she puts up with your shit and was fine with hiding things from all of us, though," Ryan tells me, a question in his eyes.

I sigh again and admit the truth about the situation. "She wasn't fine with it and I'm pretty sure that it hurt her to do it. I told her about Amber and explained to her the same reasons I just told you guys. She agreed to give me time, but I know that it has been hard for her. She's-she's amazing and I don't know how I got lucky enough to have her in my life, but I'm not going to let her go. I've never felt this way about anyone, even Amber. I know it's fast, but I am pretty sure that I'm in love with her." I drop my head and wait for the ribbing to begin.

It doesn't come. I look up and see that I have shocked my brothers into silence. Owen is the first one to recover. "Have you told her that?" When I shake my head, he continues. "Well, you should. After what you just said about her being hurt and upset, I think she needs to hear it." I know he's right but I'm not sure if I'm ready yet.

My mom and Yas come back outside a few minutes later. They're both smiling, which makes me smile, too. I walk over and take Yas' hand. "You ready to go?"

"Yeah, I am. It was great seeing all of you." She hugs my mom and brothers goodbye then we head inside and say goodbye to my dad and Alex too. We decide to take my car and pick up hers in the morning.

I notice that something is wrong as soon as we get in the car. Yas lets me take her hand but she looks out the window instead of at me. I want to ask her what is wrong, but traffic is a little rough so I decide that I'll wait until we get home. I mean her house. It's not my home. But as I think that, I realize that I feel like it *is* my home.

I barely stop the car in her driveway before she opens her door and says, "I'm so sorry." Then she is out and running up her steps. I catch up to her as she's fumbling for the right key to her front door.

"Baby, what are you sorry for?" She doesn't turn around so I keep trying. "Yas, I need you to tell me what's wrong. What do you think you need to apologize for?"

She turns then, tears glistening in her eyes. "You didn't want anyone to know about us and I screwed that up."

Shit. I thought about how I hurt her by keeping our relationship from my family. But, I never imagined that she would think that I was mad at her for comforting me in front of them. The proof of just how big an asshole I am just keeps adding up. There is no way that I am going to allow her to think that she did something wrong.

"You saw me start to fall apart and you came to me. You comforted me. Don't ever be sorry for that. If anyone should apologize, it's me. I shouldn't have asked you to keep us a secret. I should have known that my family loves you and would be happy for us. I know that I hurt you and I am glad that everyone knows now."

"Your mom asked me if I was serious about you and told me to not break your heart. I told her that I was more serious about you than I have ever been with anyone in my life and that the last thing I would ever do is break your heart." I can't say those three words yet, but I want her to know how I feel so I take her inside and spend the rest of the night showing her.

CHAPTER 13

<u>Yas</u>

If the two weeks with Scott before his family knew about us were great, these past two have been even better. We have dinner with his parents a few times a week. The whole family has been great and I know that they really like me. I feel like I'm becoming a member of their family and although I will never forget my parents, it is nice to have a sense of family again.

The store is still struggling and Erika keeps bugging me about the software. I let her set up meetings with the local banks as well as some private investors for the end of next week. I'm heading to Chicago with Scott tonight. He's become tenser and more stressed out in the last couple of days. I don't blame him *at all*. Even though I can't really afford the extra payroll, I asked Erika, Danny and Sam to cover for me while I am gone. They were more than happy for the hours, although Erika teased me about the fact that she has never met Scott. He never seems to come by when she's there. I promised her that she could meet him soon, as long as it's on a double date with her and Sean.

I'm talking with Sam at the cash wrap while I wait for Scott when she says, "I hate to bring this up, Yasmin, but is the store going to make it?"

I sigh heavily as I tell her honestly, "I don't know, Sam. I am trying to keep it going and Erika has this idea for some miracle software, but I can't promise you anything. If you need to start looking for something else, I understand."

"I am not at that point yet. I have some savings just in case you need to cut my hours. I love it here and I'll stay on as long as you can keep me," she tells me, then pulls me in for a hug.

"Thanks, Sam," I say, hugging her back.

"Do I get a hug too?" I hear Scott ask from behind me. I turn from Sam and walk over to give him a hug *and* a kiss.

"Are you ready to go?" he asks when I pull away.

"Yep. Let me grab my bag." I turn toward my office.

"Hey Sam, how are you?" I hear him ask as I open the office door. He really is a nice guy. I come back out and he takes the suitcase from me.

"I'll see you Friday, Sam. Thanks for helping cover the store."

"No problem, Yasmin. Have fun." My friends think that this is an all pleasure trip. Scott's story is not mine to tell and I won't betray his trust.

"We will," he answers before I have a chance to. We head out the door to the waiting car.

* * *

Scott

I can tell Yas is a little freaked out by the jet. I'm used to traveling this way, but I know that most people aren't. We get settled into the leather seats and Velvet brings us some drinks. She has been part of the flight crew for years and I ask about her family before we take off.

"That was really nice of you to ask about her kids," Yasmin says to me after Velvet goes up front to take her seat.

"She's been with us since *I* was a kid. I used to be scared to fly and she would sit next to me and tell me jokes while we took off."

"Aww, that's sweet. Your family is really nice to everyone who works for you. At least from what I can see. And you all do your own dishes and stuff."

"Yeah. We didn't always have a ton of money. My dad always believed in his company and my mom always believed in him. But, we had some lean years. My mom never let us forget that or think that we were better than anyone else."

"Things got better, though."

"Yeah. Like I told you, Dave's investment helped us. About three years ago, it was almost not enough. One of my dad's competitors was wooing away our best architect. Ryan was working under him, learning the ropes, because that's what he was studying in college, architecture. Ryan knew that he was about to leave us and it would have crippled the company since he was designing a new building that we had already won the bid for. At the last minute, the competitor withdrew their offer and we kept the architect. My family was really scared, though. Our reputation had been on the line and it would have been really bad."

"Wow. Well, I am glad that it worked out."

"Me too. Now, let's talk about our plans for tomorrow. Is there anything else you would like to see besides the Art Institute?"

"About that. Are you really sure that you are okay with going out with me tomorrow? I mean, I know how hard this trip is going to be for you. If you want to prepare or stay in bed all day or what-ever, it's fine." I see that she is sincere and would do whatever I asked.

I reach up and caress her cheek as I tell her, "Yes. I'm sure. As much as I would love to stay in bed all day *with you*, I want to have some fun with you in my hometown. So, tell me what you would like to do."

"Can we go to Navy Pier? It looks like fun." I nod and she continues. "I would love to have some pizza and then just see the city. Wherever you would like to take me. I can't wait to meet Zane, too."

"We can go to the Art Institute in the morning and then head over to the Pier. We can have pizza for lunch and have some fun. After that, I would love to show you the neighborhoods that I grew up in, if you want. Then, we will pick a good restaurant for dinner and after we eat, we can go see Zane."

"That sounds perfect." She's right. It does sound perfect. I can't wait to show her my city.

* * *

Yas

The hotel is in a cool older building with arches and luxurious furniture. Our suite is black, purple, gold and white with modern art on the walls. The bathroom has a sunken tub with a separate, glassed in shower. I haven't experienced this kind of luxury since I was a little girl.

"Do you like the room, Yas?" Scott asks me.

"Yes, I do," I tell him and then decide that I want to share *my* story with him, the way he has shared his with me. "When I was younger, my family was pretty wealthy. Not as well off as your family but we had a nice life. We went on trips and stayed in hotels like this. About 9 years ago, our store's business started to slow down and we had to cut back. I haven't been in a hotel this beautiful in a long time. It's beautiful."

He moves to me and takes me in his arms. "I'm glad that I get to be the one to share this with you." Then he turns serious and pulls back to look at me. "Is everything alright with the store? I know that you have alluded to it being slow and how you can't take off or go in too late. Is there anything that I can do to help? I want to be there for you, Yas."

"I'm glad that we're here together, too. The store is not doing great, but Erika and I have come up with some ideas. I know you want to help, but I can't think of anything that you could do right now. Thank you, though."

"I could give you money, if you need it. I have more than I could ever spend."

My heart fills, but I know that I can't let him bail me out. "No, Scott. I can't take your money. It will be okay." I am not sure if it will, but I can't tell him that.

"Alright, but the offer stands. I may have something else that can help, but I want it to be a surprise." He smiles at me and I see a sparkle in his eyes.

"A surprise? When do I get it?"

"Hopefully in about a month."

"A month?" I pout. "I was hoping for something more immediate."

"Well, I do have something that I could give you right now. Something that I know you love." He starts to move backward, pulling me into the bathroom with him. "I think we need a shower after that long flight."

He is already pulling my shirt up and I lift my arms to help as he raises it over my head. He stares at my breasts encased in a black lace demi bra for a moment or two. Then he reaches around me to remove the bra as he growls in my ear. "I fucking love your tits *and* your choices in lingerie." Heat pours through my body into my already wet center. He reaches into the shower to turn it on before twisting back towards me.

I push his shirt up and he takes it the rest of the way off. "I love your chest, too." I say as I lean forward and lick his nipple. I get another growl for that and then he is pulling down my skirt and panties together. I kick off my shoes and stand bare before him. "You still have too many clothes on."

"Then take them off." His eyes are the dark emerald I love as he looks at me. I reach forward and unbutton his jeans and pull the zipper down. I push them down to his calves and stare at the bulge in his grey boxer briefs. There should be a law against how good he looks in his underwear. The only thing better is Scott naked, so I snap out of it and pull his briefs down too. He kicks off his shoes and then his clothes join them on the floor. I lick my lips as I take him in. "Like what you see, Yas?"

"You know I do. If I didn't, we wouldn't have gone through all of those condoms in my drawer, plus that jumbo box from Costco in the last month." We have been together in every room of my house, and my back porch too. He's kept his promise that we would try all different positions. Some have been fun and some have just been awkward, but we just stopped those and moved onto something that felt right. I've had more orgasms than I ever thought I would have in my entire life.

"Shit. Condoms. I didn't bring any. Fuck, what is wrong with me?" Scott knocks his head against the shower door.

I leave him there and walk into the bedroom to get the condoms that *I* remembered to bring out of my bag. I walk back into the bathroom and hold a strip up to his bent head. "Good thing your girlfriend didn't forget." Oh, God. I just called myself his girlfriend. I think I am but he has never said it.

I shouldn't have worried. "Best. Girlfriend. Ever." He grabs me and pulls me into the shower with him. The warm water washes over me as he pushes my back against the wall and drops to his knees, spreading my legs open. "Now let's see if I can win the best boyfriend award."

He places a closed mouth kiss on top of my mound and then lets his tongue out for a long lick. I jerk forward and moan. I drop the strip of condoms and grasp his head in my hands, pushing him further into me. I can feel him smile against me as his tongue circles my clit. He still won't come out and say that he likes going down on me, but he does it often, so I know that he does. I start thrusting my hips as he puts his tongue inside of me. It feels so good, especially with his lip ring rubbing against me, but I need more. "Scott, put your cock in me. I need it."

"Not yet. I want you to come on my fingers and mouth first." he says as he replaces his tongue with two fingers and starts swirling his tongue around my clit again. His fingers are moving in and out and I am matching him with my thrusts. The pressure starts to build and my legs begin to shake. If Scott wasn't holding my hip, I would probably collapse onto the shower floor. Then, he curls his fingers just right and sucks my clit into his mouth at the same time which is all it takes. I scream his name as I try to thrash from side to side. He holds me steady and he continues with his tongue and fingers, pushing me to a second climax almost immediately. My legs give out and he has to stop so that he can stand us both up.

"Oh my God, Scott. That was-that was...I don't even have words. Best. Boyfriend. Ever. Without a doubt."

He smiles, kisses me passionately for several minutes, holding me up until my legs feel strong enough to stand on again. I slide down him so that he knows I'm good to continue. He turns us around and heads for the small seat in the shower. It is a ledge up against the outer window. A pane of frosted glass is inside the shower that reaches to the bottom of my chin. He has me turn with my back to his front. "Grab the glass and hold on, Yas. You wanted my cock and you are going to get it. But it's going to be hard and rough. I can't go slow right now." I spread my legs wide and tilt my ass up to him as I hear him tear open the condom wrapper. He grabs one of my hips and whispers. "Are you ready?"

"Yes," I tell him and then he thrusts up into me. He's fully inside of me and I nearly come apart again from the sensation. I arch back into him and that's all it takes. He starts thrusting in and out hard and I have to grip the glass to keep from falling.

"Is this how you wanted it, baby? Did you want me hard inside of you?" he growls in my ear, then bites my earlobe. His other hand moves up to my right breast and he's kneading it and rubbing my nipple between his fingers.

It feels so good to have him inside of me and know that he has lost control because of me. "Yes, Scott, yes. I want it like this."

He moves back and pushes into me even harder. I know that I will probably be sore and bruised tomorrow from how hard he's holding my hip but he isn't hurting me. He keeps pounding into me until I can feel him getting close. "Are you close, Yas?"

"Yes, but don't worry about me. I already came twice. Let go and come for me Scott."

He thrusts into me again and then he lets out a roar as he comes hard, biting into the top of my shoulder. He is jerking so hard that his legs go out and I lose my grip on the glass as he leans forward and we tumble onto the shower seat. "Fuck, I have never come that hard in my life." He plants kisses along my spine as he turns us so that he is sitting on the seat with me on his lap. "Did I hurt you, Yas? I know it was rough." He looks so worried.

"No, Scott. You didn't hurt me. I would have told you if you were hurting me. And you would have stopped." He nods earnestly and I continue. "I'll probably be a little sore tomorrow but it's alright. Plus, now you've marked me again, which is pretty hot. I love the fact that I made you so out of control. That you wanted me so bad."

"I want you more than I have ever wanted anyone, ever. I don't know how I got lucky enough to have you." He stands up with me in his arms and I reach over to turn off the shower. "Can you grab the towels?" he asks as he bumps open the shower door with his shoulder and steps into the bathroom. He pauses by the stack of towels and I pick them up. He carries me into the bedroom and I lay the towels on the bed. He puts me down on top of them and then lies on his side next to me.

* * *

<u>Scott</u>

I'm lying here in a bed in an Extreme WOW Suite at The W with this amazing woman who just made me come so hard that I nearly blacked out. I prop my head up on my hand and look down at her. Her skin is still glistening with droplets of water from the shower. It's so sexy. She's so sexy. I bend down and lick the water from her breast. She arches up and gives me one of those moans I love much. I lean over her further and lick the other one dry too. "You are so beautiful."

She reaches up to push my hair of off my forehead. She runs her finger across the barbell in my eyebrow. "You make me feel like I am. Thank you for that."

"You don't have to thank me for telling you the truth, Yas. I meant it." I sit up and start using the extra towels to dry her off, starting with her legs. By the time I reach her face, I see the tears falling from her eyes. "Yas? What's wrong?"

"No one except my parents has ever said that I was beautiful and made me feel like they meant it before. I mean, yeah guys have said it. But, I knew that they just wanted to get with me."

"Well, I also want to *get with you* as often as I can." I tell her, try-ing to lighten her mood. "But that's not why I said that to you. You are a truly beautiful person, inside and out. I am humbled by the fact that you want to be with me. That you are here with me, help-ing me and giving me strength."

Tears start to glisten in her eyes again as she says, "There is no place that I would rather be. I love you, Scott."

I look into her eyes and know that she means it. I also know that it's time to tell her the truth. "I love you too, Yas. More than I ever thought that I could love someone."

She slowly sits up and kisses me. It is sweet but passionate at the same time. I move my hands into her wet hair as she runs hers up and down my biceps. We kiss until we're both panting and then I gently lay her down in the middle of the bed. "I want to make love to you, Yasmin."

She nods yes and points to the bedside table. I see that she put some condoms there, too, and I chuckle. She really is the best girl-friend ever and not just because of the condoms.

I rip one off and slide it over my erection. Her legs are open for me already so I lean over and guide myself in slowly. I'm afraid that she might still be too sore for me but she thrusts her hips up, letting me know that she's not hurting. I move in her slowly, rain-ing kisses up and down her neck. She wraps her legs around my waist and pulls me closer. I'm not going to rush this time and she knows it. Her hands lightly scratch my back as I keep up my rhythm. "You feel so good inside of me, Scott."

"In all of my experimenting, I never made love to a woman, Yas-min. I didn't ever want to go slow before. But, now that I'm inside of you like this and knowing that you love me, I want to be like this with you often. I mean, I also want to take you hard. I don't think that will change. But, that can be making love too and not just fucking, can't it?" I ask her, hoping that she wants that too.

"Because we love each other, I think whenever we're together, however it is, it'll be making love."

Fuck, that's hot. Like, really hot. Who knew that being in love and having the person you are in love with talking about it could be an erotic experience? Maybe a lot of people, but never me. All I can think about is making her come so I tilt my head down and suck her nipple into my mouth, feeling her start to writhe beneath me. I nibble and suck at her breasts, taking turns while she starts to move faster. She's close. I go up on my knees pulling her hips up with my hands, while still bending forward and tonguing her nipples. The new angle has her thrusting her hips into me and as I bite down on her soft flesh, she goes over the edge, shaking and clawing at my chest. Seeing her like that is too much for me and I follow her over. I think I did black out this time because I don't remember rolling off of her. When I open my eyes we are lying next to each other, panting hard.

"This making love thing is not too bad," she says, laughing. I look over at her and laugh along with her.

We order room service and eat it in bed, wearing the hotel robes. After, we lie on our sides facing each other. We talk and kiss and caress each other into the night. Normally, I would be jumping her. But tonight, I just want this.

CHAPTER 14

<u>Yasmin</u>

I wake up wrapped in Scott's arms. I can't believe that he actually told me that he loved me last night. Scott Griffin loves *me*, hips and all. In fact, I think he loves my hips the most. That thought brings a smile to my face.

"What are you smiling about? Are you thinking of my cock again?" He tilts his hips into me so I can feel his erection. "Because it is definitely thinking of you."

"I can feel that and as much as I love that part of your body, I wasn't thinking of it when you caught me smiling."

"Then what were you thinking of?" he asks as he moves over me and starts kissing my neck.

"Honestly? I was thinking about how great it feels to have you say that you love me." His mouth stills on my neck as I continue. "Oh, and also about how I think you love my hips the best."

He lifts his head to look into my eyes and his are sparkling with amusement. "I don't think I have a favorite part of you, but your hips would definitely be a contender if I did." I lean up and kiss him lightly on the lips and then he adds. "It feels great to know that you love me too, Yas. Really great."

I kiss him again, more passionately this time and one thing leads to another. When we are done and trying to catch our breath, Scott looks over at the clock and says that we need to get a move on. "As much as I would love to stay in this bed, I want to show you my city today. I want to experience it through your eyes."

"I can't wait," I tell him as I jump off the bed and start getting dressed.

* * *

Scott

We walk to the Art Institute since it's only about a half mile from the hotel. I hold Yas's hand and watch her as she takes in the city. We have to stop a few times so that she can take pictures and I laugh at her a couple of times. "*I* am a tourist. I want to take pictures and that building is cool. If I am embarrassing you, you can walk behind me or something," she says in frustration after I ask her why she is taking a picture of a random building.

I pull her into my arms. "You aren't embarrassing me. I just want to make it to the museum before it closes." I laugh and she punches me in the stomach. "Ow! You have a mean punch."

"Don't you forget it, Griffin." She tries for a stern look but is soon laughing too. She takes my hand and starts down the street again.

When we get to the museum, she asks someone to take our picture by one of the lion statues before we go in. I have her text me the picture and I set it as my phone background while we are walking in. Yas insists on buying the tickets since she says that it was her idea but I get her to promise that she will let me buy her whatever she wants in the gift shop.

We spend a couple of hours walking through the collections and I can tell how much she is loving the art. I have never been a big fan of museums—that's Owen's thing—but I am having a great time because I can tell Yasmin is enjoying herself. After we've looked at everything that she wanted to see, Yas excuses herself to use the restroom and I tell her that I will meet her in the store.

I know her well enough to anticipate what is going to happen in there and I want to be prepared. I talk to the manager and he readily agrees to do what I ask. When Yas joins me, she looks over everything and I see her eyes brighten at many things. When I ask her what she wants, she tells me that she would just like a Museum t-shirt and a Seurat poster. I'm glad that I planned ahead as I nod at the manager and we head out to catch a cab.

Navy Pier is really crowded. I knew it would be because it's summer, but I didn't want to say no to her. We're hungry so we head for the food court and get some mini pizzas. "This is really good," Yas says around a bite of her cheese pizza.

"Chicago pizza is the best. It's a known fact."

"I think Chicago men may be the best too, at least one of them is." She covers her face. "Oh my God, that was really cheesy, wasn't it?"

"Yeah, it was," I say with a laugh. "But it was really cute, too." I pick up her hand and kiss it, bringing a smile to her face.

After we eat, we walk through the shops because neither of us wants to get on a ride just yet. I insist on buying her some t-shirts and other souvenirs. I like buying her things, especially because she doesn't expect me to. It's not like she's asking me to hit up Harry Winston like Amber did all the time. Shit, why am I thinking about Amber? That bitch has taken up too much of my life already. I won't let her interfere with Yas. I stop to clear my head.

"Are you okay, Scott?" Yas is looking at me with concern in her eyes.

I give her a genuine smile. "I am. How could I not be when the woman I love is holding my hand?" And, it's true. I feel better just thinking about Yasmin's love for me.

We head to the rides. We go on the swings, the Ferris wheel—where I kiss her at the top—and even the carousel. I stand by her horse as it goes up and down, looking at her in awe as she laughs and smiles, having fun.

We are walking back towards the entrance when she sees the sign for the dinner cruises. "That would be so cool!" she exclaims, clearly excited.

"Do you want to do that for dinner?" I ask. I've never been on a dinner cruise, although I have been on a yacht on the lake before.

"Could we? I mean are we dressed up enough?" She looks down at her t-shirt and shorts. I'm dressed the same. "And do we really have time? I would still like to see where you grew up."

"Let's do this. I'll get the tickets now." I put my hand over her mouth when she starts to protest. "I *want* to pay, Yas. I let you pay for the museum, the pizzas and the rides, let me take care of dinner. Do I have to resort to a please or are you going to honor our agreement and not make me beg?"

"No, you don't have to beg," she grumbles.

"Thank you. Now as I was saying, I'll get the tickets now for the latest cruise that they have. Then I'll take you to my neighborhoods and we can go back to the hotel to change. We should have plenty of time to make it back for dinner."

"What about Zane and Windy City Tats? Will we still be able to do that?" She looks so anxious that I can't help but to lean forward and kiss her.

"You really want to meet the man behind the tats don't you?" When she nods vigorously, I put her out of her misery. "Zane works late so he will be there until at least 1."

Her smile lights up her face. "Okay, go buy me dinner so we can get out of here." She smacks me on the butt and then walks past me."

"Hey," I protest weakly. "I thought that there was no spanking allowed in this relationship!"

"That was a slap and not a spank. Plus, I told you playful was acceptable."

"I think that I am more a fan of groping," I say as I grab her ass. She turns and kisses me. I want to push her against the wall and make out with her right there but I don't want to get us kicked out. So, I settle for holding her hand while we walk over to the cruise desk.

* * *

Yasmin

We walk out of Navy Pier, but instead of heading for the cab line, Scott turns toward the self-parking area. I decide that he must know a shortcut or something when he lets go of my hand to embrace an older man standing next to an idling electric blue Mustang.

"John. It's good to see you. Thanks for bringing my car."

"Of course, Scott. It's good to see you, too. I just wish it was under better circumstances." The man turns to me holding out his hand. "You must be Yasmin. It is truly an honor to meet you. I have heard so much about you and how you have been helping Alex *and* Scott."

I shake his hand, having no idea who he is. "It's nice to meet you too. I love Alex *and* Scott, so it has been my pleasure to help them." Seeing my confusion, Scott steps in.

"Shit, I'm sorry. I should be the one doing the introductions. Yas, this is John. He has worked for my family since we had enough money to hire people to work for us. He's like another member of the family to us, but he didn't want to leave Chicago since his daughters live here. He lives at my parents' place and checks in on my place, too. John, this is my girlfriend, Yasmin. But you know that already."

"How does John know about me, Scott?" I quirk an eyebrow at him.

"I might have told him about you," he mumbles, biting down on his lip ring.

"When did you tell him about me?"

"About a month ago."

"A month ago? Before your family found out?" I ask, not even trying to hide my surprise.

"Yeah, I couldn't tell my family yet but I had to tell someone and John has always been the one I confided in. He knows all of my secrets." Scott gives him a sheepish grin. "He's like a vault."

"I am. You know that your secrets are safe with me, Scott. All of them." He winks at me.

I don't know what to say. It was so hard for me during that time. When I thought Scott might be ashamed of me, even though he insisted that he wasn't. But he did tell someone, the person that he trusts more than anyone. My eyes tear up and I turn away.

"Yas? What's wrong? Are you mad that I didn't tell you about John?" Scott asks, frantically. I shake my head no but can't get any words out.

John seems to understand, though. "I think Yasmin is overcome by the fact that you told me about her during the time when you were telling her that no one could know. Correct me if I am wrong my dear, but I think that despite Scott telling you that he wasn't ashamed of you, you thought that he was because he wanted to hide his relationship with you."

"You're not wrong." I choke it out on a sob.

"Fuck, no. You really thought that? How could you think that?" Scott tries to pull my chin up but he sounds angry so I turn away and wrap my arms around myself.

"I think you now realize the importance of Scott telling me. Especially knowing that I keep all of his secrets. Knowing how close we are. That is why you started crying. You know now that he was never ashamed of you. He just couldn't tell his family. But, he told me."

"Yes," I whisper.

"Why won't you look at me then, if you aren't mad?" Scott demands.

"Because you are acting like an ass and yelling at her instead of trying to understand," John tells Scott and I am so startled that I turn back around and look up with wide eyes.

Understanding dawns on Scott's face. "I'm sorry, Yas. And I'm sorry again for making you think I was ashamed of you. I could *never* be ashamed of you. You know that I love you. Don't you?"

"Yes. Yes, I do and you know that I love you, too. You don't need to apologize, though. If you haven't figured it out already by now, I am pretty emotional. Sometimes I just need to cry a little. It doesn't always mean that I'm sad." I walk over to him, put my arms around his neck and kiss him. He wraps his arms around me, too, and we stay together, kissing and hugging for several minutes.

"I hate to break this up, but I need to catch a cab back to the house," John says, laughing.

"A cab? Why aren't you riding back with us? We *are* going to see where you grew up, aren't we?" I look up at Scott.

"We *are*. But I was planning to start with the neighborhood that I lived in before my family had a lot of money." He sees my stern look and adds, "But we can go backward so that John can catch a ride with us."

I turn to John who is silently laughing at our exchange. "You can have the front seat so that you two can catch up and I can take pictures without Scott teasing me about it." I turn back to Scott as he opens the car door and pushes the seat up so I can climb in.

"Thanks, Yas," he whispers as I get in.

* * *

Scott

My parents' house isn't too far away but I take the scenic route. Partly so that Yas can play tourist and partly so that I can talk with John. We talk on the phone at least once a week, but I am really happy to see him in person.

"Are you ready for tomorrow?" John doesn't pull any punches.

"I think so. I had some Skype sessions with the prosecutors. They said that I was as ready as I can be. We have no idea what Amber's lawyer is going to bring up or ask me."

"That woman is going to try to use her lawyer to hurt you. You know that, don't you?" I nod and he continues, lowering his voice. "Are you sure that you want Yasmin in the courtroom? When Amber sees her and realizes that she really has no hold over you anymore, she is going to lose it."

"She won't know how much Yas means to me."

"Yes, she will. Anyone can tell that you two are in love. The way you look at each other is a dead giveaway. By the way, I like her Scott. I like her a lot."

"I'm glad you like her. It means a lot to me to have your approval. You never gave it to me with Amber and you were right. I don't know what will happen in court, but I do know that I can't do it without having Yas with me. Just having her next to me gives me strength."

"I can take whatever she wants to dish out," Yasmin says from the backseat. I meet her eyes in the rearview mirror briefly before looking back at the road. "I didn't mean to eavesdrop, but I am right here in the backseat. Oh, and I like you too, John. Thanks for your approval."

I pull into the driveway of my parents' house and park near the front door, ignoring the six car garage. This house is more traditional looking than the Vegas house, but they are about the same size. John gets out and then helps Yas out. "Your house is beautiful," she says.

"It's not my house. It's my parents' house."

She rolls her eyes. "Okay, your parents' house is beautiful."

John chuckles as he walks to the front door. "I'll unlock the door for you and then head up to my apartment. Just set the alarm when you go. It really has been great to meet you, Yasmin. Scott needs someone to keep him in his place." She reaches out and hugs him tightly and my heart feels like it will burst. After he unlocks the door and shuts off the alarm, John turns to me and we hug each other, too. "That girl is a keeper, Scott. Don't fuck this up," he whispers in my ear.

"I'll do my best. I *want* to keep her," I whisper back. He walks toward the garages and his apartment above them with a wave.

CHAPTER 15

<u>Scott</u>

"Come on in," I tell Yas, stepping through the door. "Do you want the grand tour or do you want to just take a quick look around before we go to my old neighborhood?"

"Umm..." She looks everywhere except for at me.

"Umm? I don't think that was one of the choices I gave you." I try to catch her eye.

"I can't ask for what I want to see." I am confused for a few seconds and then it hits me.

"You want to see my room?" She finally looks at me and nods. "Well, I always did want to get a hot girl in my room when I lived here. It never worked out for me back then, but I guess today is my lucky day." I grab her hand and lead her to the stairs.

When we reach the top of the stairs and I turn towards my room, she pulls me back. "Are you sure, Scott? I mean, I know how you feel about letting anyone into your spaces. I don't want you to feel like you have to do this. It's fine if you aren't ready."

I know that she means what she says and that is why *I* say, "I want you to see my room, Yas. Just try not to laugh too hard." I add as I open the door and step inside.

Yas comes in behind me and I watch her as she takes it all in. My room is large and spacious. One wall has floor to ceiling shelves holding computer programming books and computer parts. I saved everything I experimented on while I was learning how to build and program computers. In between the shelves is a 60" flat screen TV with a cabinet under it housing my different game systems. The wall with the windows has my desk underneath it, covered with papers and notebooks. Next to it is the built in bookcase. It isn't holding books, though. It has various video game controllers that I collected. Even an old Atari one. There are also character statues from my role playing games and even some stuffed Marios, Luigis and Yoshis. To my left, is the wall that my bed it jutting out from. There are nightstands covered in more papers and notebooks as well as lamps made of game consoles. The last wall is one giant wall to wall closet. My dresser is in there because I didn't have any free wall space to put it on. The middle of my floor is dominated by bean bag chairs.

She walks around touching the shelves and TV lightly. She makes her way past my desk, smiling at the clutter and stops at the bookcase. "Your friends?" she says asks, picking up a game controller and one of the Marios. I nod and she places a kiss on each before putting them back on my shelf. Then she bends down. "Thank you all for being there for my guy. I have started playing more video games to show my appreciation."

My feet take me to her in seconds. "Yas, shit, are you for real? I mean, damn, woman. I can't believe that you just thanked some toys and game controllers for being my friends."

"You told me they were your only friends in high school. Why shouldn't I thank them? I am glad that if you didn't have human friends, at least you had something to make you happy. I know that you are happy when you play video games. I've seen the look on your face. You love it. Now, as for the part about being real, I think you know that there is nothing fake about me." She pulls on my belt loops, drawing me closer to her. "You said that you always wanted to have a hot girl in your room. Was there anything in particular that you wanted to do once you got one in here? Do you want me to dress up as Slave Leia?"

I reach up and pull lightly on her ponytail. "I would love to have you dress up for me, but I don't have a costume lying around. There *was* something else that I thought about a lot though. Remember I told you that I would like to tie you up?" She swallows hard and nods. "That is what I wanted to do in here. I wanted to tie a girl to my bed with my game controllers and have sex with her."

"Umm...I-I don't know, Scott." She lets go of my shorts, starts rubbing her arms and looks around like she is trying to decide if she needs to escape. I stand still, waiting to see if she is going to bolt. She takes some deep breaths and seems to steady her nerves. She looks up at me, a mix of fear and shyness in her eyes. "You won't hurt me, will you?"

"Never, Yas. I would *never* hurt you. I know that you know that. We don't have to do this, I was just answering you honestly."

A determined look crosses her face. "I *do* know that you won't hurt me. This is just scary for me. I am glad that you were honest with me." She takes another deep breath and reaches out to cup my cheek in her hand. "You can tie me up. Scott."

* * *

Yasmin

I can't believe that I just told Scott that he could tie me up. I've never been into that, but, I *know* with every fiber of my being that he won't hurt me. I can do this for him. I walk away from him and towards his bed, shedding my clothes as I go. I kick off my shoes and lie on his bed, grabbing the metal headboard. "Is this where you want me?"

He looks at me for what feels like forever and finds his voice. "Yeah, baby, that's good." He grabs two controllers off the bookcase. "My new controllers are wireless so I'm going to have to use my old friends here." he explains as he tosses them on the bed then removes his clothes.

Scott climbs up on the bed and when he reaches the headboard, he starts wrapping a controller around my left wrist. "Is that too tight?" he asks. I shake my head no and he does the same to my right hand. I am lying here bare and bound to his bed. I close my eyes and try to steady my breathing, but I am starting to freak out a little.

"Easy, Yas. It's okay. I'm not going to do anything different than we've already done. It's exactly the same except for the fact that you can't use your hands. I promise. I'm going to make you feel good."

"Okay. I will be alright. Just give me a minute to get used to this. I-I don't really like it, but I will be fine. There are condoms in my purse if you don't have any in here." I swallow again and try to control my breathing.

"There are definitely none in here," he tells me as he walks over to my purse on the floor and grabs the foil packets. "Your purse is a mess. How do you find anything in there?" He laughs and I know he is trying to lighten the mood and make me more comfortable.

I laugh and tell him, "I can find things just fine." I *do* feel a little lighter but I am still nervous.

"Are you wet, Yas?" Scott asks and I can tell that he is not asking to be flirty. He wants to know if I am ready for him.

"Not really," I answer honestly.

He sits down on the bed next to me as he nods, placing his hand on my stomach. "I'm going to untie you now, Yas. I know that you don't want it like this and I can't make love to you knowing that you are scared of me." He starts to reach forward and I put on my big girl panties—figuratively—and tell him to stop.

"I am *not* scared of you, Scott. Giving up control is hard and I feel vulnerable. But I know you won't hurt me and I want you to live your fantasy. I am going to take you up on your offer to tie you up one day, too. I want you to understand how hard it is." I pause. "Oh, I just realized that you might have been tied up when you were experimenting."

He shakes his head. "I wasn't tied up, ever. I told you it was all about my pleasure and being tied up never interested me. You can tie me up whenever you want. Now I'm going to make you wet so that you are ready for me." he says as he starts moving his hand down my stomach.

I nod and close my eyes and I feel his fingers slip between my folds and down into me. A few pumps of his fingers and I'm wet. He swirls his thumb over my clit and I start straining against the controllers. "I'm ready for you, Scott," I rasp out.

"You're not wet enough yet." He bends over and starts licking one nipple while his hand pinches and kneads the other one. He sucks hard and then pulls his mouth up, letting my breast pop out of his mouth. "Come for me, Yas. I want you to be dripping when I enter you."

Then he's switching nipples and giving one the other one the attention that it wants. His fingers are still pumping in and out while his thumb presses on my clit. I'm thrusting my hips pushing his fingers in deeper. I can feel the pressure building. "Come on Yas, come for me, baby." Those words send me over the edge and I'm crying out as I spasm. He moves back from me taking his fingers with him and I hear him tear the condom open. I'm still coming down when he slams into me.

He is thrusting hard. I'm still a little sore from yesterday but I am also dripping wet, so he's slipping in and out with ease. He reaches next to me and grabs one of the pillows. Sitting back, he places it under my ass and then goes up on his knees. He continues his fast rhythm as he leans forward and reaches his hands up to clutch mine while he sucks and nibbles on my neck. I thread my fingers through his and we hold hands as he comes hard inside of me.

It takes him a few minutes to recover and then he's letting go of my hands and sliding out of me. He immediately unties my hands before he even takes the condom off. He starts kissing both of my wrists repeatedly and then looks into my eyes. "Thank you, Yas. That was better than any fantasy I had as a teen. I love you so much. Are you okay?"

"Yes, Scott, I'm okay. It wasn't too bad. I just hated that I couldn't touch you. Thank *you* for making me feel safe. I love you, too."

He leaves me briefly to get rid of the condom and then he is back, holding me. He hugs me to him and we stay like that for several minutes, while he kisses my head and rubs my back. I didn't lie to him. I don't know that I will ever want to do anything like that again, but he made me feel safe and loved. I'm glad that he didn't try to wait for me, though. I am not sure that I could have come with him pounding into me while I was bound.

Scott groans and then says, "I would love to stay here, holding you, but we should get going."

We get up and put our clothes on. He puts his controllers back and then we walk downstairs and out of the house. He holds my hand the whole way, only letting go when he opens the passenger door for me and gets in the car himself. He immediately grabs my hand again and holds it tight.

* * *

<u>Scott</u>

I can't believe I just had Yasmin in my old bed, tied to it with my game controllers. Every time I think that something we do together is the hottest, most erotic thing I have ever experienced, we do something to top it. I don't think anything will ever top what we just did. At least for me. I know that Yas wasn't completely into it and I really would have untied her. But, I won't lie. I am so fucking glad that she told me not to. I need to let her take the lead the next time we are together, though. I want to give her back some control. I think she may need it. God, I love this woman so much.

We get stuck waiting for a train to pass and I tell her. "Hey, baby, you're in charge next time. We'll do whatever you want. Wherever and however you want. Anything." I pull her hand to my mouth and kiss her knuckles.

"Thanks." I can see that I made her happy. And that makes *me* happy. "So, if I ask you to just go down on me for hours *and* tell me how much you love the taste of me, you'll do it?" I can see the mischief in her eyes when I glance over.

"Do I have to say I love it? I don't want to sound like one of your books," I groan. I will though, if that's what she wants.

She laughs so hard that I think she is going to pass out. "No, you don't have to say it and I wouldn't make you do that anyway. I'll think of something." It's her turn to pull our joined hand to her mouth and kiss mine.

"I would do it for you."

"I know."

It takes a while to get to the other side of town, where I spent my toddler and elementary school years. We don't talk much. Yas looks out the window taking in another part of my city while I concentrate on driving in the busy traffic.

When we reach my neighborhood, I pull up outside my old house and get out. I run around and open Yas's door as Mrs. Johnson comes down the steps.

"Scott Griffin as I live and breathe. Come over here and give me a hug."

"Hey Mrs. J. How have you been?" I grin as I envelope her in a hug.

"I'm sure that you don't want to hear about my problems. Especially when you have a pretty girl with you."

I reach behind me for Yas's hand and she moves forward to put it in mine. "Yas, this is my kindergarten teacher, Mrs. Johnson. Mrs. J, this is my girlfriend, Yasmin."

"It's a pleasure to meet you Mrs. Johnson," she says, sticking out her hand.

"Girlfriend? You finally managed to get yourself one of those? This calls for a hug, not a handshake." She pulls Yas into her and after a second of hesitation, my girl hugs her back. "Wait until I tell the rest of the neighborhood that little Scotty Griffin has a girlfriend."

"Yeah, yeah, you've had your fun. And please don't call me Scotty, I am almost 22 years old for Fu-God's sake."

She reaches out to ruffle my hair and totally undoes my faux hawk. "Why are you pulling your hair up into that peak? If you want a Mohawk, you should shave the sides like you are supposed to. I always taught you kids that you should do something right or don't so it at all."

"No!" Yas practically yells. "I like your hair Scott, please don't shave the sides."

I can't resist playing with her a little. "So, you wouldn't want me if I had a real hawk?"

"I didn't say that. Stop teasing me. I wouldn't care if you were bald. Well, I mean, I would care but I would still love you. "

"I like this girl, Scotty. You better treat her right."

"I'm trying to Mrs. J," I tell her ignoring that she called me Scotty again. "That's why I brought her by to see my old house." I turn to Yas. "When we moved to the bigger house, my parents didn't want to sell this one. Mrs. J was about to be evicted because her building was being torn down, so she moved in here."

"That's great."

"What he didn't tell you is that they let me live here for free."

I shift from side to side, embarrassed. Like my parents, I don't want attention on me for my good deeds. The awards ceremony in a few months is an exception to our rule and we wouldn't be doing that if it wasn't for it being given to us by Erin and Dave's favorite charity. I still can't believe that I have to wear a tux.

Yas brings me back to the present. "I'm not surprised that they did that for you. The Griffin family is very special."

"Yes they are. Now, why don't you two come in for some tea?"

"We don't have time for tea, but can Yasmin have a quick look around?"

"Of course she can."

We go inside and Yas walks around saying that she loves this house too. The sincerity in her voice makes me believe her. She runs hers finger over my growth marks in the kitchen and takes a picture of them. We say our goodbyes and get several more hugs before we are on our way again.

"Thank you for showing me where you grew up. Both places are so beautiful and I feel like I know so much more about you."

"I'll tell you anything you want to know about me. You just have to ask."

"Anything? Even the secrets that John is keeping for you?"

"Alright, maybe not everything."

CHAPTER 16

<u>Yas</u>

Today has been amazing. The Art Institute was beyond words and Navy Pier was so fun. But, meeting John and Mrs. Johnson has been the best. Getting to see how much these people love my man was just so special. Seeing the homes that he grew up in was pretty cool, too. I wouldn't call being tied to a bed by game controllers a highlight, except maybe it was. I mean, I wasn't really into it, but it meant a lot to Scott and he made me as comfortable as possible. Especially after, when he told me that I was in charge next time. He knew I needed to have control after feeling so vulnerable. I love him for that. I can't wait for the cruise and Windy City Tats. Zane has covered Scott in all of those beautiful tattoos and I know that he's important to him.

We get back to the hotel and as we walk through the lobby, the concierge intercepts us. "Your packages have arrived, Mr. Griffin. I had them taken up to your suite."

"Thanks," Scott tells her, smiling and pulling some money out of his pocket for a tip.

"What packages?" He is carrying my souvenir bags and I can't imagine what else he could have had delivered today.

"Surprise packages." He leans down to kiss me lightly. "Let's get upstairs so that you can see them."

I'm excited and a little nervous as we take the elevator upstairs. Scott opens the door and motions for me to go in first. I walk in and see several bags from the Art Institute covering one of the couches. "Wh-what are those, Scott?"

"Everything you wanted from the museum store," he tells me quirking the eyebrow with his piercing, causing the barbell in it to raise up, too.

"Everything I wanted? I only wanted the t-shirt and poster that I had you buy me."

"No, you only *asked* me for the t-shirt and poster. You *wanted* many other things. I saw your eyes light up and you bite your bottom lip several times in that store." He walks over and cups my face with his hands. "I knew you that you were going to do something like that. That you would tell me only a couple things because you don't want me spending money on you. But, I *want* to spend my money on you. There's no one I would *rather* spend my money on. So, I planned ahead and talked to the store manager while you were in the bathroom."

"Scott." I start, but he leans down and kisses the protest from my lips.

"Yas, I wanted to do this. Let me do this. Besides, I don't even know when your birthday is, so maybe this could be part of that, too, if it will make you feel better."

I see the love in his eyes and I can't deny him. "Thanks. It means a lot to me that you would pay attention to what I liked. My birthday is February 2. When is yours?"

"It's August 2."

"August 2. That's only in a few weeks!" I say, a little panicked. I already have a plan, I've had one all day even though I didn't know when his birthday was. But, I need to go online to find the finishing touches.

"You don't have to get me anything, Yas. I buy myself pretty much whatever I want. My family always tells me how hard I am to shop for."

"I happen to be an excellent gift giver and I already know what I'm going to give you. I just have to get it put together."

"Put together, huh? That sounds intriguing. Do I get a hint?" he asks while kissing my neck.

I push him away from me because we really need to get ready for the cruise. "No, no hints. Now, let me see what you got me. Because, maybe it's *not* what I wanted." I am teasing him, but I'm actually a little nervous. What if he thought I liked some hideous things?

I shouldn't have worried. As I take things out of the bags, I see the beautiful pieces of jewelry I had admired. The purse made of sari pieces that I had run my finger over and even the glass wall tiles I had looked at, knowing exactly where I would hang them in my house. There are many artwork prints and an umbrella covered in water lilies. There's more, too. He really *was* paying attention. I turn to look at him and he is shifting back and forth looking a little nervous.

"Did I get it right? That was the stuff you liked, wasn't it?"

"Yes, Scott. This is everything that I liked but didn't want to ask you for. Thank you." I kiss him again and then remind him that we need to get ready.

"You can use the dressing salon and I will get ready in the bedroom, Yas."

"You don't want to get ready together?" I ask him, confused.

"Actually, no. I think it might be cool if we get ready separately so that we can surprise each other. Is that weird?"

"No, that is definitely not weird. And for someone who once told me that he didn't know how to be romantic or woo me, you are doing an amazing job of both," I tell him honestly as I grab the bag filled with the museum jewelry so that I can wear some it tonight.

"Yeah? I guess I am better at this than I thought. I do have a wonderful muse who inspires me though. I wish I had time to show you just how much you *inspire* me."

I dodge his hands as I remind him of his promise. "I'm in charge tonight, remember? And I plan to show you how much I appreciate the romance and wooing. Now go get ready so that you can dazzle me." He already dazzles me but I can't wait to see him dressed up for dinner. I have never seen him dressed up and the thought makes me dizzy.

"Yes, ma'am." He salutes me and then heads to the closet while I go behind the curtain into the dressing salon. This suite is beyond amazing.

I go to one of the mirrored wardrobes and pull out the black Bettie Page dress I brought in case I needed to dress up while we were here. It has a high neck, landing just above my clavicle, and three quarter sleeves. It lands just below my knee and hugs my body like it was made for it. So, basically I am covered up but sexy. I was a little worried that it would be too hot to wear it, but I brought it just in case. I have other dresses but I want to wear this one, because I feel hot and sexy in it. Sam and Erika were with me when I bought it and they both said that it was a must buy. I'm banking on it being a little cooler on the water. If not, I will just suffer in silence. I pull a chunky, grey mother of pearl necklace out of the museum bag. It is the perfect style for the dress. I put my hair up, but leave a few curls falling, and do my makeup. I don't normally wear much, but I want to look extra special tonight. I slip on strappy black heels, grab a black clutch and I'm ready to go.

"Are you ready?" I ask through the curtain. I want us both to be fully dressed and ready for our date when we see each other.

"Yep. I am."

I move the curtain aside and nearly pass out from the sight in front of me. Scott is in a black suit with a green shirt underneath, open at the collar so a hint of his Griffin tattoo is showing. His hair is gelled up into its usual faux hawk and he has a smile on his face. He looks so good that it almost hurts to look at him. I mean I love him in t-shirts and shorts or jeans. Oh, and naked, especially naked. But this is Scott on a whole other level. As much as he hates suits, his body is made for them. Wow, just wow. The green compliments his eyes, which are encased in the glasses that he knows I love, and makes them pop even more than usual. Or maybe they're popping because his eyes went impossibly wide when I walked into the room.

"Holy fuck, Yas. You look so fucking hot. I mean, damn. I know you're hot, but damn. I can't even form a coherent sentence."

I laugh at his reaction, which warms me all over. "You just did."

"Huh, what?" he says still looking at me like his next meal. He seems to collect himself and chuckles. "Oh, yeah, I did. But, seriously, baby. I am going to be glaring at other guys all night as they check you out."

"They can check me out all they want. This dress is only coming off for one guy. And I am going to be glaring at a bunch of women tonight too. You are beyond hot in that suit. I know you don't like wearing suits, but holy fuck to you too."

"You're right. I don't like wearing suits, but seeing the look in your eyes right now is making me rethink my wardrobe choices."

"No. You should wear your t-shirts on a daily basis and just wear suits on occasion. Any more than that might cause me and every other woman who sees you to have a heart attack." I joke as I reach him and finger the lapels of his jacket. I'm not joking, though. I probably would have a heart attack if I saw him like this every day. "And with your glasses on, too? I am swooning right now. Oh shit, did I just say that out loud?"

"Yeah, you did. But I won't hold it against you since I think that I'm doing the male version of swooning, whatever that is called." He reaches out with one hand and fingers the built in belt that crisscrosses around the dress.

I step away because I know if I don't, we may not make it out of the room. "Come on, sexy man, we have a cruise to catch."

"I know you're looking forward to it. But, just know, I would love to stay here and peel that dress off of you." He reaches out and takes my hand, leading me to the door.

"You can do that later." I promise him as we head out the door.

As we walk into the lobby, I see many heads turn our way, both male and female, so I guess we are both being checked out. I feel so happy with his arm around me as he guides me towards the valet parking booth. I stop him near the concierge desk and ask her to take our picture. She takes several as we pose for her. I go to tip her, but Scott beats me to it with a smile. Then we are outside, getting in his Mustang and heading for Navy Pier.

* * *

Scott

I valet the car at the Pier and place my hand on Yasmin's back as we head to the boat. I don't know what to expect and don't think that this will really be my thing, but I know Yas is excited for the cruise, so I'm happy to play along. A photographer takes our picture as we board. He hands me a ticket with instructions on how to purchase the photo online. I'll do it because I know Yas will want one and hell, I want one too. I can't wait to put a picture of us in my place. I will have to ask Yas to text me some of the ones from earlier today.

"Can we go outside on the deck or did you want to eat right away?" she asks me.

"I'm good. We can go outside if you want." I smile at her as she clasps my hand and leads me outside. There are couches around the outside of the boat and we manage to snag one. I put my arm around her and hold her close as the boat pulls out into the lake. I kiss her temple and she looks up at me, her eyes shining with something. No, not just something. She is looking at me with love in her eyes. "I love you, Yas. Thanks again for coming here with me."

She turns her body towards me as she kisses me. It starts out sweet, but soon her tongue is teasing my lip ring and her mouth is opening for me. I slide my tongue in and explore her mouth. Her hands are in my hair and I am running mine up and down her arms. I pull her further towards me, wanting her on my lap, when a throat clears behind us.

"Excuse me, but there are children on board." I look up into the eyes of a nervous looking teenage employee.

"Sorry, man," I say with a smile as Yas stands up smoothing out her dress and placing herself in front of me to hide my erection. "But, if you were here with her, could you resist?" I add and the kid turns bright red.

"Behave," Yas says as she swats me on the shoulder. She turns to the kid. "You'll have to excuse him, he's not used to being around people. He's more comfortable with his computer."

He laughs and I want to be mad, but I can't. My girl is just too cute when she's trash talking me. "I'm pretty comfortable with you. And last time I checked, you're not a computer. But maybe I need to check you over again just to be sure." The kid looks ready to freak out again.

"Come on, let's go inside and get some dinner." She pulls me to my feet and in the door. "I think you scandalized that poor boy," she scolds me.

"Me? You're the one in the dress that will give him wet dreams for days."

"Just days?" She stares at me, pretending to pout.

"Years, baby, years. I, for one, am going to remember you in this dress for years."

"I can't show you how much I like that answer while we are on this boat where there are children present, but I promise that I'll show you later." My cock, which is still hard from our outdoor activities, twitches against my pants. I pull her firmly in front of me as the hostess shows us to our table.

I made sure that we had a two person table when I booked the cruise. I didn't want to share our night with anyone else. After we're seated, a waitress comes to the table. She is around Yasmin's age and is looking at me like I'm what *she* wants for dinner.

"Hi. I'm Amy. What can I get you to drink?" she asks looking only at me.

I look at Yas as I tell her, "My girlfriend would like a Coke and I'll have a scotch on the rocks." She leaves the table to get the drinks and Yas tells me how cool she thinks the boat is and thanks me again for doing this for her. "Of course. I love making you happy." I place my hand over hers on the table.

"Here are your drinks." Amy is back and as she places my scotch in front of me, I see a phone number on the napkin. I pull it out from under my drink and hold it up to her.

"You should save this for someone who wants to use it. You need to be respectful to my girlfriend or send someone else over here to take care of us." I know that I'm coming across as an ass for calling her out, but I'm pissed that she tried to give me her number after I called Yas my girlfriend.

"I'm sorry," Amy says turning to Yas, who nods at her. "I can take your order now if you are ready." She is subdued and embarrassed, but I'm not sorry.

After we order and she moves away, Yas smiles at me and says, "Thank you. I have never been out with a guy who did something like that."

"You were never with the right guy before."

We spend the next couple of hours enjoying our dinner, sharing a plate of desserts and dancing. We dance inside to some oldies and then go upstairs to the lounge where the DJ is. We steal some kisses in the dark corners of the ship and then we dock and head back to the car.

CHAPTER 17

<u>Yas</u>

The cruise was so much fun. The food was great and dancing with Scott was pretty amazing. I can't believe he told that waitress off for giving him her number. It was sweet and hot at the same time. We're heading to Windy City Tats now. I can't wait to meet Zane and see where Scott got all of his tattoos. Before we got in the car, Scott took off his jacket and glasses. He also rolled the sleeves of his shirt up. I don't think he wants to walk into the tattoo shop looking so straight laced. I like how he looks with his sleeve tattoos showing but still pretty dressed up. Honestly, I like him in whatever he's wearing. I am that far gone.

We drive for about 30 minutes and I think that we are near where he lived as a boy, but I'm not sure I do know that Scott and Zane were friends when they were kids, but lost touch until a few years ago. We pull into the parking lot of the shop. There's a neon sign outside, shaped like a gust of wind with that name of the shop flashing inside of it. It's pretty cool. We get out of the car and head towards the front door. There are a few guys outside and Scott nods and fist bumps with a couple. I see them checking me out and Scott does too. "This is my girlfriend, Yasmin," he tells them in a possessive voice, pulling me close. They say hello and then we head inside.

I'm overwhelmed when I walk inside and see the walls covered in tattoo designs. I have never been in a tattoo shop and it is fascinating. I'm looking around when I hear a female voice yell, "Scott!" I turn and see an absolutely gorgeous, tatted up blonde pull him into a hug and kiss him on the mouth

Scott hugs her tight. "I missed you so much, Quinn. How are you?"

"I'm doing great and I missed you too," she tells him, squeezing his biceps. I would be jealous or a little freaked out if I didn't know that Quinn is Zane's girlfriend. Scott has told me a lot about both of them.

A tall, handsome guy with brown wavy hair and big muscles straining against his t-shirt comes around the corner. "If you are going to put your mouth and hands on my woman, then I think I should get to put my mouth and hands on yours." He smirks at Scott while nodding towards me.

Scott and Quinn turn toward me and in the next second, I'm the one engulfed in a hug by Quinn. "Oh my God, you're Yasmin. Wow, I love your dress."

"Thanks, Quinn. It's great to meet you. Scott talks about you and Zane all the time."

"Don't tell them that, Yas. They'll think that they are important to me," Scott teases and he and Zane do the whole half hug guy thing. He looks at Zane and adds, "You can hug Yasmin, but any other touching would not be in your best interest."

"You think you can take me, Griffin?" Zane asks, flexing his biceps.

"I *know* that I can't, but that doesn't mean I wouldn't try." And then the tension is broken and they are both laughing.

"They are such boys," Quinn tells me. "But I love them –Scott like a brother, I mean." she adds hastily.

"I know, Quinn." I laugh. "Scott has told me how happy you and Zane are together."

"We *are* happy." It's Zane who answers, walking over to us. He turns to me. "Can I have my hug now?" He opens his arms and I step into him, laughing. "I hear that you're making Scott happy too. Thank you for that Yasmin," he whispers in my ear before letting me go.

"So, Yas, what do you think of the shop?" Scott asks me.

"It's really cool. I love all of the pictures of tattoos on the walls." I really do think it is cool. There are so many styles on display.

"Scott says that you like his ink," Zane says and I nod. "Would you like to see where the magic happens?"

"I would definitely love to see where you do his tattoos."

"Follow me," Quinn says, grabbing my hand. "Zane is wicked talented, isn't he?"

"Yes, he is. I love Scott's tattoos. They are beautiful."

"Do you have any tattoos, Yasmin?" Zane asks as we enter his space.

"No. I've never thought about getting one," I answer honestly. I look around the space. A chair that reclines dominates the space. There is a desk with a computer and printer as well as a drafting table in here as well. There are what I think are tattoo guns and cabinets too.

"If you ever decide to get one, I would love to do it for you."

"So, you really do want to get your hands on my woman, huh?" Scott tries to look angry, but I know he's not.

"Shut the fuck up, Scott. Would you really want me to go to someone else other than Zane for a tattoo?" Both Zane and Quinn burst out laughing.

"No. I wouldn't."

"Thanks for the offer. I may take you up on it one day," I tell Zane. "Is it okay if I take some pictures in here? And can I take some pictures of you guys and Scott?"

"Sure, go for it."

I take a bunch of pictures of everything and then of Scott, Zane and Quinn in different combinations. Scott takes some pictures of me with Quinn and Zane and then Quinn takes some of Scott and me. I enlist one of the other tattoo artists to take one of all four of us.

We stay at the shop for a couple of hours, talking and laughing. Zane said that he cleared his schedule for us and I can tell that Scott appreciates it. We are sitting in the employee break room on a couch and I have my head resting on Scott's shoulder when I can't hold back a yawn. "Are you tired, Yas? Why didn't you say something?"

"You are having fun with your friends. But, yeah, I am exhausted."

"Let's get you back to the hotel and into bed." He kisses me on the forehead and then pulls me up with him.

We say our goodbyes and there are hugs all around. Quinn and I exchange phone numbers and I promise to keep in touch with her. We head out of the shop and get back in the Mustang. I'm asleep before we pull out of the lot.

* * *

Scott

Yas looks so peaceful sleeping in the passenger seat and I hate to wake her up, but I have to get her upstairs. I get out of the car and go around to the other side, where the valet guy has opened her door. I hand my keys off to the guy and grab the ticket from him before I undo her seat belt and lift her out of the car. She stirs and then puts her arms around my neck before closing her eyes again. I carry her into the hotel and through the lobby to the elevator that will take us to our room.

When we get upstairs, I fumble a little getting the room key in, but I somehow manage it. I walk in and carry her to the bed. After I set her down, I run back to put the deadbolt on the door. I walk back into the bedroom and stare at her for a minute. She looks so beautiful lying at the edge of the bed in her sexy dress, with her knees over the side. She told me that I could peel her dress off of her when we got back to the hotel, but I was hoping that it would be in a different context.

I don't really mind, though. We have the rest of our lives together for that. Wait. Did I just think about spending the rest of my life with Yas? Yeah, I did and I know then that this is what I want. To be with Yas always. I should probably be scared or freaked out, but, I'm not. I'm not ready to ask the question yet but I *know* that I will ask her one day. I honestly can't imagine going back to a life without her.

I reach down and unclasp her necklace first and put it on the bedside table. She stirs and opens her eyes. "Scott, I'm sorry. I really did plan on seducing you tonight. I just felt so tired all of a sudden." Her eyes still look tired, so I reassure her.

"It's okay, baby, we will have plenty of other nights together. Today *was* amazing. Let me get this dress off of you so you can sleep comfortably." I turn her to her side so that I can undo the belt on her dress and unzip her. I pull it down and gently move her arms out of the sleeves. She is wearing a lacy black strapless bra that dips low and closes in the front. Fuck, it's hot and her tits are practically spilling out of it. I have to stop for a minute to adjust myself and take a few deep breaths. I need to let her sleep, but my cock doesn't agree with my decision. Once I've gotten myself a little under control, I turn her so that she is lying on her back. Then, I hold her up with one arm while I pull the dress down past her hips and all reason leaves me as I see that she is not wearing any panties.

My mind is on the same page with my cock and I stare, trying to decide how I can do this without being a total bastard.

"Like what you see, Griffin?" Yasmin says to me. I look up and see her eyes are open and she has a sexy smile on her face.

"Fuck, yeah, I love what I see!" I exclaim, pulling her dress the rest of the way down. My conscience makes me add, "Are you sure that you're awake enough?"

She looks up at me standing between her knees. "Yes, I am. Power naps are underrated."

I lean over her and kiss her belly button and then work my way up. When I get to her bra, I unclasp it and it falls to the side. Her awesome tits are free in front of me and I take them in my hands, loving their weight. I knead them and remind her. "Tonight is your show. What do you want?" She is moving between my legs as I run my thumbs over her hard nipples. "Do you want me to go down on you?"

"I always want you to go down on me. You are very good at it despite pretending that you don't like doing it." I chuckle as she continues. "But what I really want to do right now is ride your cock. First, I need to get all of these clothes off of your hot body." She sits up and starts to unbutton my shirt, pulling it out of my pants.

I continue playing with her tits while she undresses me. I know she's getting wetter by the second because her breasts really do it for her. She's already breathing hard. I could probably make her come again like the first night we were together, but I want to be inside of her first, so I loosen my grip and whisper my fingers across her instead. She leaves my shirt on me after it's unbuttoned and starts on my pants. She makes quick work of my belt and before I know it, she is pushing my pants down, but leaving my underwear on. She moves back, reaching for her purse.

"Baby, what's wrong?" I ask, because she usually doesn't move away from me while I am playing with her tits.

"Nothing. Everything is perfect," she says as she turns and I see her phone in her land, lifting up to take a picture of me standing there in my unbuttoned shirt and boxer briefs. "You look so damn hot, I wanted a picture." I smirk as she gets up on her knees and takes a couple more pictures and then puts her phone back in her purse and throws it on the floor. She moves forward and pushes my shirt off of my shoulders and down my arms where it falls to the floor. "I love the way you look in your boxer briefs." That doesn't stop her from reaching out and pulling them down. They pool at my feet with my pants. I push my shoes off and step out of everything.

I get on the bed and lay down on my back. "Okay, Yas. I'm all yours. Have your way with me, woman."

"Oh, I will, don't you worry about that." She grabs the condoms from the bedside table and tears one off. "You just lay there and look pretty." she adds with a wicked grin.

"Pretty? I do not look..." I start to say but lose all train of thought when she takes my cock into her mouth. My hips jump off the bed as I thrust into her mouth.

She sucks for a few seconds and then releases me with a pop. "Do you have a problem with being pretty?" she asks, quirking her eyebrow.

"No, no. I can be pretty. I'm really pretty." I would say anything right now.

She throws her head back and laughs. Then, she tears open the condom and rolls it on me. She positions herself over me and guides my cock to her entrance. She slides down and takes me fully into her. If there is a better feeling in the world, I haven't felt it. My hands go to her hips as hers move up my chest. She leans down and kisses me. Our tongues meet and we kiss for a few minutes. My cock won't take me sitting still for long and I can't fight the urge to thrust. Yas pulls back from me with a smile on her face. She starts to ride me, rolling her hips. I meet her with my thrusts.

She starts moving faster and I move my hands from her waist, knowing that I don't need to help her. She'll ride me hard on her own. I use one hand to pinch her right nipple in between my fingers and move my other hand to her clit. I pinch and rub her as she starts to go faster and soon she's slamming up and down on my cock. My spine is already tingling and I'm trying to hold back when she starts screaming my name and comes hard. She's still moving on me and holding onto my shoulders for leverage as she shakes. I grab her hips again and thrust hard twice before letting my orgasm take me. A string of curse words leaves my mouth as she collapses on me.

"Maybe you should be in charge more often, Yas," I get out between breaths.

"We can take turns being in charge, Pretty Boy," she says and then pulls herself up to look me in the eyes. "But, I-I don't think you can tie me up again."

She looks away and I pull her face back to me. "I don't need to do that to get off. Obviously. Thank you again for making my fantasy come true, though. I love you Yas." I kiss her lightly and then move her off of me so that I can go and take care of the condom.

"I love you too, Scott. I am glad that I could do that for you." I can hear the honesty in her voice.

Although things are god right now, I still want to lighten the mood. "So, Pretty Boy, huh? Is that your new nickname for me?" I tease her as I walk back to the bed.

"Maybe, it is," she replies saucily as she takes off her shoes.

"I think I like it." I pull back the covers and we climb into bed. I cuddle her close and again thank God for bringing Yas into my life. I know that tomorrow is going to be hard for me and depending on what Amber's lawyer comes at me with, it may be hard for Yas too. But, I know that I can handle anything with her at my side. I will do whatever I can to protect her. That is my last thought as I drift off to sleep.

CHAPTER 18

<u>Yasmin</u>

I wake up and see the sun starting to light up the sky. I carefully wiggle out of Scott's arms, trying not to wake him up. He stirs but then turns onto his stomach and continues to sleep. I check the clock and see that he doesn't need to be up for a couple more hours. They want him at the courthouse at 10. He'll be the first prosecution witness but they aren't sure exactly what time they will need him. We'll wait in a room there until it's time for him to testify. I'm glad that I can be there for him but I'm a little nervous about what I may hear. I know the defense attorney will try to dis-credit him. I also know that he was with Amber for a year and I know that they were together in every way, despite her having a "real" boyfriend. I think I can handle whatever I hear, but it may be hard. I know Scott loves me and that he hates her and would never want her again. I just have to remind myself of that when I'm in the courtroom.

I use the time I have to take a shower and go over some of the loan applications that Erika slipped in the pocket of my suitcase.

I'm hoping that I can get at least one so I can buy the software she keeps telling me about. I also order us breakfast. I'm waiting for room service when I remember that I still haven't looked at the article about the software that I shoved in my purse weeks ago. I don't know that I really need to since Erika and Sean have told me everything they know about it, but they said that I should know about the guy who designed it, that he seems really cool.

They're dating now and really cute together. We're still planning on a double date since they keep missing Scott whenever he is in the store. I'm just reaching for the article when the room service guy knocks at the door. Oh, well. I've waited this long, I can wait a little longer to find out about this mystery guy.

I am setting our breakfast on the suite's dining room table when Scott wraps his arms around me from behind. "Morning, baby," he says, moving my hair out of the way and nuzzling my neck. I love it when he does that. The barbell from his eyebrow always feels good rubbing against me. "Thanks for taking care of breakfast."

I turn around and kiss him lightly. "You're welcome. I wanted to let you sleep as late as possible. You should probably jump in the shower so that you'll have time to eat."

He nods and I notice that he looks a little subdued. It is what I would expect. He is about to walk into his own version of Hell today. I kiss him again, trying to convey how much I love him and support him. He lets me go and smiles down at me. "I'll be back in a few. Don't eat all of the bacon," he yells over his shoulder before closing the bathroom door.

We eat and get dressed without saying much. I think that we are both trying to mentally prepare ourselves for the day. I put on a pink button down blouse with a black trumpet skirt and low black heels. I reach into the museum bags again for some pearl and leaf earrings and a pearl necklace. Scott is in another suit, this time grey. He pairs it with a bright blue shirt and a grey and black patterned tie. I'm practically drooling again but keep it in check as I know that we need to get to the courthouse. Scott holds my hand the entire drive and I can feel the tension in him mounting as we get closer.

We park and walk inside, still holding hands. After we're through the metal detectors, we take the elevator up to the correct floor. The doors open and we step out. I can't believe what I see and I can tell Scott is surprised as well since he stops walking with a jerk on my hand. Gary, Maggie, Ryan, Owen, Luke, John, Zane and Quinn are all waiting in the hallway.

Maggie rushes over and hugs us both. "Wh-what are you all doing here?" Scotts asks, swallowing hard.

"We know you have Yasmin, but we wanted to be here for you as well," Gary says.

Scott looks from one person to the next and smiles, tears forming behind his eyes. "Thank you. I appreciate it. I love you all."

"We love you too, Bro," Owen speaks first and everyone nods.

The prosecutor comes up to us and tells us that Scott cannot enter the courtroom until he is called to testify. He shows us to the room where he wants him to wait. Everyone else says that they're going to go inside and get seats, but I choose to wait in the room with Scott.

"We'll save you a seat, Yasmin," Luke tells me, squeezing my arm.

"Thanks, Luke. I'll see you guys in there."

Scott pulls me to him when they leave and we hold each other for several minutes. "Is it okay if I don't let you go until they call me?"

"Of course, Pretty Boy. You can hold me as long as you need to."

He pulls me over to a chair and sits down, bringing me onto his lap. "I see the nickname is staying."

"You said that you liked it."

"I said that I *think* that I like it," he says, in a teasing tone. I am glad that I am helping to ease some of his tension.

"So, you want me to stop using it?"

"I didn't say *that.*"

"Because I can come up with something else."

"Oh yeah, like what?" he asks, nuzzling my neck again.

"Hmm, maybe Game Boy?"

He bursts out laughing. "You know that Game Boys were hand-held devices right?"

"Yes, I even had one." I stick out my tongue at him. "It does fit you, though. You like to play games."

"Not with you, Yas. Never with you."

"Pretty Boy it is then." I kiss him until a bailiff knocks at the door.

* * *

<u>Scott</u>

I am so glad that Yas and my family and friends are going to be in the courtroom. She just went to go take her seat while I wait with the bailiff until they call me in. I tap my fingers on my thigh, nervous and wound tight. I'm ready for the prosecution questions, but I have no idea what the defense attorney is going to come up with.

The courtroom is quiet as I walk in. I see everyone sitting in the row right behind the prosecutor's table. Yas meets my eye and smiles. I smile back and then look to the other side. I see Amber, but she's not looking at me. She's glaring at Yas. She seems to sense me staring at her and looks me in the eye with a sneer. Then, she leans over to her lawyer, whispering in his ear. His eyes go wide but he nods, bringing something up on his computer. That makes me nervous but I don't have time to think about it as I reach the witness stand. I am sworn in and take my seat.

The prosecution questions go as expected. We have rehearsed these so there are no surprises. Then, the defense attorney gets up and I notice Amber smirking. Shit! What has that bitch got up her sleeve?

"Mr. Griffin, you stated that you knew nothing about Miss Montgomery's plans, is that correct?"

"Yes."

"Can you explain to me how you could be in a relationship with someone for a year and yet claim not to know anything about that person?"

"I believed what Amber told me about herself. I had no reason to doubt her."

"Your honor, I have a new piece of evidence that I would like to enter into evidence."

"Go ahead," the judge says as the defense lawyer hands a copy to the court clerk and another to the prosecutor.

The prosecutor immediately jumps to his feet. "I cannot see how this is relevant, your honor." What the fuck?

"I can assure you that it *is* relevant," the defense attorney says.

"I will let this be admitted," the judge says looking over the document. "But, you need to get to its relevancy quickly."

"Yes, your honor." He turns to me, handing me a copy of the document. "Do you recognize this as a text conversation between Miss Montgomery and yourself Mr. Griffin?" I look at it and wonder why the hell he would think that this is relevant. But, I nod, because I do recognize the conversation.

"Yes."

"Please read the document to the court, Mr. Griffin."

"What? I am not going to read this out loud."

"Son, you need to do it." The judge has a stern but somewhat sympathetic look on his face.

I look to Yas and try to convey how sorry I am. Then I start to read it out loud.

Amber: Can you come over tonight? I miss you and your dick.

Scott: I wish that I could but I have to finish this project for my dad. My dick misses you, too.

Amber: You're at your parent's house? Are you alone?

Scott: Yeah, I'm alone.

Amber: What would you like to do with me if I was there with you?

Scott: Amber, I really have to work.

Amber: I've got my hands inside my panties...

Scott: Shit. OK, I guess I can take some time away from my work.

Amber: Good, because I am pretending that it is your fingers inside of me. Are you unzipping you pants?

Scott: Yes, I am. I wish my fingers were inside of you and it was your hand stroking me.

Amber: Do you want to take me on your bed?

Scott: No, I want to bend you over the garden wall and fuck you senseless.

Amber: Ooh, outside. What if your parents saw us?

Scott: They are out at a party. There is no one here.

Amber: Then, why won't you take me in your room?

Scott: I just wouldn't.

Amber: I think you just like to keep me your dirty little secret. You haven't introduced me to your family or friends yet.

Scott: I will when the time is right.

"You can stop there, Mr. Griffin. You said that you were waiting for the right time. Was this because you were finalizing the plans you were making to rob your sister's house?

"What? No! Are you fucking insane?" I jump out of the chair as the courtroom goes wild.

"Order! Order! the judge yells, banging his gavel. "Sit down, Mr. Griffin." I sit down but I am seething. I look to Amber who is smirking again and then to Yas who is looking at the defense attorney like she wants to kill him.

"Mr. Griffin, did you buy an engagement ring for Miss Montgomery from Harry Winston jewelers."

"Yes, I did."

"Did you give Miss Montgomery that ring?"

"No."

"Why not?"

"I was planning on giving it to her the night that she murdered my sister and brother-in-law. In fact, I was waiting at my apartment for her when my parents called me with the news of what she had done."

"Isn't it true that you were actually waiting at the apartment for her to return after the robbery? The ring was part of your celebration plans, wasn't it?"

I start to rise up again but catch Yasmin's eye. She shakes her head and looks at me wide eyed. I get what she is trying to convey and sit back down. I'm not going to let this bastard rile me up so that I look bad to the jury.

"No and no," I say calmly. "I loved my sister with everything that I have. I would never steal from her. Besides, why would I need to? I have plenty of money."

He looks a little shaken at how calm I am. I have to fight the urge to smirk. That won't look good to the jury either.

He recovers and hits me with another hard question. "So, you say that you are waiting at your apartment to propose to the woman that you love when you get the call from your parents. If that happened to me, my first instinct would be to return that engagement ring so that I would never have to see it again. Did you return that ring, Mr. Griffin?"

"No. I didn't," I sigh.

"You didn't return the ring. Is it because you still love Miss Montgomery and are hoping that she is acquitted so that you can continue your relationship with her?"

"I didn't return the ring because it is in my apartment, which I have not returned to since that night. I do not want to have any kind of *relationship* with Amber. I do not love her and have recently realized that I never really did. I thought I did, but it took me *really* falling in love to realize that what I shared with Amber wasn't it." I look Yas in the eye as I say those words.

"You bastard! You dumb, stupid bastard!" Amber is out of her seat yelling. "You think you're in love with her? The fat chick?" She points at Yas and my blood begins to boil. I have never hit a woman, but I want to now. The other lawyers at her table try to get her to sit down, but she shoves them off. "Thank God I didn't share my plans with you! You are too stupid for words." She realizes what she just said and her eyes go wide. Her lawyer turns pale.

"No further questions, your honor."

The prosecutor says that he has no further questions and the judge calls for lunch recess. As I'm walking from the witness stand, I see Yas walk towards Amber, a steely resolve in her eyes.

She reaches her just as the bailiff takes Amber's arm to lead her from the room. I reach them just as Yas starts to speak.

"Listen to me, bitch. This *fat chick* could and will kick your ass if you ever come near the Griffin family again. Especially Scott. He is *mine* and I will protect what's mine to the death. Do you understand?" The fierceness in my girl's eyes is something I have never seen before and I see Amber go pale. She nods as the bailiff takes her away.

I grab Yas and kiss her passionately.

"Damn that was hot!" I hear Luke say. "You are one scary but hot woman, Yasmin."

"She is *my* woman," I remind him with a growl.

Ryan is the one who answers. "We are all very aware of that, Scott." He places a hand on my shoulder and continues, "If we weren't already, we are now." He looks at Yas with admiration in his eyes and I relax.

The prosecutor walks us out and tells us that it went better than expected. Amber's outburst has pretty much sealed her fate. He won't need me again so he says that we can go back to Vegas. My parents and brothers are heading back but I want to stay one more night. There is something that I need to do.

We have dinner with everyone at one of our favorite Chicago restaurants. After, my family heads to the airport. Zane and Quinn head to work and John goes back home. During dinner, I thanked them all for being there for me and many hugs were shared before they left. I am truly lucky to have all of these people in my life, especially Yas. Now it is time to take her home. To my apartment.

CHAPTER 19

<u>Scott</u>

After seeing Yas tell off Amber, I realized that it's stupid of me to keep her out of my places. She loves me and I need to trust her, fully, with my heart. I didn't plan on going to my apartment, but I know that I's time for me to face it. With Yas by my side, I think that I can face anything.

As we're driving, she notices that we are not turning towards the W. "Are we not going back to the hotel, Pretty Boy?" she asks and I smile at the nickname.

"No, baby, I wanted to take you somewhere else if that's alright."

"Of course it is." She pulls her joined hands to her lips and kisses my knuckles.

As we pull up to the underground garage, I let go of her hand to pull the parking card out of the center console. I touch it to the sensor and drive in when the arm lifts. I wave at Jerry in the security booth as I drive in. He's surprised to see me and waves to me with a smile on his face.

I get out and run around to open the passenger door for Yas. I guide her to the elevator and we take it to the lobby. As we step out, Bobby jumps up from his seat. "Scott! It is so good to see you. It's been too long."

I walk over and shake his hand. "It's good to see you too, Bobby." I turn back to Yas and can tell from the look on her face that she knows where we are. "This is my girlfriend, Yasmin. Yas, this is Bobby, one of the doormen here in my building. And a friend."

"It's great to meet you Bobby," Yas says walking to us and holding out her hand.

"Yeah, you too." Bobby looks at me with a curious expression on his face. "I don't know if I should let out this guy's secret, but I have never seen him bring a woman here."

"It's not a secret," I tell him laughing. "Yas knows that she is the first."

"I do. But thanks for telling me anyway." She smiles at Bobby and then we say our goodbyes as I take her hand and lead to the elevators. We get in and I punch the button for my floor.

"Are you sure about this?" Yas asks, placing her hand on my forearm as we step out into the hallway.

I turn to her and cup with face with my hands. "Yes, I'm sure. I want to show you my apartment and when we get back to Vegas, I want you to stay over at my house there. I love you, Yas. I should have let you in sooner and I'm sorry that I made you wait. But, I want to share everything with you now."

She places her hands over mine. "You are worth the wait. But, I am glad that you want to share all of yourself with me now. I love you too and I can't wait to see your apartment and the rest of your place in Vegas."

I let go of her face and walk to my door. I take a deep breath and unlock it.

* * *

Yasmin

Scott holds the door open for me and I walk past him into his apartment. I know that this is a big deal for him, so it is a big deal for me too. The setup here is similar to his guest house in Vegas. It is definitely a guy's place with modern furniture and some cool metal sculptures. I walk over to one.

"That's Owen's work."

"Wow! I didn't know he was a sculptor!" I am amazed that someone I know made this beautiful piece of art.

"He paints too. His pieces are in our company's buildings around the world."

"That is so cool."

I must sound too excited because Scott pulls me against him from behind and whispers in my ear. "Computers are cooler."

I laugh. "I don't know about that but a certain computer guy I know is pretty cool." He kisses my neck. "And sexy."

"Sexy, huh? How sexy is this guy?" He moves his hands down and starts unbuttoning my blouse.

"So sexy that I think my panties melted the first time I met him," I admit, shivering as he pulls my shirt out of my skirt and rubs my stomach.

He spins me around, mischief in his eyes. "Even though I tried to steal your pen?"

"Even then," I tell him, honestly.

"Well, then I should probably confess that this sexy, pen loving bookworm I know made me harder than I have ever been in my life the day that I met her, too. I had to go next door to the coffee shop for a cold drink to cool off."

"I wanted to grab you and push you against the bookshelves and kiss you." I can't believe I just told him that, but it's true.

"You did that a few weeks ago."

"I know and it was better than I imagined. You are better than I could have ever imagined."

"I feel the same, Yas. So, what do you think of my place so far?"

I walk around and look at everything. It is so *him* and I love it. I'm about to tell him this when I round the corner of the kitchen island and see it on the lower counter. The little black velvet box. I can't resist picking it up and flipping it open. One of the most beautiful rings that I have ever seen stares back at me, sparkling in the light. I don't know how many carats the round diamond is, but it's huge. It's definitely not my style but I can appreciate the beauty of it.

"Baby, you didn't answer me yet. Do you like—oh shit!"

"It's beautiful." I'm trying to breathe normally. I know I'm being stupid. He's with *me*. He brought *me* here. But, seeing the ring that your boyfriend was going to give to another girl is not exactly easy.

He takes it out of my hand and closes the box. "It's way too big and just, ugh. I mean yeah, it's from a fancy jeweler and technically it's pretty high class, but I only bought it because I knew that she wanted it. I wouldn't have bought something so flashy otherwise." He opens a drawer and throws it inside. "I need to have John return that for me."

He runs his fingers through his hair and I can tell that he's frustrated and nervous. "How about you show me your bedroom?"

He smiles, taking my hand and leading me up the stairs. His bedroom is all black and grey. There is no desk here or computer parts. Just a giant platform bed, a dresser and some side tables. Oh, and of course a giant TV. "I know it's not fancy. I wasn't sure how I wanted to decorate it, so I didn't."

"You don't have to explain to me. I'm not interested in you for your design skills."

"Oh, really? What *are* you interested in me for?" he asks, moving close.

I spend the next few hours showing him a big part of what I am interested in him for. We go back to the hotel and cuddle for the rest of the night before heading to the airport to take the jet back to Vegas. We're settled with drinks and snacks when Scott reaches into his messenger bag. He turns back to me with a bunch of pens arranged in a bouquet.

"I thought that you would like these better than flowers." He smiles at me, looking a little bashful.

"You know me so well." I look at them closer as I take them from him. "Wait, these are from the places we visited in Chicago. Oh my God, thank you Scott."

"Yep, they are. The plain ones are from Mrs. J's and the court-house. They didn't have any special ones there."

"You stole me some pens?" I ask laughing.

"*No*, I asked for them. I promise. I don't want the bookworm pen police after me."

I punch him in the arm and then start taking the bouquet apart to look at each pen.

A Water Lilies pen from the Art Institute.

One with the giant Ferris wheel from Navy Pier.

A Nintendo themed one. I look up at him, "From your room?" He nods and I kiss him lightly.

A plain black Bic.

A ship themed one with the logo of the cruise company.

A Windy City Tats silver one with the swirling logo.

A plain blue Papermate.

One from the restaurant we ate at with his family and friends.

A fancy brown one. I quirk an eyebrow at him. "Oh, that one's from Bobby," he explains.

Finally, there is one from the W.

"Best. Boyfriend. Ever." I lean over to kiss him. We make out for the rest of the flight as Velvet keeps herself busy in the front of the plane.

* * *

<u>Scott</u>

We've been back from Chicago for two weeks now. I jumped right back in to the software project and Yas has been taking care of things at the bookstore. We alternate our nights between her place and mine and things are as good as ever. My dad and Ryan didn't want me to stress out about the project in case I had to stay longer for the trial or go back again so they pushed back the release date of the program. Amber was convicted last week and is awaiting sentencing. I am not going back for that. I said all that I had to say. I have a month before the program has to be ready but I'm still on track to have it done in two weeks. I asked to meet with them today at the new Vegas office to talk to them about something that I would like to do.

My dad's secretary, Angie, shows me into his office where they're both waiting for me. "Wait, are you Scott? My brother? I think it's you but between your computer and your girlfriend, I haven't seen you in a long time," Ryan jokes.

"Shut up smart ass. We just had dinner with everyone last night." I punch him in the arm which hurts me more than him. Damn, my brother is *built*. All that construction work he did for a few years hasn't worn off, I guess.

"I know but I had to give you shit. I've never seen you this way before. It's actually pretty cool. Yasmin's pretty cool."

"Yeah, she is. She's also the reason that I wanted to talk to you guys today."

"Is everything alright with her, son?" My dad asks, concerned. My mom and he have really taken to Yasmin and I know they think of her as part of the family already.

"I don't think so," I tell them honestly, pulling on my lip ring with my teeth. "I don't think the bookstore is doing well. She doesn't really talk about it with me. I offered her money but she said no. So, I have another idea to help her."

"My opinion of her just increased. I knew she was a good person, but to refuse your money when your relationship is so new and you seem to think that she needs it, just tells me how good she is. You want to give her the program don't you?" Ryan says.

I look at them both and sigh. "Yes. I know we lowered the price for independent bookstores and agreed to give it to them early but I'm not sure that she can afford it, even at the lower price." I take a deep breath and continue. "I will have it done in two weeks. I would like to give it to her then, before everyone else."

I wait anxiously until my dad speaks. "I wish we could, son. But, we can't show blatant favoritism like that. I am perfectly fine with you giving her it for free, though. That is you giving a gift to your girlfriend." Ryan nods his agreement.

"Thanks, guys. I knew giving it to her early was a long shot. And, I can pay the fee for the program myself if that would look better."

"No, it's fine. You created it and you should be able to have at least one free copy," Ryan says.

"I just had a thought. We're having that joint birthday and project completion party for you in three weeks. Why don't you give it to her then if it's done? If you ask her not to use it yet, I'm sure that she'll agree. Do you think she will agree to the program if she wouldn't take your money?" my dad asks.

"Yeah, I could do that. That would be cool. She *is* the best present I've ever gotten. I hope that she'll take it. I haven't talked to her about it. She is not very computer savvy. Do you think Mom would be okay with me inviting her friends that she works with and maybe her other friend, Candi?"

"Are you kidding? You know that your mom loves entertaining, as long as it's casual and not our business associates."

"Cool, I'll call and tell her. Thanks again guys."

* * *

Yas

I had my meetings with the bank and the private investors. They didn't go well. It looks like I may have to get a second mortgage after all. Erika and Sam convinced me that I should go that route instead of just selling the house. A part of me thinks that I should've taken Scott up on his offer, but I know that I made the right decision by saying no to his money.

Things are going so well with him. He did what he promised and took me to his house. It's nice to be able to stay over there when we have dinner with his family instead of driving back to my place. His deadline for the project that he's working on is coming up fast too, so it is easier for him to already be at his place. And next week will be the party to celebrate the completion of his project along with his birthday.

"I can't believe that I finally get to meet this mystery man of yours," Erika tells me as she comes in to work.

"He's not a mystery, Sam has met him. You just keep missing him."

"I have and he's pretty hot," Sam says as she comes out of the back after her shift is over.

"Speaking of hot, why are you taking this Justin guy to the party instead of putting Danny out of misery and going with him?" I ask her.

"Danny doesn't like me like that."

"Oh, yes, he does," Erika tells her. "You just never give him a chance. You always find these jerk guys to date instead."

"Justin is not a jerk!"

"Umm, yeah he is."

"Let's just agree to disagree about Justin," I say before they start fighting and scare away the few customers that we have in the store. "But I do wish that you would give Danny a chance. A good guy is not a bad thing."

"I'll think about it," she tells me and then hugs us goodbye.

"So, Sean told me that the company that is doing the computer program has pushed back the launch date for two weeks. The programmer had some personal things to deal with apparently. So, you should get your loan payment before then," Erika tells me.

"Oh wow. That is good news. I was worried that I would be last to get it which would suck since I'm counting on the extra business you guys think that I will get from the website to help with expenses."

"Speaking of hot, I saw a picture of the programmer the other day. If I wasn't in love with Sean, I would have to think of a way to meet him."

"That good, huh?" I ask. "Good thing I'm in love, too!"

"I don't know, maybe you could get a free program if you dated him."

"You know I would never do something like that."

"I *do* know that and it is one of the reasons that we are such good friends. You would never think of using someone."

This Hallmark moment is getting a little intense and Emotional Yasmin is threatening to come out. Thankfully, Alex and Maggie arrive to distract me.

"Hi Yasmin! Hi Erika!" Alex says.

Maggie comes over, too. "It's good to see you, Erika."

"You too, Maggie. You know I always think that you look familiar every time I see you."

"I have one of those faces, I guess." Maggie turns to me. "Is now a good time to stop by your friend's bakery to talk about the cake?"

I look to Erika who tells me she will be fine without me for a couple of hours. I grab my purse and we head to Drago Sisters Bakery. My friend Eliza, and her aunt Doreen, help us design the perfect cake for Scott. We go to the party store to pick out a few decorations and then they drop me back at the store.

It's still slow so I head to my office to work on my present for Scott, telling Erika to call me if she needs me. While we were in Chicago, I decided that I wanted to make him a scrapbook type album of our trip. I covertly gathered napkins and little things from the places that we visited while we were there. I bought some cool video game papers and stickers from Japan through Ebay to use with the pictures from the houses and apartment and they arrived a couple of days ago. I have also kept in contact with Quinn and she sent me some stuff too. I think what I have done is pretty cool and I can't wait to give it to him.

CHAPTER 20

<u>Yasmin</u>

Today is Scott's birthday and I wake him up with my mouth. I'm on my knees between his legs and he has his hands in my hair, thrusting into my mouth as I take him deep. My fist is wrapped around his base, matching the rhythm of my mouth as I bring him to his climax. He jerks up off the bed as he comes. "Fuck Yas. Baby, yes. Shit."

I move up his body, peppering him with kisses as I go. When I reach his mouth, I tell him, "Happy Birthday, Pretty Boy," and then kiss him hard. His hands are moving up and down my spine and then grabbing my ass. We make out for an hour or so before taking it further. We actually enjoy making out like teenagers and do it often. I took the day off from work and Scott is done with his project, so we stay in bed all day. I lose count of how many orgasms he gives me and I have to remind him at one point that it's his birthday and not mine. He laughs and tells me that he likes watching me come so it's all good.

We finally get out of bed to shower and dress separately. Ever since we got dressed separately for the dinner cruise in Chicago, we've been doing it for every date. It's fun to get ready and then see the look of surprise and appreciation in Scott's eyes when he sees me. I use the master bath and bedroom and he uses the guest room and bathroom down the hall. I realize that I forgot my new hair clip in my purse so I run out of my room to get it stopping in my tracks as Scott walks out of the bathroom in only a towel. I have seen him in a towel many times, but it never gets old.

"We have to go to the party, Yas," he reminds me. "You can't look at me like that." He sprints into the guest bedroom and slams the door. I break out of my trance and go grab the clip.

I'm wearing another Bettie Page dress. They flatter my figure and I know that I look good. This one is a halter style that is fitted all the way down into a pencil skirt. It is covered in light blue flowers with gold centers and trimmed in black. I do my hair in a 50s style with big curls and waves framing my face and clip the blue flower into the side. I've got on black wedges with ankle straps. I clip on the firecracker earrings Scott bought me at the Art Institute and I am ready to go.

Me: Ready?

Scott: Yep.

Me: OK. I'm coming out.

* * *

Scott

Yas walks into the living room and as usual, I have to catch my breath. I have a similar reaction every time I see her, no matter what she's wearing. But, when she wears those retro dresses, I feel like I'm going to come in my pants like a kid. I am one lucky bastard. I can't wait to give her the program tonight. I hope that she isn't too proud to take it. It didn't cost me any money and since it's something that I created, I think that she will accept it.

"There are no words for how good you look," I tell her honestly. That dress has got to be illegal in some states.

"You look good too." I see her look me over, appreciatively. I dressed up a little, but didn't go all out. It is *my* party, after all. I am wearing a blue button down with the sleeves rolled up to my elbows, untucked over dark long slacks. I have my combat boots on my feet.

"I told you that you can't look at me like that," I growl. We have spent all day in bed and I still want her like we have been apart for weeks. I know that she feels the same way. We can't get enough of each other.

"I can't help it," she insists.

"We better go while we still can." I drive to my parents' house in my Mustang, which I had shipped out from Chicago last week. I love my car and since we are settled here in Vegas now, I wanted it with me.

We arrive at the house and head out to the patio where everyone is gathering. Sam is there with some guy, while Danny looks at her like she kicked his puppy. Yas told me that he's in love with Sam, but she won't give him a chance. The guy she brought looks like a douche, but I'll be nice to him. Sam is a cool girl so I don't want her to feel uncomfortable. Yas' friend Candi is there too and she's flirting and laughing with Owen. Hmm, that's an interesting development.

Yas runs up to my mom and Alex and quickly apologizes. "I am *so* sorry that I wasn't here to help decorate."

"It's fine, Yasmin. We had it under control. Your friend dropped off the cake earlier, too," my mom tells her.

"How did it come out?" Yas asks anxiously.

Alex answers her. "It looks so good! You picked the perfect design."

"You and your grandma helped."

"We just agreed with you. You designed it. Don't shortchange yourself," my mom admonishes her.

"Can I see this amazing cake?" I ask.

"When it's time. No peeking," Yas scolds me and turns back to my mom. "We will have to keep him out of the kitchen."

"I'll be good. I promise." I chuckle as I kiss Yas's temple. "I can't wait to see what you came up with for me and what's in that package you're carrying."

"After dinner, you can have it all."

I lean down to her ear. "All? Really? I already had it several times today, but I want it some more."

She turns red, but whispers back, "You can have it all you want later."

"I'll take you up on that," I tell her and then say loud enough for everyone to hear, "Let's eat."

Dinner is great. My mom made all of my favorites and I have fun talking and laughing with everyone. My family makes Yas' friends feel welcome and included in our conversations. The plates are cleared and we're waiting for Erika and Sean to arrive to have the cake. Erika had to close the store and Sean stayed with her.

They're at the door and my mom and Alex go to start preparing the cake. Yas tells them that she will join them in a few minutes, after she greets her friends. A pretty blonde who I assume is Erika steps through the sliding door first and freezes when she sees me. I'm not sure why she is looking so shocked.

"Whoa, Erika, let a guy know if you are stopping that fast. What happ-." Sean stops as he sees me too. "You're Scott Griffin."

Erika snaps out of it and looks to Yas. "Your Scott is Scott Griffin? Why didn't you say anything? We have been talking about his computer program for weeks!"

"Computer program? You mean the bookstore one?" Yas looks confused but I am starting to feel uneasy.

"The computer program that you are salivating over, Yasmin?" Justin says. "I know Sam said that you would do anything for it, but fucking a guy to get it is pretty low. I'm impressed."

Yas's eyes go wide as she looks at me. "No. I didn't. I swear I didn't know. You know that we never talk about work, Scott. I thought your family business was all real estate and architecture. That your program had to do with buildings." She looks at me with pleading eyes.

I want to believe her, but I can't. Not again. My heart is splitting apart and I lash out. "That's why you snuck into my workroom all those weeks ago isn't it?" I advance on her and she shakes her head, crying. "I *trusted* you. In fact I was going to *give* you the program tonight. That's what you wanted all along. I can't believe I was so stupid. *Again.*"

"You weren't stupid, Scott. I didn't know. I love you. You *know* that I love you."

But in that moment, I don't.

* * *

Yasmin

"You said that you would never be like Amber, but you're worse." I flinch back like he punched me. It feels like he did. My heart just exploded. "You really took your role far. Were you laughing when I offered you money? Were you waiting for the bigger payout? You made me fall for you. I have never felt like that before about anyone and it was all a lie. Again. I must be the dumbest guy on the planet."

I reach for him. "It wasn't a lie, Scott." I am starting to feel anger mixing with my hurt. Did he really just say that I am worse than Amber?

"Don't touch me, bitch. You had a good time manipulating me, didn't you? Just doing what you wanted while you played me."

I lose it and don't even know what I am saying until it is out of my mouth. "What I wanted? Really? Because I don't remember ever *wanting* to have you tie me to your bed with game controllers and fuck me so that you could live out your teenage nerd fantasy."

"Whoa, man, you did that?" Owen says, breaking the silence around us.

"Yeah," Scott says with a sneer. "The slut will probably live out your fantasy, too, if you ask since you own part of the company. You want to put some paintbrushes up her pussy? Owen's art is so cool, isn't that right Yasmin?"

"Scott!" Gary says sharply.

I am slapping him before I even think about it. "You goddamn bastard."

"Get out of my house," he says through clenched teeth, rubbing his jaw.

"You think that you can talk to her like that and get away with it? I can have some guys here to kick your ass in minutes," Candi snarls at him.

"No, Candi. Leave him alone."

I look over at her and make sure that she sees that I mean it. "Fine. He's not worth the call, anyway."

I grab my purse and turn to go as Alex and Maggie come outside carrying the cake. "We thought that you might have gotten caught up with your friends, so we decided to head out," Maggie says and then notices the tension. "What's wrong? Did something happen?"

"I need to leave, Maggie. I'm sorry." I look at the cake, covered in video game controllers and characters and wish that things were different.

"You can't go, Yasmin. We haven't had cake and it looks like Uncle Scott hasn't opened your present yet." Alex looks so confused and my heart aches, thinking that I may not see her again.

"I have to go, Alex. But, I need you to know something. No mat-ter what happens and what you hear, I love you and I will always be here for you if you need me."

"I don't understand. Yasmin, please don't go." Alex is crying now.

I pull her close. "I have to, sweetie, I have to go." I turn to Danny. "Can you give me a ride home?" He nods yes and I start to walk out of that house, leaving the broken pieces of my heart behind.

"Before you go, Yasmin, I want you to know that you can't buy the software. We won't sell it to you," Scott says to me in a cold voice.

"She needs that program, Scott. Don't do this to her." I can hear the pleading in Erika's voice as everything starts to spin.

"I don't give a fuck what she needs."

"You really are a bastard," Sean says as I collapse against Danny.

"Yasmin? Are you okay?" I think it is Danny asking me, but I can't tell. I am barely holding on right now.

"Just take me home, please." I manage to say the words and make my feet work long enough to get out of there. Danny drives me to my house and walks me to the door. I convince him that I will be fine and he leaves. I fall to the living room floor and cry un-til I can no longer keep my eyes open. As I start to fall asleep, I re-alize that without the program, I am going to lose everything soon. Not just Scott, who I lost tonight. But, the store and my house, too. What will I do then?

CHAPTER 21

<u>Scott</u>

It's been a week since my party and we're officially launching the software today. I haven't had any contact with Yasmin and really anyone else since the party. I have stayed in my house, playing video games and looking for the signs I missed. I'm having trouble finding any, but I know that they are there. She is just a better actress than Amber.

My phone rings and I see Zane's name on the screen. "Hey, man what's up?"

"Just wanted to call and congratulate you on your launch. I know you have been working on this for a long time."

"Congrats Scott!" I hear Quinn yell in the background. "Put him on speaker."

"Thanks you guys, I appreciate the support."

"How are you, Scott?" Quinn asks.

"Great for a guy who fell completely in love for the first time in his life only to find out that the woman he is in love with was us-

ing him. Oh, yeah and the girl before that used him too. I never realized how fucking pathetic that I am."

"Are you sure that she was using you? She seemed really into
you when she was here. And she told Quinn that she loved you,"
Zane says.

"Her friends said that she has been talking about that program
for over a month and planning on using it to save her store. How
could she not have known who I was?"

"I don't know, Scott. But that scrapbook that she was making
you looked pretty awesome. She sent me some pictures of it,"
Quinn tells me.

"What scrapbook?"

"The one that she made you for your birthday."

"Oh, I never opened her present. We didn't get that far."

"You should look at it, Scott."

"Lay off him, Quinn. He doesn't need to forgive her just so you
can stay friends with her," Zane says to her.

"Guys, don't fight because of me. Please. I will get over this and
everything will go back to normal."

"Don't worry about us. When will you be back in Chi-Town?"

"The whole family will be there in about three months. The
charity that Erin and Dave supported wants to honor them and
we're accepting the award."

"That's cool, man."

"It would be if I didn't have to wear a tux and take out my piercings. The company PR people say that I should look presentable at
this thing. I *am* proud to be accepting this award, though. My family is going to continue Erin and Dave's contributions."

"That's bullshit about the tux, but at least your family accepts
you how you are even if your company doesn't."

"I know. I lucked out in the family department. Listen guys, it
was great to talk to you but I have to go get ready for the press
conference. I'll talk to you soon."

We say our goodbyes and I go put on a suit. I glance at Yasmin's wrapped present on my hall table. What Quinn said has me curious, but, not enough to open it. Seeing whatever Yasmin did just feels like looking at another lie.

* * *

<u>Yasmin</u>

"I can't believe that Scott hasn't called you to apologize," Erika tells me.

"I said things that I should be apologizing for too," I remind her. "I can't believe I told everyone about him tying me up." I groan and drop my head into my hands.

"That was pretty intense. I will never look at a game controller the same way again. In your defense, he did push you to say it," Sam chimes in. I groan again and keep my head buried.

We are having a girls' night at Erika and Sean's. They moved in together a couple of days ago. It may have seemed fast to me if she hadn't admitted to me that they had been circling each other for the last couple of years and had even hooked up a few times before officially getting together last month. I'm really happy for them. They're a great couple.

It has been two weeks since the party. I feel the loss of Scott every day and I feel like it is slowly killing me. I also miss the rest of his family, especially Alex. She hasn't been back to the store. I hope that she is okay and that if she is not, that she calls me. I meant what I told her, even though her family pretty much hates me, I care for her—and them.

"That was some freaky shit, though. I didn't know you had it in you," Candi teases me. "You wouldn't go to the sex shop with me but you act out some kinky fantasy?"

"Can we talk about something else please?"

"Back to the apologies, I still can't believe that he would think you were using him. You are *so* not that type of person." Erika rubs my back as I start to sob.

I look up at my friends. "That is what hurts the most. That he could think that I am capable of that. That I'm like Amber or in his words, worse than her. I love him so much."

"I want to apologize again for Justin starting this whole thing. You guys were right, he is an asshole," Sam tells me.

"Does that mean you are finally willing to give Danny a chance?"

"Maybe I already have." Seeing our shocked expressions, she continues, "We went out last night and it was awesome."

I reach over and hug her. "I am so happy for the two of you!"

"What you need to do is find another man to fuck and get Scott out of your system. I know he is one hot guy, but there are plenty of better ones out there," Candi says with certainty in her voice.

"Like Owen?" I ask her. I know that they have seen each other at least once since the party.

"I don't kiss and tell. Well, I do, but not this time." And that is all she will say.

"I'm not ready for someone else yet. Besides, I need to focus on the store." Everyone gets quiet and Erika turns on While You Were Sleeping. We watch it in silence. I don't think anyone knows what to say to me. I don't blame them.

I honestly don't know what I am going to do. Since I can't buy the software, I didn't take the second mortgage so I don't have to worry about that at least. But ever since the other indies got the program, my internet sales have dropped. Online customers keep asking when we will get it and so do some of our regulars in the store. Everyone knows that in 3 weeks Amazon and B&N will have it. I am going to fight for my store with everything I have left in me, but there's not even much of that.

If my parents were alive, they would know what to do. I feel like a disgrace to their memory. Rationally, my brain knows that I am doing all that I can to save the store, but my emotions are not rational. I feel like if I lose the store *or* the house, that I will be losing a piece of them. I don't have too many of those left.

* * *

Scott

"I need some new books," Alex says as we are eating breakfast.

"I can take you to Barnes and Noble before I start to work on my new program," I tell her.

"Can't we go to I Heart Books? Barnes and Noble has a good selection and the people are nice, but I miss Erika, Sam, Danny *and* Yasmin."

"No. We are not going there." It has been three weeks now and what she doesn't know, what no one knows, is that I drive by that store every night and watch Yas close up. I don't want to do it and I even tried to skip one night, but my body didn't get the memo and I was in the parking lot across the street before I knew it. I think that she saw me one night, she knows the Mustang, and I saw her stop for a moment and look straight at me. She shook her head and walked to her car, without another look.

"Please. You can wait in the car. I miss it so much."

Before I can say anything else, my mom speaks up. "Do you want to go back to volunteering there, Alex?" I look at her like she is crazy.

"Yes, I do. I miss the kids from story time and the other regulars. Can I please?" Alex looks so hopeful and I don't want to take that away from her.

"If Yas-Yasmin will have you back, I am okay with it." I can't say her nickname out loud. It's too much.

"Alright, then. School is about to start so you can't be there too often, but maybe you can do one day after school and Saturdays," my dad says.

"Can we go ask her right now?" Alex jumps up out of her chair.

"I can't take you there, Baby Girl. I just can't."

"Whatever happened, I'm sorry you are so sad, Uncle Scott. She's such a good person, though."

I snort and my mom steps in before I can say something that will upset Alex. "I'll take you, honey. Just let me grab my purse."

I hope that Yasmin will take Alex back. I know that she cares for her. Wait. How do I know that? I thought that she cared for me and I was wrong. But, I don't think that I'm wrong about her feelings for Alex. She *did* stop and tell her that she would still be there for her when she was leaving the party. If she is just playing Alex too, she better be ready for Hell to rain down on her. I would destroy her without a second thought and I know that my family would back me up.

* * *

Yasmin

I'm sitting at the cash wrap, staring at my empty store. I sent Danny home early since we have had maybe five people in to shop so far today. I officially canceled my registration for school. If I have any hope of staying open, I am going to have to work open to close and only have someone with me for a few hours a day. I asked everyone to meet me at the store tomorrow morning so that I can tell them that I have to cut their hours even more. I know that they are expecting it, but it still kills me to have to do it.

The door opens and I slap a smile on my face to greet a customer. It's not just a customer, though. It's Alex and Maggie. I jump off of the stool and run for Alex. She meets me halfway and we hug, holding each other tight. "I missed you so much, sweetie."

"I missed you too! My grandparents said that I can come back and help one day a week and on Saturdays. Is that OK?"

"Yes, of course. I would love for you to come back." I kiss her on the forehead and taking a deep breath, turn to face Maggie.

"Hello, Maggie."

"Hello, Yasmin." Her voice isn't as cold as I thought it would be, but it's not exactly warm.

"Thanks for letting Alex come back here. I truly did miss her and she's always welcome here."

"I believe that you do care about my granddaughter. I don't think your reaction to seeing her could be faked." She pauses and then sighs before continuing. "But, as much as I like you, my son has to take priority. He believes that you deceived him and I have to take his side. Gary and the rest of the boys feel the same way. None of us will have anything to do with you, other than dropping off and picking up Alex. That's just the way that it has to be."

"I understand." And I do. I can't stop the tears from forming, though. I look away, but I know that Maggie can see. I don't want to make this any more difficult for her than it has to be, so I force myself to smile as I say to Alex. "Do you want to start this Saturday? You can do story time."

"That would be awesome. Can I look at books for a few minutes, Grandma?"

"Yes, I will wait for you in the coffee shop next door. Take your time." Maggie gives me one last, sad smile and walks out of the store.

Alex spends an hour looking at all of the new books that have come in and brings a stack to the register. I ring her up and she turns to go, but then stops. "No one will tell me what happened between you and Uncle Scott, but I know that he thinks that you betrayed him. Did you, Yasmin? Please tell me the truth."

I look her in the eye and reply honestly. "No, sweetie, I didn't."

"I didn't think so." She hugs me and heads out the door.

I slump against the counter. At least someone in her family believes me.

CHAPTER 22

Scott

I am hanging out with my family today at my parents' house. It has been three weeks since Alex went back to working at the bookstore. I know that she is happier and I am glad. I haven't gone into the store and I can't even take her there for her shifts, but I still drive by every night. My dad just dropped her off there about a half hour ago, so I am surprised to see Alex walk into my parents' kitchen with Erika.

"Are you okay, Baby Girl? Why are you home so early? And why didn't you call one of us to pick you up?" I move toward her, worried.

"Stay away from me. I kind of hate you right now." My eyes go wide and I know that my jaw drops.

"Alex, what is wrong with you? Apologize to your uncle!" my dad orders her.

"I should go. Alex asked me to bring her home because she wasn't feeling well when she got to the store." Erika starts to back away and Alex grabs her arm.

"What I am feeling is pissed. I heard you and Yasmin talking."

"What did you hear, Alex? I thought you just came into the backroom when the door slammed."

"No, I was back there putting my purse away when I heard you. I know I shouldn't have eavesdropped but since everyone treats me like a baby and won't tell me everything that was said the night of Uncle Scott's party, I had no choice."

"Trust me, Alex, you don't want to know everything that was said that night." Owen is laughing and I glare at him.

"What did you hear, Alex?" Erika asks her again, ignoring him. "Maybe you misunderstood what we were saying."

"I didn't misunderstand. You said that Yasmin has sold most of her furniture and her car and that you didn't want to take a pay-check because you knew that she wasn't eating and couldn't afford groceries. You also said that she is going to take an offer on her house that will give her only enough money to keep the store open for another month. And that if Uncle Scott had let her buy his program, this wouldn't have happened."

"Holy shit." I look at Erika. "She sold her car? How is she getting to and from work? And she's not eating?"

"She takes the bus as far as she can and walks the rest of the way. And, no, she doesn't eat unless we force her to. She has no extra money."

"She *walks* at night, alone? Her neighborhood is nice but the surrounding area isn't. She can't do that."

"She doesn't have a choice, Scott."

"I heard more," Alex tells us and then continues. "You said that my family should have seen that you were surprised when you realized that Uncle Scott was her boyfriend. Then, Yasmin said that he should have seen how shocked she was, too and everyone should have believed her when she said that she didn't know that he created the software program that she needed. You called Uncle Scott a bastard, but Yasmin said that he was a good man and she hated the thought of him being hurt because he thinks she used him. And that even if it's not true, that the hurt was real to him. She was crying really hard by then."

"She really said that?" I ask. "She said that I was a good man? She defended me?"

"Yeah, she did. Oh and then you guys talked about her meeting Sean's friend tonight because she knows that Uncle Scott will never believe her and so she has to move on."

"Wow, you really did hear it all," Erika says, looking a little dazed.

"She really didn't know? How could she not know?" I am sure that I look a little crazed right now. I grab Erika's shoulders.

"You know that she isn't that computer savvy. Sean and I gave her all the details about the program. We never told her your name because we didn't think it mattered. She always just called you Scott, so we didn't know. You have a common name. She honestly didn't know, Scott. None of us did.

"How could you not know that she loves you? She flew all the way to Chicago to help you through something that was hard for you, even though she couldn't afford the extra payroll it took to cover her being gone. She refused money when you offered it to her and even insisted on paying for some of your dates. She went way out of her comfort zone with you and from what I hear, she threatened that bitch, Amber, when she tried to have her lawyer accuse you of being in on things with her. And what did you do in return? You destroyed her. I'm not just talking about the store, either. Oh, and by the way, the fact that you told her that she is worse than Amber was seriously not cool."

"Wait, you said that she was worse than Amber? How could you do that, Uncle Scott?" I am ashamed when she asks me that. I don't have an answer for her. She looks to the rest of my family. "And how could all of you stand by and let him call her a bitch and a slut? I know we have family loyalty, but she was never anything but nice to all of us. More than nice."

"You're right, Baby Girl," I tell her. "I messed up but I am going to fix this." I look around at my family and then I look at Erika. "I'm going to need your help. And Sean's. Can you call him and ask him to come over here. Oh, and he can tell his friend that Yasmin isn't available for a date tonight *or* any other night."

My family is made up of great people. What happened to Yasmin, because of me, because I was hurt, is horrible. I know that they are upset about it. I'm going to need their help to fix this. We need to help her and I need to show her how sorry I am and how much I love her. I just hope that it's not too late. I go outside to sit by the pool and think things through while we wait for Sean to get here.

CHAPTER 23

<u>Scott</u>

It shouldn't have taken my niece telling me that Yas didn't betray me for me to believe it. I should have known it myself. I think I *did* know it. After all, I couldn't find those signs I was looking for. I transferred the anger that I felt for what Amber did onto Yasmin, because I could never yell at Amber, never protect my family from her. But, Yas did. In that courtroom, she told Amber to stay away from us. That she would protect me because I was hers. Even if we are apart, Yas is *mine*. It's time for me to man up and take care of her. I know that under normal circumstances, she wouldn't take the amount of help that I'm about to give her. She would protest. But, while I can't take all of the blame for her bookstore struggling, I definitely hurt it by not letting her even *buy* my software. So, I have to hope that she won't hate me even more when she finds out what I'm about to set into motion. What do people say? Ask for forgiveness instead of permission.

I have to earn her forgiveness. What I am planning to have my family and I do will help. But, money isn't going to do it for her. I need to woo her again. The things that I said to her were horrible. My woman is only a bitch when she has to be. When she is protecting the people that she loves. She is definitely not a slut. Yas let me tie her up because she loves me and wanted to do that for me. I wish she hadn't yelled that out in front of my family and her friends, but it's not like it's going to kill me. So what if my brothers tease me about being a perv while my dad laughs? I had no right to say that she would do Owen, that she would let him... Shit, I *am* a bastard. But, I'll do anything I need to in order for her to forgive me.

I'm still sitting outside by the pool, lost in my thoughts when my mom comes out to tell me that Sean has arrived. She tells me that whatever I have planned, the family will support me. She also says that she is glad that I realized that Yas loves me, because she already knew that. I kiss her on the cheek and we walk inside. It's time to lay out my plans and get everyone started on what I need them to do.

"Thanks for coming, Sean," I tell him holding out my hand. He looks to Erika, who nods and only then does he take it.

"If this will help Yasmin, I'm happy to be here. What's the plan?"

"The most pressing things that we need to take care of are getting her food and making sure that she is not walking alone at night. Erika, do you know if Yas changed the locks on her house?" When she shakes her head no, I continue. "Mom, can you go grocery shopping for her? I can meet you at her house to take everything inside. She gave me a key the day of the party."

"Of course, I would love to fill her house with food for her. Let me go grab my purse." She hugs me as she walks by.

"Next is the car situation. I can't just buy her a car yet. She wouldn't take it. She's closing every night, Erika?" I ask, even though I know the answer.

"She works open to close every day and just has us one of work for a few hours during the busy times. She can't afford to have us there anymore than that. I've offered to work for free but she won't let me."

Fuck. It's even worse than I thought. I take a deep breath and it comes to me. "She won't let you work for free, but she will let Alex volunteer as much as she wants. Dad, if Alex took her homework there and promised to do it, could she stay in the store until 9:30? Then, when one of you picks her up, you could insist on driving Yas home. If she protests, Alex could ask her. She can't say no to our girl."

"If it's okay with Alex, then yes, we can do that." He looks at Alex. "But, you don't have to do this, honey. I know you've made friends and they may want you to go out sometimes."

I answer before she can. "If her friends ask her to do something, she should go with them instead. We can come up with some reason why one of you happens to be near the store when it closes and sees her waiting for the bus. Does that work for everyone?" They all nod and I continue.

"On to her house. Do you know who her realtor is?" Sean nods and then gives me the name of his friend who he says is her realtor. "You know the guy? Perfect. Can you call him and tell him that I want to make an offer today?"

"You're buying her house? She is *not* going to be okay with you giving it to her." Erika looks worried.

"I'm not planning on giving it to her." When I see the startled looks on everyone's faces, I chuckle. "I'm planning on asking her to live there with me once I win her back. I love that house." They all visibly relax and smile.

Sean gets out his phone and after speaking to his friend for a couple of minutes, hands it to me. "Hi Tony. I would like to make an offer for twice the asking price on the house." I pause while he lets out a string of curses. His commission on the sale is going to be really good. "I want to close immediately but you can't tell her that I'm the one buying it. Also, I want you to tell her that the buyer can't move in right away so I want to let her stay in the house for sixty days to watch it for me because I don't want it sitting vacant. Can you do that?" He agrees and I hang up.

"You're pretty good at this planning stuff, bro. We could have been using your talents at the company all along. I'm impressed," Ryan tells me shaking his head.

"I am perfectly happy with my computer, Ry. I can't work at the office. But thanks for saying that. It means a lot to me." I tell him what I need from him. "Can you find out if the owners of the strip mall where I Heart Books is located are willing to sell?"

"You want to buy the strip mall?"

"Yeah, I do. You know that I have the money and that way I could lower the rent."

My dad steps in then. "The company can buy the strip mall if it's for sale. We can use a good tax write off and lowering the rent for all of the businesses in the center would be something that we can do to help them out as well. I have visited many of them when dropping off or picking up Alex and there are some great people struggling there." He turns to Ryan. "Do your thing and find out what they can't refuse and then make the offer."

Ry nods. "I'm on it." He pulls out his phone and starts dialing. My brother is a genius when it comes to architecture and commercial real estate.

"Thanks, Dad." I hug him too. Damn, I'm turning into a Hallmark movie. But, it feels good to have my family helping me. I knew they would.

"I am obviously going to give you guys the program. Sean can you install it on the website without Yas knowing?"

"I should be able to get it past her. She doesn't know how to code and I don't think she has looked at the site itself lately. She just checks the orders."

"Good. I'll get you it before you go. I would love to put it in the store system but I don't think we could hide it there. Erika, is there anything else that we can do to get people in the store right away?"

"Do you know anyone at any of the Big Five publishers? Yasmin was trying to get a big author in to do a signing, hoping that it would bring new customers in. They all turned her down."

I smile and look at my dad, who nods. "Actually we do know people. The publishing houses have been after my dad to write his life story for years. After what happened with Amber, they want my story, too. I think that we can leverage that to get some authors in."

I look at Owen and Luke. "Now, for you two. Don't think that you are going to get out of helping. I need your help too."

"Anything, bro, you know that." Luke looks excited.

I smirk at my little brother. "I need you to get some of those chicks that you hook up with to the bookstore. I know at least some of them have to read. I don't care what you have to do—buy them books with my credit card if that's what it takes. We just need to get more people into the store."

"Blaine has blacklisted me from the fraternities and sororities since the pool party, but I think I can find some girls who are willing to let me buy them some books. And I mean *me* not you. I want to help Yasmin too. She was always cool to me and I know what she's done for Alex."

"Do you have anything for me to do or are you afraid that Yasmin might *want* to help me live out my teenage fantasy?" Owen asks me before ducking behind my dad.

"You're going to hide behind Dad? What are you, ten? If you're going to say something like that to me, you better be man enough to back it up." I tell him with a glare, looking pointedly at Alex.

His eyes go wide when he gets it and he says sheepishly, "Sorry. I couldn't resist. But, seriously, is there something that I can do? I really want to help."

"Yes, there is something that I would like you to do." I am smiling now, because I know he is going to like what I am about to tell him. "I need you to channel your old street art ways and paint a mural on the front of Yasmin's store. She really does love art and I'm hoping that you can somehow convince her that this will be a favor to you. Then, I need you to social media it up and let all of those fans of yours know that you're going back to your roots for this one."

"I can definitely do that," Owen tells me. "I can also tell my fans that the store is special to me and get them to shop there."

"Not to be rude, but you have fans?" Erika asks him.

"Yeah, I do. I have 5 million twitter followers and over a million Facebook fans," he says. My brother is one talented guy and people know it. I know he misses doing his street art. Once he started doing the commercial work for the company, he gave it up. I'm glad to have a way for him to do what he loves *and* help Yas.

"Whoa. I had no idea," Erika tells him, impressed.

I rein them back in. "So, is everyone good with their assigned tasks?" They all nod. "Great, then let's get started with whatever we can right now. I know some things will have to wait until Monday but I would like to have as much in place as possible today. Thank you all for helping. It means a lot to me and it will mean a lot to Yas too."

My family heads off to get started and I walk Erika and Sean over to my place to get the software disk that I had made for Yas. When we get inside, Erika sees the wrapped present on my hall table. "You never opened that?"

"No, I didn't. It's not a big deal. I don't need a present from Yas. I just need her."

"It *is* a big deal. She spent a ton of time on it and was so excited to give it to you."

"Yeah? She always told me that she wasn't very crafty. I'll open it when you guys leave, I guess."

"She isn't crafty but she wanted to do it for you."

I want to kick myself. No, I want to beat the shit out of myself. I have ruined the best thing that ever happened to me. What if despite everything that I am doing, I can't win her back? I know I don't deserve her and that she probably shouldn't forgive me. But, I want her to. I *need* her to.

Sean clasps my shoulder and startles me out of my thoughts. "She'll forgive you. I mean, what you have planned for her is awesome, but even if you weren't doing all that stuff, you love her, right?" I nod. "I know she loves you, too. Which means that she will want to forgive you. You can make this work."

"Thanks, Sean." I take a deep breath. "Let me show you my workroom and I'll give you the drive with the program on it."

I take them into the room, where Sean and I start talking computers. Erika just wanders around touching things, which would normally freak me out. But, I know that I can trust them. I get the program for them and then offer Sean a job, if he wants it. I've been toying with the idea of hiring an assistant to help with some of the easy coding and finishing touches of my programs. After talking to him, I know he can do it. And like I said, I trust him.

"Are you serious? I would love to work for you! You're a genius."

"I'll take that as a yes. Just go by the company office on Monday and ask for Ellen in H.R. She'll get you all the paperwork."

Erika hugs me as they leave. "I'll do what I can to help you."

I thank her, close the door and walk over to the package on the table. I pick it up and sit on the couch. I turn it over in my hands and then slowly tear the wrapping paper off of it. I nearly drop it when I see what it is.

It's an album with Yas and me on the cover. The picture is one of the ones that we took at the tattoo shop. She is sitting on my lap and my arms are around her while we look at each other with our foreheads touching. We look so happy and in love. We *were* so happy. We *are* still in love. At least I am and from what Erika and Sean said, so is Yas. I really need to not screw this up again.

I open the album and see a message written inside.

Pretty Boy,

Thank you for showing me your city. The time that we spent there gave me some of the best memories of my life. I will never forget the places we went or the things that we did. I am honored that you wanted to share so much with me, including yourself. I made this scrapbook so that you could see just how much the trip and YOU mean to me.

I love you more than words can possibly express.

Yas

P.S. I used your Nintendo pen to write this!

I could stop right there at the first page and be happy for the rest of my life, but I continue because I want to see what she chose to commemorate our time in Chicago. The pages are in order of where we went every day. By the time I'm done, I want to just run to the store, get down on my knees and beg Yas to take me back. But, I know that she's not ready for that yet. I need to work on fixing some things and not just with Yas. I need to work on fixing myself. I open the scrapbook back up and start again from the beginning.

A map of the Art Institute along with a Seurat postcard and the picture of us from outside by the lion. The background paper is of letters in various fonts.

A visitor's guide to Navy Pier along with a napkin from the pizza place and a picture of us that we had someone take. Our arms are around each other and we're looking at the camera. Lake Michigan is behind us. The paper is covered in Ferris wheels.

Pictures of me and John hugging by my car, a picture of the house and the three of us in a selfie there. This paper has Mustangs on it.

Pictures of my room—the computer shelves, the bookcase with my controllers and figurines, my desk and a selfie of us in my bed, cuddling. The paper for this one is really cool with Mario characters and Japanese writing all over it.

Pictures of me and Mrs. J., the three of us and the marks in the kitchen showing my growth. This paper is similar to the last one, just with different colors.

A napkin and matchbook from the cruise ship along with pictures of us arriving and dancing. Ships cover the paper on this one.

A flyer for Windy City Tats along with photos of us with Zane and Quinn. The paper is covered in drawings that I recognize as Zane's.

A napkin and to go menu from the restaurant we ate at with my family and friends along with a group picture of all of us from the table. The background is of various types of food.

Pictures of my apartment—Owen's sculptures, my staircase taken from a cool angle and me playing video games on the bed after we made love. The background is another one of those cool Japanese ones.

The last page has a background of hearts and features the picture of us in the hotel lobby as well as various papers and cards from the W.

I go through the album several more times before my mom calls to tell me that she is done shopping. I tell her that I'll meet her at Yas's house, grab my keys and head out the door. I drive to the house and arrive just before my mom. I unlock the door and prop it open with one of the planters from the porch so that it will be easier to carry in the groceries.

We carry the first batch to the door and then both stop just inside. Yas really did sell her furniture. There is nothing left. Even the walls are mostly bare. Except for the wall tiles that I bought her at the museum in Chicago. She kept those.

"Oh, Scott." My mom looks anguished.

"I know, Mom. I will make this right, I promise."

"I know you will." She looks at me and a smile replaces some of her sadness. "Now, let's get these groceries put away so I can start cooking."

"You're cooking?" I ask as we walk through an equally bare dining room and into the kitchen.

"I know that Yasmin can't say no to my mac and cheese so I thought that I would make some. I want to make sure that she eats."

"Thanks, Mom."

"You don't need to thank me. I love Yasmin, too. Do you want to leave the key with me so that I can close up?"

"No, I have something that I want to do while we're here."

It takes a little while to bring in all of the groceries and put them away. I think my mom bought the entire store. I leave her in the kitchen and head to Yas's room. I'm kind of freaked out to see it. I don't want to see that sexy bedroom taken apart. It was where we were first together and we spent many other nights there as well. I take a deep breath and walk down the hall. I nearly fall over when I walk into the room and see that nothing has changed. She kept this room intact. I'm glad that I just bought this house so that she won't have to sell anything. I head over to the loveseat by the window, take out my notebook and get ready to write. My mom is leaving her some mac and cheese and I am leaving her a letter. And some pens.

CHAPTER 24

<u>Yasmin</u>

I managed to make it through the rest of the day without falling apart. I was glad when Erika said that Sean's friend couldn't meet with us after all. They insisted on coming by to drive me home and I was too tired to argue. I just want to get back to my house and take a long bath. I don't have much time there. Tony called today to say that he got an offer that he wants to talk to me about. I put him off until Monday because I am not ready to deal with leaving the house yet. Getting rid of the furniture wasn't too bad because I had been wanting to pick my own new stuff for the last year but couldn't afford it. Now, I can start new in an apartment. I will take my bedroom furniture with me, though. I couldn't give it up, especially after the memories that I made there with Scott. I know that it shouldn't matter and that I said that I was moving on, but I want to remember him there with me. I *need* to remember those times when he still loved me and we were happy. Remembering them keeps me from falling completely into the darkness that wants to overtake me.

We pull into my driveway and I say my goodbyes and head into the house. As soon as I walk in, I smell something good. Something like Maggie's mac and cheese. I follow the scent into the kitchen where the light is on and there *is* mac and cheese in the oven. A note on the stove from Maggie tells me she heard that I wasn't eating much so she made this for me and it's warm so all I have to do is take it out of the oven. She tells me that my cupboards and refrigerator are full as well. She also said that I'm welcome at the house for dinner anytime. And that she loves me. I choke back a sob and wonder what changed, why she would suddenly want to be in my life again. And how did she get in? I can figure that out later. Right now, I need to eat because I'm a little dizzy and I don't want to pass out.

After I eat, I feel better but I still want a bath. I put away the leftovers and wash my plate in the sink. I'll call Maggie tomorrow and thank her. I just want to get these clothes off and try to relax. I walk into my room and stop in my tracks. There are a bunch of silver Bic pens in the shape of a heart on my bed. I had wanted those pens forever but you can only buy them if you live in England. I told Scott that once and it looks like he remembered. That's how Maggie got in, I realize. I had given him a key the night of his party. I'm still trying to process the pens and figure out what has changed when I notice the envelope in the middle of the heart. *My* heart starts beating hard and I walk slowly to the bed and pick it up.

Yas

I walk over to the loveseat and sit down. I swallow a few times before pulling the paper out and reading.

Beautiful, honest, amazing Yas,

I need to start by telling you how sorry I am. I should have believed you when you said that you didn't know that I designed the software program. I should have never even considered that you would use me. I know you better than that, but I let my insecurities and fears take over. I projected my anger at Amber on you. I never had the chance to tell her off or yell at her for what she did. So, when I heard Justin say that you would do anything for the program, all rational thoughts left my mind and I lashed out at you without giving you a chance to explain.

I knew that I was upset about what Amber did, but I never realized just how messed up I am over it. How insecure I felt, thinking that no one could really love me. Yet you did and instead of treasuring you and our relationship, I destroyed what we had between us. After everything happened with Amber, my parents wanted me to go see someone to talk about what I was feeling and help me deal with it. I told them that I didn't need to do that and they supported my choice. I realize now that I do need help. I need to talk to someone and try to believe that I am worthy of love, your love. I 'm going to get better for me and then I am going to come to you as the man you deserve and ask you to give me another chance. Until then, I'm going to woo you again. You deserve that and so much more.

I have some specific things that I need to apologize to you for. I called you a bitch and a slut. You are neither. You stood up to Amber for me and my family but that doesn't make you a bitch, it makes you a beautiful, loyal woman who cares for us all. You let me live out a fantasy because you loved me and that doesn't make you a slut, it makes you the best girlfriend a guy could ever hope for. You are an amazing, compassionate, smart, sexy, gorgeous woman. One that I am lucky to have met.

Thank you for the scrapbook. It's the best birthday present that I have ever received. I love you more than words, too.

I know that I don't deserve anything from you, but if you could just text me to let me know that you got this letter, I would appreciate it.

Yours always,

Scott

I'm crying so hard that I am shaking. Scott still loves me and knows that I didn't use him. I'm so happy, but so scared at the same time. I want to drive over to his house and hold him tight but I am worried that something else will happen to make him doubt me. I don't know how his mind works and I don't want to always be afraid of saying or doing the wrong thing. If this happened again, I don't know if I would survive it. He says that he is going to get help before he comes for me. That he wants to woo me again. Will that be enough? Will I be ready to give him my heart again? I honestly don't know. But, I am willing to give it a chance. I won't make a decision now. I'll wait until he comes to me and see how I feel then.

I know that I have to text him, but I don't know what to write. I don't want to shoot him down, but I also don't want to give him false hope. And right now, I feel that it would be false because, even though I love him, I'm not sure that I can be with him again. I finally decide on something and send if off before I change my mind again.

Me: Thank you for your letter. I'm glad that you're getting help. When you are ready, I will hear you out. I can't promise you anything but I'm willing to listen to you. I need to apologize too. I should never have told everyone about what we did. I am really sorry that I did that.

A reply comes almost immediately.

Scott: Thanks for agreeing to talk to me. And thanks for the apology. Prepare to be wooed :)

I spend Sunday working as usual. It's not too busy and I'm happily surprised when Alex and Maggie walk in. I rush over to hug them and Maggie holds me tight.

"Thank you so much for the food, Maggie. I really appreciate it."

"It was my pleasure. I am so sorry that it took my family so long to realize that we were misjudging you. We should have known better."

"You did know better, though, didn't you? When you brought Alex back, it seemed like you knew."

"Yes. I did believe you. I didn't think that you could fake the love I saw in your eyes when you looked at my son. But, I had to side with him."

"It means a lot to me that you believed me. I understand that your loyalty had to lie with Scott."

"But, now she can be loyal to both of you," Alex says, looking excited. "Uncle Scott told us that he is going to see a therapist to help him. I know he loves you and you two can be together again!"

I sigh and look at her. "Sweetie, I am happy that Scott is going to talk to someone and try to get past the things that are hurting him, but that doesn't mean that we will be together."

"You don't love him anymore? He hurt you that much?" Tears are pooling in her eyes.

"I *do* love him, Alex. More than I ever thought that I could love someone. But, that doesn't mean that I can just forget how much he hurt me. Because, he *did* hurt me very badly. I don't know if there is anything worse than having the person you love not trust you or your love for them. I promised him that I would talk to him when he is ready, but that is all I can promise right now."

I wipe my eyes to clear the tears that are now falling. Maggie pulls me to her as I sob into her shoulder for a few minutes. "I understand, Yasmin. Just please give him a chance. He wants to get better for himself *and* for you."

I nod and try to put a smile on my face. "So, did you come by for some books, Alex? And, oh my God, I didn't even ask how you are feeling today. Are you still sick?"

"Sick?" she asks puzzled and I see a look pass between her and Maggie. "Oh yeah, I am better. Once I got home, I felt better. I should have come back to help. In fact, that's why I'm here. My grandparent's said that as long as I can bring my homework here, I can come every night and stay until close if it's okay with you."

"I would love to have you here every night, but are you sure you don't want to hang out with the new friends that you made at school?"

"I do, actually. Can I tell you on a daily basis if I can be here?"

"Of course, sweetie. You're doing me a favor by being here."

"Now that that is settled, I have some things that I need to do. Owen will be by at 9:30 to pick her up." Maggie hugs us both again and then she is on her way.

The rest of the day and night are quiet in the store. I check the online orders, not expecting much, but there are 30. How did that happen? I don't have time to check as Alex and I fill them all and I box them up while she watches the store. It's nine before I know it and I lock the door and get the small deposit done. I put it in the safe and we head outside where Owen is waiting for Alex in his car.

"Hi ladies, are you ready to go?" He comes over and hugs Alex and then me. It's a little strange that everyone is now accepting me since Scott did, but I *did* always know how close they all are.

"Goodbye you guys. I'll see you tomorrow Alex. It was nice to see you Owen."

"Wait, where are you going? Don't you want a ride home?"

"What makes you think that I need a ride?"

"Well, you're heading towards the bus stop with a bus pass in your hand." I forgot that I had taken my pass out so that I could have it ready.

"I'm fine. I take the bus every night."

"Yasmin, can I please give you a ride? I actually want to talk to you about something. I need to ask for a favor."

"You need a favor from me? If it's about the party..." I look warily at him.

He laughs so hard that I think he might fall over. "No, it's not about that. I know that you're not into me and I am kind of seeing someone right now." He turns serious. "But, I do have something to ask you."

"Then, yes, I would love a ride. Thanks."

We all get in the car and the drive to my house is filled with small talk and catching up a little with each other. When we pull into my driveway, Owen shuts off the engine and turns to me. "So, this favor I need from you is something really important to me." He takes a deep breath and continues. "I know that you've seen my sculptures and paintings, but my real love lies in street art. I stopped doing it when I started doing the more commercial stuff, but I love it. Creating something on the side of a building where everyone will see it is just the best for me."

"Umm, isn't that sometimes illegal?"

"Yeah, it is." He chuckles. "And I *have* gotten in trouble before but then some of the businesses that we ate or shopped at started letting me make murals on their buildings. I'm actually kind of fa-mous."

"Oh wow, Owen. I had no idea. That is really cool."

"Yeah, it is. But, I haven't done any murals in a couple of years. I've been focusing more on the company art. I was thinking that I would like to do one on your building, though. Maybe some flying books and people reading or something. Since your store stands alone in the middle of the center with three walls, I think that I could do something cool. Would you let me?"

I'm momentarily stunned. He wants to paint my building? That would be so cool. But, then I remember that it may not be mine for much longer. "I would love for you to do that Owen. But, honestly, I'm not sure how much longer I can stay in business. Things have been kind of rough lately."

"I'm sorry that you are having a rough time. How about I do it and it can stay as long as you're there. If something happens and you have to close, the new tenant can leave it or not. I just really want to do this." He reaches out and grabs my hand. "Is there any-thing else that I can do for you? Do you need money? Because I have it if you need it."

I see the sincerity in his eyes, so I answer honestly. "I do need money, Owen. But, I wouldn't feel right taking it from you. Thank you for offering, though. And yes, you can paint my building." I lean over and kiss his cheek and then open the door to get out. Alex gets out and gives me a hug. I head into my empty house for what may be the last time. I have to make that call to Tony tomor-row.

CHAPTER 25

<u>Scott</u>

It has been 2 weeks since I set everything in motion and things are somewhat surprisingly going according to my plan. Owen started the mural last week. I drove by and it is looking really cool already. He's been posting updates to his Facebook and Twitter and his fans are going nuts. Ryan is finalizing the paperwork for the purchase of the strip mall. That took some work on his part. The owners didn't want to sell at first and Ry had to really negotiate hard. But, he managed to make it happen. Letters will be going out this week to the tenants letting them know that their rent is going to drop significantly.

My parents and I have been in touch with the publishers who want us to do books with them. We have been honest and let them know that we're not ready yet. We told them that it would make our decision easier if they helped us out. Some said no, but there were a couple that are willing to send their biggest authors to I Heart Books. Yas should be hearing from them soon.

Tony called me after he talked to Yas about the sale of the house. He said that she couldn't believe the price that was offered. He had to tell her something about the purchaser wanting to make sure the offer wasn't beaten by anyone because he loved the house. It's true. I do love Yas's—I guess now my—house. I would have paid ten times the asking price for it if I had to. Tony also said that she was happy that she can stay in it. If my plans work out, then we'll be living there together. If they don't, I'll figure out somehow to get the ownership of it back to her.

Business at the shop is steadily increasing. Luke has been taking girls there almost daily, buying them books. He said that when Yas commented on it, he told her that he wanted to spread the love of reading. Alex says that Yas doesn't believe him, but she's not complaining about the extra business. Owen's fans have also started to drop by and he tells them that the least they can do is buy a book if they want to watch him work. Many of them have been doing just that. The online business has started to boom as well. Sean told me yesterday that Yas is starting to get suspicious about why they are getting so many orders when they don't have my program. Everyone has been distracting her when she tries to go on the website, but I know that it is only a matter of time until she sees it. I am hoping that she will not be too mad at us for going behind her back. We all did it because we love her.

I am walking into the kitchen to grab some sodas for Sean and me, when there is a pounding on my front door. You have to have a gate code to get into our driveway so it has to be someone in my family, although they normally use the doorbell. I walk over to open it and when I do, Yas barrels past me into the living room.

"How did you do it? Did you hack my website?" She spins on me as I close the door.

"What? Of course I didn't hack your website. Why would I do that?" I ask, but I think I know where this is going and my earlier worry about her not being mad seems to have been validated right now.

"Then how did your program get onto my website. I didn't put it there."

I have to snicker at that. "Of course you didn't."

"You think this is funny? You can just mess with my livelihood and it will just be okay because you are Scott Fucking Griffin?"

"No, Yas. I don't think the situation is funny. The thought of you coding a website was funny. I'm sorry I laughed." I am seriously screwing this up.

She relaxes a little. "It *is* funny to think of me trying to do that. But if you didn't do it, who did?"

"Me." I didn't notice Sean step out of the hallway but he's in the living room with us now.

"Sean? What are you doing here?" Yas looks confused now and I hope she takes this well.

"I work here. Scott hired me as his assistant."

"You did?" she asks me and I nod. "That's great. I'm so happy for you." She hugs Sean and then her face falls and she looks at me. "Oh my God, please don't fire him, Scott. If he took the program, it was just to help me out. I'll pay you for it or he can remove it since I know that you didn't want me to have it."

She looks so worried. I scratch my neck and admit, "He didn't steal it, Yas. I gave it to him to put on your website. I would have liked him to install it on your store system but you would have noticed it right away. I wanted to help you, but I wasn't sure if you would take help from me. I'm sorry that we deceived you. It's my fault for convincing Sean so please be mad at me and not him."

Now, she looks torn. "I should be mad at you. At *both* of you. But, the internet sales have been really good and helped me a lot. Thank you for doing this for me." She looks at Sean. "Can you please put it on the store system when you get a chance?"

"Yeah, I can stop by later and upload it." He hugs her goodbye and I see him whisper something in her ear. She gives him a re-signed smile.

"I'm sorry that I just barged in here. I should go and let you guys get back to work. It was nice to see you, Scott." She leans up and kisses me on the cheek. "Thanks for helping me out."

"Let me walk you out to your car. Wait, I heard that you didn't have a car. How did you get here?"

"I borrowed Sam's car. You don't need to walk me out."

"I want to. Is that okay?" She nods and we walk out into the backyard.

I put my hands in the pockets of my jeans and wait to see if she will break the awkward silence. I haven't been doing too good a job of talking to her today without it all coming out wrong so I would rather have her start the conversation. We're almost to her car before she finally says something. "How are you doing? Alex said that you are going to see a therapist. Is it helping you at all?" She looks at the ground when she asks instead of looking at me. I want her to look at me so I reach out and pull her chin up.

"It's going really well. I've been going in 3 times a week to talk to Mike. I'm comfortable with him and I don't feel like I'm in a doctor's office. I feel like I'm talking to a friend, just one who can be impartial and talk things out with me. We do a lot of talking and I am starting to realize that I might be lovable." She starts to protest but I put my hand over her mouth. "I always knew that my family loved me, but I'm talking about romantic love. Not just with Amber, but even in high school when no one wanted to be friends with me, much less date me. And later in college, when girls were perfectly fine with just hooking up with me and not having any kind of relationship. I mean, yeah, it was fun, but I never stopped to think about how what I was doing, what I was settling for, was feeding my insecurities."

She moves my hand from her mouth. "What about me? Do you believe that I loved you?"

"Yes, I do." But, my heart has just plummeted. She said "loved" not "love." "It is one of the first things that Mike and I talked about. How I let my insecurities ruin what we had. We talk about you every session. I know I fucked up and having him point things out to me has been really hard. But I need it. I need someone to call me on my shit. My family just sided with me because that's what families do, but I needed to be told that I was wrong. Mike doesn't tell me that, but hearing him repeat what I tell him, makes me realize it. I'm not completely better. That is going to take a long time, but I have started to realize my self-worth. It feels really good."

"I'm really happy for you, Scott. You are a wonderful man and I am so glad that you are realizing that." She smiles up at me. "I want to thank you for the wooing. I loved the cupcakes, candy, flowers and of course the pens. You don't need to keep sending me stuff, though."

Does she know that she's killing me? That I'm slowly dying inside. First, she used the past tense when she talked about loving me and now she's telling me to stop sending her things. It's over. I didn't do enough to convince her. I didn't get better fast enough. I am starting to panic and she must see it because she grabs my shoulders.

"Scott, what's wrong? Tell me. What happened?" Yas is looking panicked now, too.

I take a few breaths to calm myself down and then I do what Mike says that I need to when I am in a hard situation. I tell her the truth. "You told me that you would give me a chance when I'm ready." She nods, still looking confused. "I thought that there was a chance for us to be together again but you just said that you *loved* me, past tense, and then asked me to stop sending you things. It's just hard to hear that it's really over. I don't want it to be over." I hang my head and fight the tears gathering in my eyes. That's all I need. For her to see me crying over her.

"Look at me, Scott." I shake my head and she lets out a frustrated sigh. "Dammit Scott, do you want me to beg? *Look* at me please, Pretty Boy." It's her use of my nickname that has me raising my eyes to meet hers. "I used the word *loved* because I need to know that *you* know that for the time we were together, I loved you. I want to make sure that you know that my love for you was real. That doesn't mean that I'm not in love with you now. I am. I can't imagine that I will ever not be in love with you. Even if we're not together, my heart will always be yours. And as for sending me things, I just meant that you should concentrate on getting better and working on your new project instead of finding things to send me."

"You're still in love with me?"

"Yes, Scott, I am. That doesn't mean that I'm just going to fall into your arms and forget how you hurt me. Or that I'm going to put up with you treating me like shit again. You nearly destroyed me. But, it does mean that I forgive you and I am hoping that we can be together again. I don't want it to be over either."

"I'm almost ready to ask you to give me that chance. Like I said, I am going to have to keep seeing Mike for a long time, I think. But, I am better. And, I love finding things to send you. It makes me happy to know that you like what I send."

"I'm here waiting for you. I probably shouldn't admit that, but it's true. When you're ready to come for me, I will be ready to listen. Your presents do make me happy. Now, I better get going. I'll talk to you soon." She hugs me and then gets into her car.

CHAPTER 26

<u>Yas</u>

It has been a couple of days since I went to Scott's house. Things are still going great with the store. In fact, business is kind of booming. Between Owen's fans, Luke's girls and Scott's program, we are looking to turn a profit this month. I got a call today from two publishers asking me to host signings for their authors. These are some of the biggest authors out there now and although I'm happy, I am starting to feel like things are too good to be true. Like there is something going on that I don't know about.

"You should just be happy that things are going well," Sam tells me.

"I *am* happy but it just seems weird that this all just fell in my lap. I mean, I just sold my house for an amount of money that makes me a millionaire, publishers are calling me to set up big signings when they wouldn't even give me little ones a few weeks ago and now I heard that the landlords sold to a new company and everyone's rent is going down. It is all a little much."

"It's more like karma, Yasmin. You are such a good person and you deserve all of this."

"Maybe I deserve it but I don't know how I started getting it," I tell her and then I find out. The mailman brings me a letter from Griffin Commercial & Technology telling me that they are the new owners and that my rent will be lowered to a ridiculously small amount. I know when I see it that the family is behind what has been going on. I want to be mad, but I'm not. They once thought of me as part of their family and families help each other. I know Owen is loving the mural and Luke is loving those girls he brings in, but I realize that they were helping me more than I realized, too.

I think about Alex. How she was here every night and whoever picked her up would give me a ride. Now that I'm doing better financially, I have been scheduling someone with me until close and Alex has gone back to two days a week. One of my friends has been driving me home. I wonder who bought my house. No, actually I don't. I know in my heart that it was Scott. I don't know how or when I am going to let them know that I am aware of what they have done. I want to call them all right now, but that doesn't seem right. I will think of something.

I tell Sam what I've figured out and she looks guilty. "Wait a minute. You knew, didn't you?"

"Yeah, I did. I'm sorry Yasmin. Erika and Sean were there when Scott told everyone about his plan and how they fit into it. We just wanted to help you and we weren't sure you would take the help if we offered."

"I probably wouldn't have. I know that I am too proud sometimes. I'm not mad, though. I needed the help and it is nice to have people care enough to do things for me."

"We all love you."

"I love you guys too. Now, tell me more about all of this being Scott's plan."

She tells me about everything. I can't believe Scott organized all of that for me, even before he started getting help from Mike. It makes me think that he already believed in me and our love. Maybe he just didn't know how to deal with it yet. I want to call him up and talk to him about it, but I don't know if I should. He told me that he would come to me when he was ready to try again and I feel like I should wait for him.

Sam is giving me a ride tonight, but tomorrow I'm going to pick up my new SUV. I can't wait to have my own car again. We set the alarm and walk out of the store. I can't believe the sight before me. Scott is in the parking lot, leaning against his car like Logan in the Veronica Mars movie. My friends and I saw that movie and we swooned together at that part. I think that I am swooning right now too.

He's wearing a black short sleeved button down shirt untucked over his jeans. His combat boots are on his feet and his glasses are on his face. I nearly melt just looking at him. He smiles when he sees me and I sway a little. It should be illegal to look that good.

I barely register Sam saying goodbye to me as I walk to him. "Hi, Pretty Boy."

"Hi, Yas. Can I give you a ride home?"

"Well since my ride just left me, I think you have to."

He smirks and says, "I always liked Sam."

He opens the passenger door for me and I get in. We're both quiet on the way to my—I guess his—house. We pull into the drive-way and he gets out to open my door and walk me to the porch. We step onto it and he takes my hands in his and finally speaks. "Will you go on a date with me tomorrow, Yas?"

"Yes, I will."

"Wow. That was easier than I thought. I was prepared to work for it."

"I never intended to make this hard for you. I just wanted to know that you were serious about us, that you wouldn't just walk away from me again."

"I have a lot of work still ahead of me, as far as my therapy. But one thing I know for sure is that once I get you back, I am never letting you go again."

"You seem confident that you'll win me back. It's good to see you being confident about that."

"Well, you *did* agree to go out with me, so I think that I have a shot."

"You might," I tease, squeezing his hands.

"I know this may be a long shot, but is there any way that I can kiss you right now?" When I hesitate, he adds, "Just kissing, I promise. My hands won't leave yours."

I pull on his hands to bring him closer and then lift my head towards his. He immediately lowers his head and touches his lips to mine. He continues to give me little kisses until I can't take it anymore. I slant my mouth and suck his piercing between my teeth. He moans and then opens his mouth to deepen our kiss. Our tongues are playing with each other and I feel myself getting lost in him. I pull away and his mouth follows me so I give him another peck and then step back.

"Goodnight, Scott. I'll see you tomorrow." I make myself let go of his hands and walk into the house. I know that if I don't, I will invite him inside and I can't do that tonight. Maybe tomorrow, but not tonight. I've just reached the bedroom when a text comes through.

Scott: I was thinking that we could go to the Maestro's restaurant at Crystals. I know that you said that you always wanted to eat in that treehouse of theirs.

Me: That sounds great. Good night, Pretty Boy.

Scott: I'll pick you up at 6. Sweet dreams, Yas.

I will have sweet dreams, because they'll all be about him. And that kiss we just had. And what he managed to plan for me. Oh, and what I plan to do with him tomorrow night.

* * *

Scott

I've been going crazy all day waiting for my date with Yas tonight. I was also driving Sean crazy so he sent me upstairs to get ready, saying that he could finish deciphering my notes on his own. I was actually glad to have extra time to get ready. I want to make sure I look good. I'm definitely wearing a suit. But which one and what color shirt? Shit, I'm acting like a girl. But tonight is important. I'm going to ask Yas to be with me again. I don't think that it will take much convincing if the way she kissed me last night is any indication, but I am prepared to do whatever I need to in order to win her back. I finally decide on a dark gray suit with a teal shirt the same color as the bra and panties she was wearing the first time we slept together. The thought of that night has me instantly hard and I have to think about wrinkly senior citizens to get myself back under control as I head out to my car.

When I get to Yas' house, I ring the doorbell and wait for her to answer it. Yes, this is technically my house, but she doesn't know that yet. I can't just walk in. She answers the door and I nearly fall to my knees.

"Sweet mother of God, Yas. Are you trying to kill me with that dress?" It's black and only one of her shoulders is covered. The dress hugs her tightly across the chest and stomach and then falls into a chiffon shirt that goes past her knees. She is wearing fuck me heels and a few pieces of the museum jewelry. Her hair is in soft waves.

"I could say the same about you." I look into her eyes and see the hunger there. I need to rein this in for both of us because I want to take her out and talk to her. I really do. And then I want to bring her back here and make love to her until neither one of us can walk.

I mentally shake myself and grab her hand. "Come on, we better go while we still can."

The restaurant is really good and sitting in the treehouse is pretty cool. I can tell that Yas likes it too. We haven't talked much yet, but after the waiter brings out our warm butter cake to share, I know that it's time for me to tell her how I feel.

I take her hand. "Yas, I want you to know that I love you. You mean more to me than anyone ever has. I know that I hurt you and that I was...am...pretty fucked up. You know that I have been working on getting better and I think that I have. Obviously I am far from done, but I have come to realize some things. I know that I am a pretty good guy who cares about the people he loves and does what he can to help others. I also know that being smart and nerdy is not bad. I can be loved by someone just as I am. I deserve that kind of love. The love that you give me. I can't promise to never be scared, but I am confident that I can stay calm and listen to what you have to say before lashing out again. You are my everything and I don't want to be without you in my life."

She reaches out and places her hands over mine on the table. "I love you too, Scott. I was hurt by you, but I've already told you that I forgive you. I also understand why it was so hard for you to believe in me. I really needed you to believe in me and I can honestly say that I think you do now. I love the smart and nerdy side of you. It's pretty fucking sexy. You are my everything, too, and I don't want to be without you, either."

"Thank you for not making me grovel. I would have gotten down on my knees in front of this entire restaurant if I had to."

"We promised each other that we would never have to beg. I don't need you to. What I do need you to do is pay for our dinner so you can take me home and make love to me. It's been too long."

I throw some money on the table and practically run to the valet parking, pulling Yas along with me. We get in the car and I force myself to drive the speed limit. We're holding hands while I drive, just like we used to. I'm so hard that it physically hurts and I'm glad that I won't be taking care of it myself again, like I've been doing for the past 5 weeks. I want to be inside Yas. I *need* to be inside Yas. The way she is squeezing my hand and squirming in her seat, I know that she wants that too.

We get to the house and I park, get out and open her door as fast as humanly possible. She jumps out and immediately reaches up to kiss me, sucking on my tongue. She slides her leg up to my hip, grinding against me. It takes an amount of willpower that I didn't know I had to not take her right here up against the car. I reach my hands under her ass and lift her up. She wraps her legs around my waist and I start walking to the front door. She moves her mouth to my neck so that I can see as I walk. She is kissing and sucking and oh shit, biting me and I almost lose control. But, I don't want to give her neighbors a show and even though the house is set back from the street, I won't take that chance. I take out my keys and get the door open. I start to walk to the bedroom but she stops me.

* * *

Yas

"Take me here, Scott. I've always wanted to have you take me against a wall."

"You never told me, baby. I would have done that for you anytime. How do you want it?"

"I want to have my legs wrapped around you while you slam me into the wall. Then, when I come, I want you to flip me around and take me from behind. The way you like it. And call me baby again. I love hearing you say that and it's been too long."

He walks me to the wall next to the fireplace. "I like it any way with you, *baby.*" He leans me against the wall and I work on his belt buckle and zipper. Then, I push his pants and briefs down while he sucks on my neck. He's going to mark me with how hard as he's sucking and I want it. I want to have his mark on me. He stops long enough to help me get his pants, briefs and suit jacket off. "Now, it's my turn." He reaches under my dress and stills when he realizes that there is nothing to remove. "Fuck, baby, you've been bare under that dress all night? So, you knew that you were going to let me come back here and make love to you?"

"I knew last night." I manage to get out as he slides his fingers into me and starts biting my nipple through the fabric of my dress. I unbutton his shirt but don't try to slide it off. "I wanted you last night but I needed you to say what you had to first. I had to hear those words from you before I could give you my body again." I arch as he twists his fingers and I almost come, but I need him in-side of me. "I need you now, Scott."

"I need a condom." he says, lifting his mouth from my dress.

"No, I went on the pill a few weeks ago. I'm clean and I know you said that you got tested before we met. I want you bare inside me. I want to really feel you."

He removes his fingers from me and finds the zipper on my dress. He pulls it down and then slides the sleeve of my dress down along with the top of my dress. "I haven't been with a woman without a condom. Ever," he says as he guides himself to my entrance with one hand while holding me up with the other. "I may not last long so I'm going to play with your tits while I take you. I want to play with your clit too but I need to brace myself on the wall so I can take you hard like I need to. I may need you to touch yourself if I am getting too close and you aren't. Will you do that for me, baby, will you take yourself over if I need you to?"

"Yes." I manage to get out as he slams into me. Oh my God, I missed his cock.

He's licking and sucking on my nipples as he pounds into me. It feels so good. Then he starts talking against my breasts. He knows I love his dirty talk. "You like it baby? You like my cock in you, fucking you hard? I know you do. Your pussy is so wet for me. When we're done here, I'm going to take you to the shower and clean us both off. It's going to be a quick shower while I soap you up and touch you everywhere. Then, I'm going to lie down on your bed and you are going to get on top of me and we are going to sixty nine." I jerk at the thought, getting close. His words are spurring me on, making me start meeting him as he thrusts into me. I'm not going to need my fingers. The pressure is building already. "Would you like that? Having my cock in your mouth while I lick and suck your pussy and clit?"

"Yes, oh fuck, yes, Pretty Boy. Yes to all of it." I tell him and as he shifts so that my clit rubs against him, he bites my nipple and I am gone. I thrash against him and scream his name as he continues to thrust hard and I'm not sure that I will come down anytime soon. He waits as long as he can with me before sliding out and moving us sideways so that I'm in front of the mantle, holding on to it. He pulls my dress from my hips and enters me again from behind. His hands are on my breasts now, kneading and pinching as he kisses the back of my neck.

"It feels so good to be inside of you like this, with nothing between us," he tells me between kisses.

"Yes, it does. Your cock belongs in me and I love feeling you like this. You're so hard for me and it's making me wetter." He likes dirty talk, too, and he's moving faster and faster as I talk, moving his hands from my breasts to my hips so that he can hold me as he starts to lose control. "After we sixty nine and you come in my mouth, I'm going to lick your tattoos while you recover. I have missed them and I want my tongue on them, all over them. When you're ready for me, I'm going to climb on your cock and ride you the way that I like." I know he's close so I turn my head and bite into his bicep. That's all it takes. He growls and then comes hard. Yelling out my name along with a string of curse words. His legs start to give out and I let go of the mantle as he lowers us both to the ground, turning me as we go. We're lying face to face, breathing hard.

"Damn, Yas. That was...that was..."

"Amazing," I finish for him. "Just like it always is."

"Yeah, it always is." He smiles and kisses me softly and then turns serious. "I have missed you so much, Yas. And I don't mean just for this. Although, I won't lie, I missed this a lot."

"I missed you, too."

We lie there for a little while, just kissing lightly and caressing each other on the living room floor. When he has his strength back, Scott stands me up with him and then picks me up in his arms, carrying me to the shower. We do all of the things that we promised each other that we would and then fall asleep in each other's arms.

CHAPTER 27

<u>Scott</u>

I wake up the morning after our night together happier than I can ever remember being. I am happier than when I was with Yas before, even. I know that I deserve her love now and I trust her. I am worthy of her and she makes me feel like I can do anything. I need her to go with me to Chicago again in a few weeks and I'm going to talk to her about it this morning. First, I want to make her breakfast. I slide out from under her and watch her move onto her stomach as she makes herself comfortable in her sleep.

When I come back in with the omelets and toast that I made, she's still asleep. I wore my girl out last night. Hell, I wore myself out. My adrenaline is pumping, wanting to talk to her about Chicago, which is the only thing keeping me awake. I don't know why I'm worried. She loves me and I am pretty sure that she will agree to go with me. But, I can't calm down because I need her there with me, maybe even more than I needed her at the trial.

I feather kisses along her spine, waking her slowly. "Hey, baby, I made you some breakfast. Hope you don't mind me using your kitchen."

"It's really your kitchen now, so you don't have to ask." I freeze as I take in her words.

"My kitchen?" I swallow, trying to calm my racing heart. She knows.

Yas turns over and looks me in the eye. "It *was* you who bought my house, wasn't it?"

"Yes," I admit because I am not going to lie to her. "Are you mad?"

"Did I seem mad last night?" she teases, sitting up.

"No, no you didn't." I smile back and kiss her.

"Thank you, Scott. And thanks for everything else that you did."

"How much do you know? Did Erika tell you? Sean and I were surprised that she could keep it from you for so long."

"Erika didn't tell me. When I got the letter saying that your family's company had bought my strip mall and were lowering the rent, the pieces started coming together. I knew that things seemed too good to be true. I can't believe that you did all of that for me. How *did* you do it?"

"My family all took on a part of the plan. We all have our strengths and when we come together, it can be pretty awesome."

"It *is* awesome. And you were the mastermind of it all, I hear?" I nod with a smirk. "Who knew that you were so talented at world domination or at least bookstore rescue? I mean, I know that you are a computer genius and have other, exceptional skills that I am lucky enough to be the recipient of, but what you did for me is beyond anything that I could have imagined. What did I do to deserve you?"

I answer her honestly. "You loved me, Yas. You love me. And there is no one that I would rather share my exceptional, as you call them, skills with. But, before I share them again, you need to eat this breakfast that I slaved over a hot stove to make you."

She kisses me lightly before saying. "Yes sir, Mr. Griffin. Give me my omelet." I hand it to her and she grabs my hand. "Is there anything that you need from me? For your therapy or anything?"

I do need something from her. "Yes, actually, I do need something. It's not therapy related although Mike would like you to come in and do a session with me if you can."

"Of course, Scott. Just tell me when. What else do you need?"

"I don't know if you remember me telling you about my family being honored by the charity that Erin and Dave used to fund." She nods and I continue, "It's in three and a half weeks and I am having a hard time with it. Not just with going, which will be hard because we all have to talk and I don't know if I can do it. But, also because my sister loved me the way I am, tattoos and piercings and all. And the PR people are still saying that I have to cover up. I mean, I don't want to go in jeans and a t-shirt. I just want to not wear a tie and keep my shirt open a little so part of my Griffin tat shows. And keep my piercings in. My parents say that I can but I know my dad and Ryan are working on a big deal with a conservative company. We don't need the money but we also can't just stop doing deals and just disappear from the world. So, I'm going to do it even though it's killing me."

"I'm so sorry, Scott. How can I help you?" Yas is stroking my back now.

"Can you go with me? Having you with me always makes things better."

"I would be honored to go with you. But, are you sure that you want me there cramping your style? I mean, what will all those society girls do with themselves if they can't get you to dance with them? I heard that they practically rush you whenever you go to one of those things. Not that I blame them. You know what you do to me when you wear a suit." She's teasing me now, trying to lighten the mood and it's working.

"They can watch me dance with the woman that I love. None of those bitches would even give me the time of day when we were in high school together. I may have taken one or two into a closet for some fun during college, but they never meant anything to me. I told you last night that you mean everything to me and I meant it."

"I know you do. Yes, I will go with you although I'm a little nervous now, too."

"You're nervous? Why?" I ask, baffled.

"Some of those girls who you 'took into the closet' are going to be there aren't they? I mean, I know you have been with a ton of girls but to be faced with them makes me a little...self-conscious." She looks down and I pull her chin back up.

"What the fuck would you have to feel self-conscious about?"

"Well, they are probably super thin and ultra-fashionable. And I'm, well... I'm not."

"Are you kidding me right now? You are the sexiest, most gorgeous woman I have ever met in my life. I love how you look and how you dress. They are going to be jealous when their dates are drooling over you." I have to be honest with her again, though. "They can be catty, though. So, someone may say something to you, but, I will shield you from as much as I can."

"You make me feel sexy and gorgeous. Thank you for that. I would love to go with you. Just give me the dates and I'll get the store covered. Will we have time to see Quinn and Zane? Quinn and I have become good friends." I nod, smiling. "Oh and John?"

"We can go a day early again to see my friends and John will be at the party. I love you, Yas. Thank you for doing this for me. Will you have time to find a dress?"

"You don't have to thank me. I love being anywhere that you are. As for a dress, I would like to have one made. I have an idea for one that I think would be perfect." Her eyes are twinkling and I know that I'm going to love whatever it is she has planned.

"I can pay for it since I'm asking you."

She laughs. "Scott, you made me a millionaire when you paid twice the asking price for this house. I can afford my own dress. We need to talk about the house, you know. I should give you back some of the money."

"No, Yas. I would have paid all of the money I have if that's what it would have taken. I want you to have what I paid. That was my choice."

She sighs but I can tell that she is going to let it go. "Okay. I have been working on accepting help better and not being so proud. I still think it's too much but if you say that you can afford it, I be-lieve you. Now that I know, should I move out sooner? I was going to start looking for an apartment."

I look at her incredulously. "You're not moving out. This is your home, Yas."

"Umm, I know that we are back together, but I'm not ready to move in with you yet." She looks away.

"That's fine. You can live here and I'll stay at my place for now."

"You don't have to do that. You bought this house and you should be able to live in it. I can find another place to stay until I am ready to move in with you." She looks me in the eye. "Because I'm hoping that our relationship progresses to the point where we move in and maybe more. I'm just not ready yet."

"I want you to stay here and I definitely want our relationship to progress in that same direction, but I have to ask for another favor while we wait. Can we buy some furniture and stuff together? You know, for when you are ready? And can I start converting one of the extra rooms into my new workroom? I won't use it yet, but I want to be ready."

"Yes, we can do that. I would love to have us both decorate the house. And I would love for you to have a workroom here too. What would you like to change in this room?"

"Here? Nothing. I love this bedroom. I don't want to change it." I pause for a moment. "Although I would like to add a bigger TV, of course."

"Of course."

* * *

Yasmin

After we eat breakfast and make love again in the shower, Scott leaves to go to work. He wants to stay but says that he and Sean are at a crucial part of the new program and he hates to stop, but, he offers to stay if I want him to. I tell him to go to work and that I'll come by later. I have something that I need to do today, too.

When Scott told me about covering up his tattoos, I got an idea. I call Zane and ask him what he thinks. "That would be cool, Yasmin. If you can find someone to do it, I can get it ready."

"I think that I can find someone but we may not have a lot of time. Are you sure that you don't mind?"

"Mind? I love this idea. Scott is going to love it, too. By the way, I'm glad to hear that you two back together."

"Thanks. I am glad too. I am going to look up some designers now and then I'll call you back."

"Okay. Talk to you soon."

I get off the phone with Zane and look up some things on my computer. I find who I am looking for and send off an email, hoping to hear back in the next couple of days. What I want is going to take some time.

I decide to head into work, even though I had planned on going in later. I want to get my work done so that I can go over to Scott's later. I have to look over the applications that I've received since

I'm able to hire a couple more people. It's nice to be able to take some time off and not be at the store from open to close.

I get to the store and let myself in. We don't open for another half hour but I don't see Sam and Danny anywhere. I walk into the backroom to find them making out against one of the tables. I yelp out loud.

They break apart fast. "Oh my God, Yasmin. I'm so sorry. We didn't think that you were coming in so early today," Sam says turning red.

"I wasn't but I wanted to get some interviews set up. You don't need to apologize, though. I'm happy that you two are finally together."

"I'm happy, too." Danny moves back over to Sam and puts his arms around her. She smiles up at him.

"I'm going to go lock myself in my office. You have half an hour until we open. So, do whatever you want until then. And come see me later. I need to ask you guys to pick up some extra shifts so that I can go to Chicago in a few weeks."

"Chicago?" Sam asks. "So, you and Scott?"

"Yeah, me and Scott," I tell her with a smile and then go into the office and close the door.

I spend the day setting up interviews and taking care of orders and bills. Owen arrives to continue his painting and I tell him that I know about the plan and thank him.

"Seriously, Yasmin. This *is* a favor to me. I have missed this. So, yeah, Scott asked me to help you, but he knew that he was helping me too." I hug him and head over to my car. I can't wait to get over to Scott's place. I know that he's probably going to still be working but I can wait in one of the cabanas for him to be done. I just want to be close to him.

I drive through the gate and see Maggie and Alex getting into Maggie's BMW. They stop when they see me. I get out of my car and walk over to them. "Yasmin! Uncle Scott said that you're going to the ball with us. We're going to look at dresses. Do you want to come with us?" Alex tells me, grabbing me in a big hug.

"I'm actually planning on having a special dress made, but I would love to go help you two pick out dresses." I *would* like to go and it will give me something to do while I wait for Scott.

"It would be wonderful to have your input, Yasmin. And I want to hear more about this special dress of yours," Maggie tells me as we get into the car.

I tell them my plan as we drive to Crystals at City Center. They're both excited and tell me that Scott will love it. I tell them that I haven't heard from the designer yet so I am not sure if it is doable, but if not, I have plenty of time to find a dress. We spend a few hours shopping. Alex ends up with a Dolce & Gabbana and Maggie finds a gorgeous gown at Valentino. I find some cool sandals with blue and green beaded leaves at Jimmy Choo that I think will look good with the dress that I'm envisioning. I find some emerald and gold earrings at Tiffany that I buy, too.

When we get back to their house, I see Sean and Scott in the driveway. I get out of the car and Scott is by my side almost immediately. "Hi baby." He kisses me lightly. "I saw your SUV but I didn't know where you were. I was about to call you."

"I came by earlier and your mom and Alex met me in the driveway and asked me to go shopping for the ball with them. I figured that you would want to work longer, so I went with them and got some shoes and earrings."

"Thanks for that. I did need to keep working." He leans in and whispers in my ear, "Do I get to see you in those shoes and earrings? *Only* in those shoes and earrings?" A shiver goes up my spine, but I shake my head.

"Nope. You can see them when you see me in my dress. And then you can see me in *only* them after the ball."

"I knew that would be your answer but I thought that I would give it a try." He laughs.

"You two need to get a room," Sean says with a grin.

"We have a room around the corner," Scott says to him with a bigger grin.

"On that note, I'm going to take off."

"Say hi to Erika for me," I tell him. He nods and drives away. We talk to Maggie and Alex for a few more minutes and then escape to Scott's place.

We order in pizza and play video games. Or I should say, he plays video games and I *try* to play along with him. We have fun, though. I love being with him like this. With no expectations and no pressure. Just having fun and making out on the couch in between games. Eventually, our making out gets hotter and I'm straddling him. Scott stands up, taking me with him and I wrap my legs around him as he carries me upstairs and makes love to me all night again.

CHAPTER 28

<u>Scott</u>

It's the day of the ball. Yas and I went to see Zane and Quinn yesterday. We all went out to eat and then hung out at their place. At one point, Zane and Yas exchanged a glance and then went into the kitchen together. I tried to follow but Quinn started asking me questions about my new program, looking nervously at the kitchen every few minutes. I was worried for a minute and then realized that they must be planning something for me. Maybe Yas is going to get a tattoo. That would be hot. I would love to see a tattoo on her awesome body.

We're staying at my apartment this time and we didn't get much sleep last night. If Owen knew that I took Yas from behind as she held on to one of his sculptures, he would never let me live it down. It was pretty damn erotic though, having her naked, pressed up against the metal with her hands above her head, holding on. Thank God and Owen that he insisted on me having his sculptures attached to the floor so that they wouldn't tip. That one would have definitely tipped last night. That was just the beginning of our night. Shit. I need to get a grip or I'm going to have to take a cold shower and I don't have time for that.

I'm in the guest room getting ready while Yas is upstairs in my room. She was nervous all day, waiting for her dress to arrive. When it did, she immediately ran upstairs with it. I can't wait to see her. It still sucks that I have to cover up and I'm not happy as I remove all of my piercings, but I get to have my girl with me so that makes up for it. I get the text that I have been waiting for.

Yas: Are you ready?

Me: Yep. I am walking out to the living room now.

I walk out and stand at the bottom of the steps waiting. When Yas walks out, I can't believe what I am seeing at first. Her dress... her dress is like nothing I have ever seen before. It almost brings me to my knees as she walks down the stairs and stops a few steps from the bottom. The top is flesh colored and covered in my tattoos. Where they are on my body underneath my clothes. But being shown on her body, on the fabric of her dress, over her curves. The bottom of the dress is stiff black material, a little shorter in front then the back and showing off her shoes which have blue and green leaves twisting around them. She has emerald earrings in her ears but no other jewelry. There's no need for any. The dress is a work of art. My work of art. And Zane's. I realize now what they were talking about. He had to have helped with this. I can't say anything. I don't know the words.

Yas misinterprets my silence. "I-I can change, Scott. I have a backup dress." She turns and I reach out and pull her to me.

"Don't you dare fucking change. I love this dress. I more than love it. I just couldn't find my words for a minute. How did you do this?"

She takes a breath, relaxing. "When you invited me to the ball and told me how you couldn't show your tattoos or piercings, I thought that maybe I could show them for you. I called Zane to see if he could help and then tracked down a guy I saw on Project Runway who had a fabric printer. Are you sure that you like it?"

"Yes, baby. It's amazing and you are amazing for thinking of this and doing it for me. I love you so much."

"I love you, too. Oh, and I'm sorry about the piercings. I thought about them, but I just couldn't do it." She looks sheepish.

"This is enough, Yas. It's more than enough. You have no idea what it feels like to see my ink on you."

"Ohh, are you feeling all alpha?"

"Yeah, I am. And if we didn't need to get to the party, I would show you just how much." I growl and then kiss her hard. I make myself pull away after a minute and lead her from the apartment and into the elevator.

We exit into the lobby and Bobby is there. "Wow, you two look amazing." We thank him and then head out to the limo.

* * *

Yasmin

When we arrive at the ball, I'm not ready for the photographers who are waiting for us. I didn't realize how famous the Griffins are in Chicago. I recover as quickly as possibly as Scott leads me onto the red carpet. We pose for pictures and even kiss. Reporters ask me about my dress and I tell them the name of designer and also give them Zane's name and tell them about his shop. We make it inside and find his family.

"Whoa, Yasmin. That dress is sick," Luke tells me. Owen and Ryan nod their agreement.

"Thanks, Luke."

"You look beautiful, Yasmin," Gary tells me, kissing my cheek. "Thank you for doing this for my boy."

"It's my pleasure."

We head to our table and have a nice dinner, laughing and talking. It's nice to see John again and I tell him that. I notice that both Ryan and he keep glancing to a gorgeous blonde across the room. She has a smile on that doesn't reach her eyes. A handsome guy who obviously thinks he's God's gift to us all keeps trying to kiss her, but she is expertly dodging him. He's holding her hand, though. Ryan looks like he wants to punch something...or cry. John just looks resigned. I will have to ask Scott about it later.

I head to the restroom before dessert. I walk out of the bathroom and start to head back to the table when two women step into my path. They are both dressed in similar bubble gum pink dresses and look like they haven't eaten in a year.

"I don't know what Scott sees in you, but he'll toss you aside soon. I mean look at that trashy dress you are wearing," Thing One says to me.

"Seriously, are you that desperate that you would need to put his last name on the front of your dress and his mom's name on the back?" Thing Two chimes in, then adds, "You don't know him like we do."

I paste a sweet smile on my face as I stare them down. "Oh, you mean like you know him from when he fucked you in the closet?" Their eyes nearly pop out of their faces and I continue. "And I think that if you really knew him, you would know that these are his tattoos and that he loves my dress. In fact he loves it so much, that when we get back to his apartment, he is going to make love to me all night in *his bed*. Just like he did last night."

"Who do you think you are, you bitch?" One sneers at me, seeming shocked that I would stand up to her.

"She's my girlfriend." Scott comes up behind me and puts his arm around my waist. "And if you don't shut the fuck up, I'll have you thrown out." They looked dumbstruck that he is defending me. "Oh, and for the record, I *am* going to take her back to *our* apartment and make love to her all night. And then, we are going to go back to Vegas and pick out furniture for our house there. Because anything that is mine is hers, too."

They stand there with their mouths open as we walk away laughing. "I'm sorry that I didn't get there faster, but you were holding your own."

"It's okay. I *was* holding my own. And you know what? I didn't feel self-conscious when they were insulting me, especially because they didn't even know that these were your tattoos. How is that possible?"

"I never took my shirt off when I went in the closet," he tells me with a laugh.

* * *

Scott

It's almost time for our speeches. I had mine written already but I would like to add something. I ask my dad and Ryan if it is okay because it might affect their deal, but they tell me that I'm more important than any deal. I thank them and look over what I wrote, deciding on where to add this in. I read what I had written to Mike at our last session and he said it was great. Yas had gone with me to meet him a couple of weeks ago and it was really good. He told me the next time I saw him that he liked her. My parents and Ryan speak about Erin and Dave and how we want to keep helping and then it's my turn.

I take a deep breath as I step up to the podium. "I want to thank you for this award and for honoring my sister and brother in law's memory. Many of you know the circumstances of their deaths and you probably wouldn't be surprised to know that I blamed myself for a long time. I don't blame myself any longer because I realize that I was a victim too. I wanted to get that out of the way but that is all I am going to say about it publicly. I would rather talk about the people who I care about, who love me and have helped me become the man that I am today.

"Dave was a great guy. He was a wonderful husband to my sister and a wonderful father to my niece, Alex. I will always be thankful to him for that. I will also be thankful to him for being like a big brother to me. When he married my sister, he took us all in as his family. His advice and love helped me though high school. I love him and I miss him.

"My good friends John and Zane helped me through some rough times, too. They were always there for me and listened when I had a problem. To this day I know that I can call them up and they will drop whatever they are doing to talk to me. They mean more to me than they will ever know.

"My dad has always supported me and let me find my own path. He didn't think that it would lead me to his company, but we have been pretty successful with my work. I will always appreciate the love that he has shown me, especially in my darker times.

"Ryan, Owen and Luke, you are the best brothers that a guy could hope to have. You have kicked my ass when I needed it and called me on my shit more than once. You've also always been there through everything and helped me with my plans, even if they were a little crazy sometimes.

"All of those guys helped me and shaped me, but it is the women in my life who have shown me how to love and be loved.

"My sister Erin was always like a second mom to me. She held me when I cried in elementary school because no one wanted to play with the nerdy kid. She taught me about girls and how to treat them, telling me that if I was a jerk, I would never get a girl who was worth it. I didn't listen to her for a long time, but now I know that she was right. I love my sister and miss her every day. I carry her love with me and I know that she is watching over me.

"There is nothing that I can say about my mom that will be enough. She is the mom that every kid hopes for. She makes the best mac and cheese and can scare us all with one look. She also let my brothers and I find our own way even when she knew we were making a wrong choice. She wanted us to learn from our mistakes. She also made sure that we stayed humble despite our wealth. My mother taught me about unconditional love and I love her unconditionally back.

"When my niece, Alex, was born and I held her in my arms, I knew what love at first sight was. I could not be any prouder of this beautiful girl who is smart, funny and honest. She told me off a few weeks ago when I was being an ass and I will be thankful to her for that for the rest of my life. She is a ray of light to everyone who meets her and I am honored to have the love that she gives me."

I pause to think of the other woman in the room who I should be talking about next. After what she did to Ryan, I can't do that, even though she did so much for me when we were younger. I take a deep breath before moving on to tell them about the most important woman of all.

"There is one more woman that I need to tell you about. She is the woman who owns my heart. I belong to her mind, body, soul and everything in between. She belongs to me, too, and I am the luckiest man in the world. From the day we met, she challenged me and didn't let me get away with anything. She loves me honestly and, although we have had some bumps along our path and will probably have more in the future, I know that I will be spending the rest of my life with her. She's horrible at video games and will never be able to code a website but she loves me and puts up with the nerd in me. She is also incredibly sexy, sarcastic, fiercely independent and smarter than me in so many ways. Tonight, she managed to do something even more amazing than I could have thought possible. When we were first told about this party, the PR people at our company told me that I would have to take out my piercings and cover my tattoos. I've done that for other events, but it didn't feel right to cover up for this. My sister loved me just the way I am and I wanted to be myself. My parents agreed with me but I ultimately decided to listen to the PR people and covered everything up. Then, my girl walked down the stairs to me wearing my tattoos on her dress. She had it made by someone from Project Runway and my tattoo artist and friend, Zane, helped them get it right. She said that she wanted to show off my tattoos for me since I couldn't do it myself. I can't imagine anyone doing anything for me that would mean more. I love you, Yas, and I can't wait to spend the rest of my life with you."

I jump off the stage and pull her into my arms, kissing her passionately. The crowd claps and then I hear Owen's voice from the podium. "You all need to hide your game controllers now." Yas laughs against my lips and I flip him off behind her back. My life is perfect now.

EPILOGUE

Yas

Six months later

We're in Paris for the wedding. Not our wedding, Erika and Sean's. Scott's new program did extremely well and as a bonus, he insisted on paying for this wedding for them and flying all of us out here. They are getting married in Monet's gardens at Giverny with just their families, Scott's family, Sam, Danny, Candi and me. Scott and I will be staying a few days after the ceremony to explore Paris. I closed the store for a week so that we could all be gone. I can afford it now.

The gardens are magnificent and Erika looks beautiful in her lacy Elie Saab gown. Sam, Alex and I are in short gold Elie Saab dresses as her bridesmaids. The guys are in black suits. There are the natural flowers growing around us and Erika brought in gorgeous white flowers, offset by gold ribbons. Her cake is a masterpiece of white and gold layers. We all eat, dance and drink into the night. Sam catches the bouquet, which is fitting since she and Danny are already engaged and will be getting married at Disney

World next year. Scott is paying for that, too. He has no reason to, but he says that he loves my friends and wants to do this for them. We head back to the little inn where we are staying and fall into bed so that we can get up early for the train into Paris.

In Paris, we are staying at the George V. I would have picked a small hotel, but Scott likes to stay at luxurious hotels with me. Yesterday we explored Montmarte and went to the Louvre and the Musee d'Orsay. I loved it all, especially the museums. I let Scott buy me a bunch of stuff from the museum shops, because I knew he would just watch me again if I didn't tell him what I wanted. I felt a little weird at first, being here with him, when I know that he once wanted to make a trip to Paris with Amber. Scott assured me that what we are experiencing is nothing like what he would have been doing with her. She would have just taken him to all of the most expensive boutiques and expected him to buy them out for her. I prefer the fun, little French shops although I did pick up a few designer things. I paid for them myself, though.

We kissed on the top of the Eiffel Tower last night. This morning, we went to the Lover's Bridge and left a lock. I know that they take them down to make room for more but I really wanted to do it and Scott thought it was cool, too. We ate at a café and looked at a flea market for things for our house.

Scott moved in with me last month. It was time. Well, actually it was past time, but, he has been patient with me as I fully learned to trust him again. He's still been having sessions with Mike, but they're now only meeting once a week. I am proud of him for getting help and working on his issues. I decided that going to school full-time wasn't good choice right now, but Scott convinced me to take a few online classes. I've enjoyed them and it's nice to do the work when it's convenient for me.

We just went to Laduree for macaroons and saw Notre Dame, standing on the spot marking the center of Paris. Now, we are headed into Shakespeare and Company, a famous bookstore that I really want to see. I want to buy a copy of *Much Ado About Nothing*, my favorite Shakespeare play.

"Why don't we just ask the guy at the counter? They probably keep all of the Shakespeare plays up there," Scott says as we try to navigate around other shoppers.

"Umm, OK," I tell him, wondering why he is in a rush. He knows that I wanted to come here and he's been acting weird today.

I ask the guy at the counter and he *does* have a copy behind the register. He smiles brightly at us as he rings it up. I pay for it and Scott hurries me out of the store. He finds an empty bench and pulls me down next to him.

"Is everything okay, Scott?" I ask him nervously.

"Everything is perfect, Yas. Open up the bag and look at your book, please."

"I can wait until later."

"No, baby, I *need* you to look at it now."

"Okay." I pull the book out and see the ring tied to a ribbon like a bookmark. It is a princess cut diamond surrounded by square purple sapphires around it and more diamonds on the band. It is big, but not huge. "Scott?" I look up as he slides off the bench and gets on one knee in front of me.

"Yasmin, I know that I should write you a big speech, but I've already done that, so I am going to keep this simple. I love you and I want you to be my wife. Will you please marry me?"

"Yes, oh my God, yes Scott!" I pull him to me and kiss him as I hear clapping around us. We pull apart and receive congratulations from the crowd.

"Do you like it?" he asks slipping it on my finger.

"I love it and I love you, Pretty Boy." I tell him and I can't wait to spend the rest of my life with him.

ACKNOWLEDGEMENTS

First, I would like to thank my daughters, Dominique and Gabrielle for always supporting me and inspiring me. They have told me that they will never read my books (because that would just be weird), but they encouraged me to go for it and write!

My two biggest cheerleaders were fellow authors Tera Lynn Childs and Erika Babbitt. When I sat down one day and just started writing this book, they gave me encouragement and made me keep writing. They also convinced me that I had to actually do something with this book and not just put it away somewhere. I am eternally grateful to them for their help as well as their friendship! And yes, Erika's husband in real life is named Sean as well!

My beta readers were a great help and I am happy that they loved Scott and Yasmin as much as I do. Velvet Wehrman, Jenn Valencia, LauraAnn Deketelaere, Cel Legaspi-Mesina, Samantha Boydman, Adylene Ascencio, Sierra Johnson, Cyndy Deleon, Sarah Erskine Vela and Lisa Dess were amazing and super helpful. Authors Jessie Evans and Jessie Humphries gave great input on technical things.

Thanks to Tracy Wolff for not only reading the book, but giving me a cover quote as well. I'm a big fan or Tracy as both an author and as a person, so it meant a lot to me that she would do this for me!

Cyndi Porter was also a big cheerleader as well as a reader-we had many conversations about my nervousness over writing the sex scenes that people would one day read. After reading book 2, she will tell you that I have gotten past that now!

Lauren Blakely gave me so much support and advice that helped me along my journey. She answered all of my questions and referred me to Helen Williams for my cover and Jesse Gordon for the book formatting.

My co-workers were a great source of support as well. Candice McCallum, Brent Surratt, Reuben Calderon, Alexandra Murphy and Julie Hayes all encouraged me, laughed with me and gave me some crazy ideas (most of which I didn't use, but I still appreciate them).

I want to thank everyone who purchased this book to read. I never had any intention of writing a book until I sat down one day and did it. I hope that you enjoyed the final product!

ABOUT THE AUTHOR

Crystal Perkins has always been a big reader, but she never thought that she would write her own book, until she did. She lives in Las Vegas, where you can find her running author events and selling books at conventions when she isn't reading, buying too many Sherlock t-shirts online or finding a place to put all of her Pop! figurines. A mac and cheese connoisseur, she travels the country looking for the perfect version, while attending book conventions and signings as a cover for her research.

You can find her on Facebook:
facebook.com/CrystalPerkinsAuthor

And Twitter: @wondermomlv

Turn the pager for a Sneak Peek of
Ryan and Chloe's story,
Building Our Love

Coming Summer 2014!

The other two books in the Griffin Brothers
series will be released later this year:

Creating a Love: Owen & Candi's story
Learning to Love: Luke & Olivia's story

Ryan

As I head to my dad's office, I can't help but wonder what my brother wants to see us about. Scott usually sticks to his computers. Or his fiancé. He's well underway with his new software project, so I don't think there's anything going on with that. It's unusual for him to ask to see us in a formal setting.

When I get to the outer office, my dad's longtime secretary, Angie, looks at me nervously. That's strange. She usually playfully flirts with me, even though she is pushing 60 and I am just shy of 25. I don't have time to ask her what's wrong as Scott storms out of the office.

"You didn't tell me that *she* would be here!" He yells over his shoulder. She? What she is he talking about?

Then, the floor drops out beneath my feet as I hear the person he is yelling at respond. "I had to bring her, Scott. Your family is her only hope." John's here. And there's only one "her" that Scott would be yelling about in relation to John. Chloe. The girl I gave my love, my everything, to. The girl who shredded my heart and never looked back.

Scott sees me then. "Ry, I swear I had no idea. John asked if I could set up a meeting but I didn't know that bitch would be here."

Before I can say anything, John is in his face. "Do not call my daughter a bitch. She may have made choices that you and I don't agree with, but my daughter was a great friend to you when you were younger and you will respect her in my presence." He then looks at me. "I'm sorry, Ryan. I wouldn't have brought her here if she had anywhere else to go. I need your help. Yours and your father's. Please just at least listen to us. If you can't bring yourself to help, we'll both leave and you will never have to see us again."

"What do you mean, both of you will leave?" Scott is panicking now. I know that John is his closest confidant and I need to calm him down. Even if it will hurt me in the process.

"No one will be leaving. We'll help you, John. You're part of our family and if that means helping Chloe too, we'll do it for you."

I walk into my dad's office to find him looking uncomfortable while Chloe sobs into his jacket. I can only see the back of her but my body instantly reacts to the sight of the only woman that I have ever loved. Her soft blonde hair is cascading down her back and she is wearing a flowered dress that hugs her thin body and perfect ass. She is wearing heels that bring her height up to six feet.

I stand there and just stare at her, wondering again about what I did to lose her. How bad I was as her first lover that made her leave me the next day for another man. No, I'm not going to do this. I don't care why she left. I don't care about her. But, I do. I still love her. That doesn't mean that I'll let her hurt me again. She will never get that close to me again. I need to take control of the situation.

"What are you doing here, Chloe?"

She turns and her beautiful blue eyes take me in. She is as gorgeous in person as she's been in my fantasies for the past three years. Maybe more so, now that she is no longer a teenager. She's still thin with soft, natural curves and legs a mile long. There's nothing fake about her body. It is just her who's fake. I make my expression one of steel as she looks at me with a hint of sadness.

"I had nowhere else to go, Ryan."

"What about your fiancé? You know, the guy you left me for."

"Adam and I are no longer together. He left me."

"Karma's a bitch, huh? Just like you."

"Ryan, I warned you-," John starts to say.

"Dad, it's OK. I deserve whatever Ryan calls me." She takes us all in. "Can we please sit down and then I can explain why I'm here?"

* * *

<u>Chloe</u>

Ryan nods and we all take seats around the table in his dad's office. I take a deep breath and my dad reaches over to squeeze my hand as I start to explain. "I graduated 3 months ago at the top of my class. I had offers from several interior design firms. Then, Adam and I broke up and what he told the press caused me to lose all of those offers. My student loan payments are due soon and I don't want dad to take on the burden of those along with helping out my sister and her family. I need a job and he thought that you might be willing to give me one. I know that it's a long shot, but I had to ask. I promise that I would be professional and work hard."

I look at Ryan and have trouble breathing. He looks so gorgeous, even as he's glaring at me. His black hair is a little long on top with a few strands hanging down into his eyes. Those amazing green eyes that all the men in his family have are like hard emeralds that are cutting through me right now. He's clean shaven and conservative looking in his designer suit and tie. I can see his muscles trying to break free under the suit. He worked construction every summer to learn that side of building. He's kept that strong physique and looks like he is carved out of marble. I remember the way it felt to be held in those strong arms and I have to stop myself from jumping onto his lap. Yeah, that would go over well.

"What do you mean you lost your job prospects after Adam went to the press?" Gary's voice breaks my trance. Ryan's dad is a good man and I hate knowing that I let him down and now I have to tell him things that will make me look even worse to him.

"You don't know? I thought that you would get the Chicago papers."

"Contrary to what you seem to think, we have better things to do than keep up with your love life," Ryan spits out and I flinch.

"Adam told the press that I cheated on him throughout our entire relationship and that he caught me and broke up with me." I say it all fast. I need to get it out without thinking about it.

"So, you made me wait 5 years and then you just went crazy and fucked everyone in sight?" Ryan's eyes are now flashing and not in the way that I used to love.

"Ryan, I love you like a son but I will not let you speak to my daughter that way." My dad is on his feet.

"Dad. Please sit down. Ryan has every right to be angry. Even if what Adam said isn't true." It isn't true. The only man that I have ever slept with is the one in front of me with murder in his eyes. I can't tell him that, though. I can't tell anyone the truth.

Scott speaks for the first time since we sat down. "I don't have any interior design work, but you can help me if you want. I can pay you to be my secretary. God knows I need one." He laughs to try to lighten the mood.

I turn to thank him but Ryan's voice stops me. It is cold and hard and when I look to him, he is sneering at me. "If Chloe is going to work for us, she's going to work for me. I happen to be in need of an assistant since mine left to get married."

"Ryan, I am not sure that would be a good idea," Gary says.

"I'll take the job," I tell them as I stand to face Ryan. "Thank you."

"Oh, don't thank me yet, sweetheart. I'm not the sweet college boy who worshipped you anymore. You saw to that. You may not like who I am now."

I swallow hard before answering. "I'm not the girl you worshipped anymore, either. And it doesn't matter if I like you. I'll work hard for you." He turns to leave, motioning for me to follow. I smile at my dad, hoping to reassure us both that this will be OK, and follow Ryan out the door.